searching for shadows

redwood coast rescue
book five

Tonya Burrows

part one
shadows

the shadow stalker

In shadows so deep, the Stalker hides.
Fear his presence where moonlight dies.
Beware his bunker, hidden and dark,
Where he preys on souls, leaving his mark.
In woods so still, his hunt begins,
Fear his presence, where moonlight thins.
One by one, his tally grows,
For in the shadows, his secret shows.

chapter
one

VERONICA MARTENS STOOD in her empty kitchen, the stainless steel refrigerator door hanging open. Pale light cast eerie shadows on the white countertops and hardwood floors.

The fridge was almost empty.

An empty fridge meant she had to leave the house.

Her heart lodged in her throat, and she looked over her shoulder toward the front door of her small seaside cabin. That door was as terrifying as the entrance to a deep, dark, endless cave, and she had no interest in exploring what lay on the other side.

But she needed to eat.

She closed the fridge with a soft thud and glanced toward her phone on the kitchen counter. She could call Dad. He'd send groceries. All she had to do was ask...

Except the ask always came with questions and concerns, and she didn't want to admit just how difficult it was for her to leave the house. He wouldn't understand the crippling anxiety that gripped her every time she stepped outside, and he'd only worry. He already worried about her too much.

Besides, she couldn't keep relying on him. She was a grown-ass woman and could take care of herself.

Not for the first time, she wished she had Wi-Fi. Her cell phone worked for calls in the cabin, but internet access was spotty unless she stepped outside. But Wi-Fi meant she had to interact with a stranger. Maybe even invite them into her home to have it installed, and the idea of inviting a man—because it would probably be a man—into her sanctuary gave her heart palpitations.

No.

She could live without Wi-Fi. She didn't need to order groceries for delivery. She could go into town like a normal person.

Taking a deep breath, she grabbed her keys and headed toward the door. She could do this. It was just a quick trip to the grocery store. Nothing to be scared of.

As she reached for the doorknob, her palms began to sweat. The impulse to bolt back into the safety of her house was nearly overwhelming, but she steeled herself, drawing on the remnants of her Air Force pilot's resolve. With trembling hands, she turned the knob and pushed the door open, taking a single step onto the porch.

The wind whispered through the trees, rustling leaves, and all she could think of was a predator hiding in the foliage, stalking its prey. The wind brought with it scents that should be comforting— damp earth, salted waves—but instead, it made her insides quake. She scanned back and forth between the dark woods to the left of her cabin and the rugged cliff that dramatically dropped into the restless expanse of the Pacific on the right. The vast horizon, painted with bright oranges and pinks from the setting sun, taunted her. Reminded her how she used to soar through open skies, fearless and free.

Would she ever be fearless again?

Probably not.

The suffocating presence of anxiety lurked like a bogeyman just out of sight, threatening a panic attack.

She couldn't breathe.

Heart pounding, she retreated into the house, slammed the door shut, and locked it with all three deadbolts. The final snick of the last lock sliding home eased the tension in her chest, calming her nerves. She leaned her back against the door, taking deep breaths to steady herself.

Her phone rang.

Dad.

Goddammit.

The man had a sixth sense when it came to her panic attacks. Somehow, he always knew. And he always called.

She drew one last steadying breath and answered. "Hi, Dad."

Shit, her voice came out fainter than she'd hoped, and of course he noticed instantly.

"Sweetheart, are you all right?"

He lived nearly ten hours away in Seattle, but she could picture the worried lines creasing his brow as if he stood right in front of her. Arthur Martens was a good man, a loving father who had always been there for her, even when she had pushed him away. And yet she couldn't stop pushing him away.

"I'm fine," she lied.

"No, you're not. I can hear it in your voice. What's wrong?"

Dammit. "I just... I'm out of groceries."

"Ah," Arthur said. "Well, don't worry about it. I'll send a delivery out to you."

"Thank you." Her gaze strayed to the wine rack in a nook under the kitchen counter, where only one bottle remained.

She shouldn't say it.

She didn't need it.

"And I need more wine."

"Veronica." His tone was stern, but under it, concern bled

through. She could almost see him shaking his head, his thinning salt-and-pepper hair catching the light. "You know that's not the solution. Your mom—"

"Please, Dad. I don't need a lecture. I just need some wine. I have a glass or two with dinner. It's not a big deal. I'm not like mom."

He exhaled, and she heard his disappointment loud and clear.

"Okay," he relented after a long moment of silence. "But if I'm going to get you wine, we need to talk about Connelly."

Shit. She'd walked right into that one. "There's nothing more to say about him."

"God, you're stubborn."

"I get it from you."

"Not one of my better qualities." He paused for a beat. "Forgive him, Vee. He didn't mean any harm."

"Absolutely not." Her jaw clenched as it always did at the mention of Connelly Davis. "Forget the wine. I don't want to talk about him."

"Veronica, please—"

"Goodbye, Dad. Thanks for the groceries." She hung up on him and tossed the phone aside. It immediately rang again. She pressed a hand to her forehead, trying to ward off the headache that threatened to engulf her.

She needed to clear her mind.

To forget about Connelly.

Her mom.

Her dad's disappointment.

Forget about everything...

She scrambled to her feet and lunged for the wine rack, grabbing the last bottle and uncorking it with a satisfying pop. She poured herself a generous glass, savoring the rich aroma of blackberries and dark chocolate that filled her senses. The cool liquid burned down her throat, easing the insistent ache in her chest. She took another long drink, relishing in the numbing sensation, and wandered over to the sliding door, peering out over her unused deck to the ocean and endless sky beyond. A storm was brewing over the mountain to the south, darkening the sky.

At one time, she had soared through those temperamental skies, pushing the limits of her aircraft. She touched the cool glass of the door and could almost feel the thrill of defying gravity again.

The familiar ache for freedom swelled in her chest.

But that was a lifetime ago.

She wasn't that woman anymore, and now staring out at the unobtainable world just made her angry. She closed the blinds, finished her glass, and went back to the bottle on the counter to pour another.

And another.

And another.

And suddenly, the bottle was almost gone, and the world grew soft and fuzzy around the edges.

She stumbled over to the couch, collapsed onto the cushions, and exhaled a deep breath. This was better. She didn't have to think about the sky, or going outside, or Dad, or Connelly. Here, in the safety of her home, she could close her eyes and let the alcohol wash away her troubles.

"Cheers," she murmured, raising the glass to the empty room before taking a deep drink.

As she finished off the glass, her inhibitions slipped comfortably away. She kicked off her shoes and stretched out on the couch, enjoying the cool leather against her skin. Her mind was hazy, her thoughts jumbled and disjointed. She turned on the TV, but the screen swam before her eyes, so she gave up trying to watch it. Instead, she allowed her mind to wander, letting it drift into places she couldn't visit while sober.

She closed her eyes and thought about the last time she had been with a man. Voluntarily, at least. She couldn't think of the actual last time when three men she thought were friends had drugged her and—

No.

No.

She stopped that thought before it could fully form. If she let it take root, she wouldn't be able to do this. And she needed it. Her body was on fire. She was desperate for something, anything, to take the edge off.

It had been years since she had felt the loving touch of another human being. The thought of someone else's hands on her skin, someone else's lips on her neck, made her pulse race with a mix of anticipation and fear.

But it wasn't really someone else, she reminded herself.

It was only her own touch. Her own imagination.

She shifted on the couch, her fingers trailing down her chest, teasing the swell of her breasts. She imagined someone else's hands there, rough and calloused, kneading and pinching. She moaned and pressed her thighs together as a thrill ran down her spine.

God, it had been so long.

She imagined being touched. She thought about the feel of a man's hands on her skin and the way his lips would taste. She thought about the way his body would feel as he laid above her, pressing her into the mattress, his warmth seeping into her.

What would he look like? She pictured him tall and strong. His hair would be dark, his eyes darker still. Eyes to get lost in. His arms would be thick with muscle, and his body would be covered in dark hair...

Her hand drifted lower, over her flat belly and down to the

waistband of her sweatpants. Her breathing grew ragged as she slid her fingers underneath the fabric and traced the outline of her panties. Pressure built inside her, the ache swirling in her belly.

Connelly's face flashed in her mind, making her jolt and open her eyes.

No, not him. He was the last person she wanted to see, but since reappearing in her life a few months ago, he was constantly on her mind.

She should stop.

She was losing control.

She traced the outline of her panties again, then slipped her hand underneath and dipped her fingers experimentally into her sex.

She couldn't stop.

She bit her lip to stifle a moan. God, it had been way too long. She pressed her fingers deeper, sliding them in and out of her tightness, her body already shuddering as the pressure built. She worked herself faster, stroking her inner walls as a gasp of pleasure escaped her lips. Her mind filled with images of her fantasy man—not Connelly. It could never be him. It was his fault her life was a mess. If it weren't for him, she wouldn't have had to quit flying. If it weren't for him, she wouldn't be here, drunk, alone, and finger-fucking herself—

The pressure eased, the orgasm slipping away.

No. Dammit. She had to focus.

She closed her eyes again and tried to imagine a different man. Someone as different from Connelly as possible, with blond hair and light eyes. Someone sweet and gentle with none of the baggage, like that lawyer she sometimes saw at Redwood Coast Rescue when she still left the house. Cal Holden. Yeah, he was a safe fantasy man because it would never, ever happen in real life.

She imagined hands teasing her nipples, imagined lips

sucking her breasts, imagined a tongue swirling around her navel. She groaned as the pressure built inside her again, her body begging for release. She pressed on her clit—

But it was no use. Her mind was filled with Connelly. His smile. His laugh.

And then his face blurred and split into three. Three leering, laughing faces she could never forget, no matter how much she drank.

And fear once again took her in a chokehold.

She couldn't do this.

Her fingers stilled, and she pulled her hand out of her sweatpants, resting her head back on the couch. She stared at the ceiling, willing her heart to slow down.

She needed to not think about them.

She needed to not think about Connelly.

Veronica shoved to her feet, the room spinning around her. She gripped the couch as the wine rushed through her head. "Shit."

She was drunk.

She stumbled to the kitchen and exchanged the nearly empty bottle of wine for a bottle of water that she drained in a few gulps.

Of course she was drunk. She had to be to think about sex. But, even wasted, she couldn't do it without seeing *their* faces. Those three fucking faces always haunting her.

Ugh, why was it so fucking hot in here?

She was suffocating and leaned over the sink to crank open the window. Cool air rushed in over her exposed skin. She leaned against the counter, closed her eyes, took a deep breath, and listened to the waves pound on the cliffs below the cabin.

After a few minutes, her heart slowed, and she opened her eyes again. Nothing had changed. She was still drunk, still aching, still scared.

She might as well finish her wine.

She reached into the fridge again for the wine and shoved the door shut with her foot. She considered just drinking it straight from the bottle, but that was too much like her mother for comfort. As long as she used a glass, she wasn't an alcoholic, right?

As she poured another glass, she heard a noise outside the window.

She froze.

The waves continued to crash against the shore, and thunder rumbled in the distance, but otherwise, everything was silent. She listened for a moment, heard her breath and heart hammering.

She was being paranoid. There was no one out there, just the wind in the trees, the brewing storm, and the waves crashing below.

She was safe.

She took a deep breath and walked back into the living room.

Safe.

She was safe.

She had to be safe.

She could stay here, alone, in her own head, in her own life.

She didn't have to go out.

She didn't have to find anyone to share that life with.

She didn't have to be anyone special.

Because she was safe here.

Veronica collapsed back onto the couch and cuddled one of the pillows to her chest, but she still couldn't shake the feeling of being watched. She closed her eyes and told herself to calm down.

She was safe.

She repeated it like a mantra.
She was safe.
She was safe.
She. Was. Safe.

chapter
two

THE WOODS SEEMED to absorb all light, casting an eerie darkness that clung to the gnarled branches overhead. Shadows danced on the forest floor as a chilling breeze, the last gasp of a stubborn winter, whispered through the leaves.

The Shadow Stalker stood in that darkness, shrouded by a thicket of brambles and undergrowth.

Waiting.

Watching.

The thorns caught at his clothes and bit at his skin, but this was the perfect vantage point to watch her.

Veronica Martens.

His muse.

Every night he would sit in silence, observing her through the binoculars that rested against his weathered coat. He would breathe in the scent of pine and damp soil and dream about the day he could have her.

She had become the Shadow Stalker's favorite pastime.

Of course, he wasn't the real Shadow Stalker of legend who lured unsuspecting victims into his bunker to suck out their souls. That was just a fairy tale.

The Shadow Stalker name was a mantle, passed down

from one predator to another for centuries. The current Stalker was more dangerous than the myth, because he didn't actually hide in the night. The Stalker blended in. The Stalker had a life and friends and nobody suspected his dark side, even as they whispered fearfully about his deeds.

And the myth lived on.

It was a tradition older than the woods themselves, and he had been chosen to carry it on. He was proud of that legacy. Someday soon, the current Stalker would retire. The name would finally pass to him and people would whisper about him, too. He'd even had a bunker ready, one he'd found abandoned up on Murder Mountain during a hunting trip. He'd spent months preparing it, readying it for his first victim. When he finally took her, it was beautiful.

Until she had escaped and her friends took it all away from him.

And then the current Stalker had called him reckless.

He clenched his fists at the thought, resentment slithering inside of him like a well-fed serpent. He wasn't the reckless one. He hadn't been the one to set Alexis Summers free to hunt her, only to lose her in the forest.

But it didn't matter now.

Alexis Summers was in the past and the more he thought about it, the more he realized she hadn't been perfect for his first kill as the Shadow Stalker.

Not like Veronica.

Just beyond the brambles, Veronica's lighted cabin was a beacon against the night's black canvas, the only human touch amidst nature's wild sprawl. She was inside, her silhouetted form pacing behind curtained windows.

Beautiful, damaged Veronica.

A woman who'd flown through the sky in supersonic jets, navigated dangerous territories in service to her country, yet now cowered inside her house, too scared to step beyond its safe confines.

A shiver of anticipation rippled through him as he watched her move, watched her exist in her self-imposed isolation.

There was an unparalleled beauty in her vulnerability. It was raw, untamed. Every night, it beckoned him closer, whispering promises of exquisite pleasure and intimacy in his ear. He could almost taste her fear. It filled him with an insatiable hunger, and he yearned for the day when her fear would be for him.

The curtain moved and his breath came in shallow, ragged pants as her face appeared in the window. Her long, dark hair was pulled up into a ponytail. Her haunted eyes—hazel, he knew, though he couldn't see the color now—scanned right over his hiding place.

"Look at me," he whispered.

She turned away from the window, tugging the curtain shut. But it didn't close fully. Through the sliver, he could see her pick up a book, her fingers tracing the spine.

His body tensed, his gaze never leaving her hands.

Touch me like that.

What book was it?

He had to know.

He waited until all the lights inside were extinguished. Waited longer until the cabin was swallowed by the inky blackness of the night. He waited until the only sounds were the whisper of the wind rattling through the leaves overhead and his own heartbeat thundering in his ears. Only then did he push himself out of his prickly shelter, his every movement precise and controlled as he expertly navigated the dense undergrowth.

The moon hid behind thick clouds, casting everything into an even deeper darkness. It didn't matter to him—he knew these woods like the back of his hand, knew each treacherous root and low-hanging branch that dared to obstruct his path.

It took only minutes to reach her doorstep, his gloved hand ghosting over the handle. Locked, of course. She had three locks, he knew, but that wouldn't be a problem. He pulled out a lock pick kit from his pocket. He'd honed the skill over years of practice and had her locks opened in minutes.

The interior was as he imagined— quaint and claustrophobic, with an unmistakable feminine touch. The scent of her hung heavy in the air, a mix of vanilla and something uniquely Veronica. He breathed it in greedily. The smell was intoxicating, overwhelming his senses until he could taste it on his tongue.

His pulse quickened as he made his way to her bookshelf. The stacks of novels with candy-bright covers made his lips curl. He'd expected better from her than cheesy romantic comedies.

But there was one shelf with darker covers, the titles in sharper fonts. And one book hadn't been pushed in all the way so that it was even with the others. He pulled it out and traced the spine as she had.

The Shadows Within by Connelly Davis.

He exhaled a quiet laugh.

It was perfect.

He slid the book back into place and moved deeper into the cabin.

Her scent became stronger, more pervasive as he neared what must be her room. The door was slightly ajar. He peeked inside, careful not to make any noise. Not that it mattered. She was an insomniac, but he knew once she finally passed out, she was a heavy sleeper.

The room was small and cozy, dominated by a queen-sized bed with rumpled sheets. Her sleeping form was just visible under the covers, rising and falling gently with every breath she took.

He paused in the doorway, his heart pounding with anticipation. He wanted to go to her, to touch her. Yet, he knew better. It was not the time. He needed to remain patient, to wait for the moment when everything would be perfect.

He turned away from her room and prowled through the rest of her tiny cabin. A small stack of pictures caught his attention, resting on a coffee table in her living room. They were mostly old photos of her and a man who looked enough like her to be her father. The younger Veronica had a radiant smile that seemed foreign to the woman he had been watching religiously.

In one picture, she was wearing a cap and gown, standing next to a different man. Or, boy, really. Floppy dark hair, dark eyes, a wide grin aimed at the camera, his arm slung around Veronica's shoulders as if he had every right to touch her. The neat writing on the back of the photo said, *Veronica and Connelly, graduation, 2012.*

Connelly?

Like the author of that book?

A surge of possessiveness swept over him, and he shoved the picture away, spilling the rest of them onto the floor.

Nausea crept up his throat as he stared down at the scattered photos. The bastard was in almost all of them. Another photo was more recent—Veronica seated with Connelly, both in Air Force blues, their heads tilted toward each other as they laughed at an inside joke. The chemistry between them was palpable, even in a static image.

Had they been lovers?

The thought filled him with a fury so intense he felt sure he would combust. He crumpled the picture in his fist. After a few deep breaths, he stuffed it into his pocket. He couldn't leave it behind now, or she'd realize someone had been in her space.

He'd overstayed his welcome.

He methodically returned the other photos to the exact place he'd found them on the coffee table, then scanned to make sure he hadn't left anything else of himself behind.

At the last moment, he walked back to the bookshelf and grabbed the book. Taking it was a risk, but he had to know more. Had to understand what drew Veronica so fervently to it, what tied her to this Connelly guy.

And if stealing the book made her uneasy, made her think she wasn't alone, all the better. That just made this little game of theirs all the more thrilling.

chapter
three

CONNELLY DAVIS STARED at the blank computer screen, his fingers hovering over the keyboard. He'd been sitting at his makeshift desk in the cabin for hours, the cursor blinking tauntingly on the empty page. His gaze strayed to the lush redwoods just outside his window. The tall trees were shrouded in mist, their ancient branches casting eerie shadows on the forest floor. It was the kind of atmosphere that had always inspired his best work, but today, it only seemed to mock him.

Connelly closed his eyes and raked his fingers through his hair. Three months at this secluded cabin on the California coast, and he had barely written a chapter. The acclaimed horror writer who had chilled readers with tales of demons, possession, and things that went bump in the night was facing his own worst nightmare...

Writer's block.

He tapped the keyboard, attempting to start a new paragraph, but the words felt hollow, the sentences disjointed.

He deleted them all with a frustrated growl. "Fuck me."

He'd come to here to find inspiration, to recharge his creative batteries, but instead, he'd found nothing but suspicious locals, a best friend who didn't want anything to do with him, and a thick mental fog that refused to lift.

"Come on, Conn. You can do this. You've done this a hundred times." But even as the words left his lips, doubt gnawed at the edges of his mind. He hadn't been able to write horror in more than a year, since finishing *The Shadows Within*, and while his recent attempt at a self-published police procedural had been fun, it had not been well received by fans or critics. They wanted horror from him, and nothing else.

He looked at the shelf above his desk, where his previous novels sat in a neat row. The spine of each book bore his name, but they might as well have been written by someone else. He couldn't believe he'd ever crafted those chilling tales of suspense and horror, not when he was struggling to form a single coherent sentence now.

What if he couldn't do it again?

What if he'd run out of darkness to share with the world?

The darkness had always been with him for as long as he could remember. He'd had paralyzing night terrors as a child, and at the encouragement of a therapist, he'd started writing his nightmares down as a way to exorcise his demons. Then he'd started crafting those nightmares into stories, and submitting those stories to publishers, and, suddenly, he was a published author before he even finished high school.

He'd always thought being a full-time author was his dream. He'd attempted other things— college, military, a string of random full-time jobs. It was all interesting for a while, but none of it held his heart in a chokehold like writing.

Except now he was starting to think it was more a curse than a dream.

Veronica used to tease that he had everyone fooled, because the girls in high school always thought he was "sweet," but she knew the truth. He wasn't sweet. He had a shadow self that thrived on terrifying people. And maybe that was true.

He always loved to hear that his books kept readers awake, staring into the dark, afraid of what lurked there.

He pushed back from the desk with a sigh and went to refill his coffee mug, his footsteps echoing in the silent house. This small two-bed, one-bath cabin was tucked away from the highway on a forested road that overlooked the ocean. The place was secluded and moody, with its dramatic views from the back deck, its thrift store decor, and cedar shake siding grayed by decades of salty ocean wind. It was supposed to inspire him, and yet his mind remained stubbornly empty. He stood at the window, gazing out at the dense forest surrounding the cabin. Just beyond those trees was Veronica's place. He hadn't seen her since the day he'd tried to comfort her three weeks ago, and she slammed the door in his face.

Connelly sipped his coffee, contemplating his next move. He knew he should try to make things right with Veronica, but she clearly wanted nothing to do with him.

His phone rang, interrupting his thoughts. Glancing at the caller ID, he silenced it without answering. His agent could wait. Right now, he needed to clear his head.

Leaving his useless laptop behind, he headed outside into the chilly air. The days were slowly getting longer and warmer, but the evenings still clung to the chill of winter. Hands in his pockets, he strolled down the dirt road that connected their cabins. Maybe he'd get lucky, and Veronica would at least agree to talk to him this time...

Connelly didn't get far before his phone rang again. Letting out an irritated huff, he fished it from his pocket, fully intending to silence it once more. But then he saw the name on the screen— Arthur Martens.

Against his better judgment, he answered. "Hey, Arthur."

"Conn, my boy! How's the writing going?" Arthur's voice was warm and booming, belying the cancer that was slowly chewing away at his insides.

"It's... uh, going," he said evasively.

"That good, huh?"

"I've had better writing sessions."

"It'll come to you. It always does."

He scuffed his boot against a rock. "Yeah."

A beat of silence.

Arthur drew a breath, and Connelly steeled himself for the question.

"So... I wanted to ask about Veronica. Have you spoken to her again?"

"No."

"Listen, I called her yesterday, and she sounded..." He trailed off as if he didn't know how to finish that sentence.

"She won't see me, Arthur. I've tried."

"Yeah, I know she's been giving you the cold shoulder, but she's still working through everything."

"I get that."

"Just give her time. But not too much time," he added after a beat. "You let her go too long and she'll withdraw completely. I really think you two reconnecting could help. Don't give up on her yet."

Connelly scoffed. "When have you ever known me to give up? I'm headed to her place as we speak."

"Oh." Arthur's laugh sounded a lot like a relieved exhale. "Good."

"But I doubt she'll even open the door."

"Nonsense, my boy. I have a feeling she'll hear you out this time. And if she shuts the door in your face, just try again tomorrow. Be patient with her. She's been through a lot."

"I know."

"And Connelly, if I may give you a piece of advice?"

"Of course," he said, grateful for any guidance he could get.

"Don't let this writer's block get the best of you. You're

too talented for that. The darkness is still inside you, waiting to be unleashed. You just have to find the right key to unlock it."

Connelly's chest tightened with emotion. Arthur had always been a mentor to him, both in writing and in life, and the thought of losing him to cancer was almost too much to bear.

"Thanks, Arthur. I'll keep that in mind."

"Good. Now go talk to our Vee. And write something that'll make my skin crawl, will ya?"

With a fond smile, Connelly ended the call and gazed up at the darkening sky, watching as heavy clouds rolled in over the peak of Mt. Humboldt, which locals called Murder Mountain. A distant rumble of thunder echoed through the valley. It made the hair stand up on the back of his neck. Northern California was like Seattle—they didn't get many thunderstorms—and he couldn't help but feel like the one rolling in now was an omen of bad luck.

The canopy of trees blocked out much of the afternoon sunlight, leaving a dappled pattern on the ground beneath him. Wind rustled through the leaves, but rather than energizing him with its freshness, it seemed to whisper caution. The birds were quiet as he continued down the path and his footsteps crunched in the stillness.

Usually nature brought him inspiration, but something about this place left him unsettled. It had an undercurrent of foreboding that should exhilarate him, but instead felt like a fingernail scraping uncomfortably down his spine.

He glanced over his shoulder at the warm glow of his rental, before tugging up his collar against the wind and trudging reluctantly down the beaten path toward Veronica's. He already felt himself bracing for disappointment as the cabin appeared through the trees, its windows dark and unwelcoming.

Connelly took a deep breath and knocked on the door.

For a moment, there was no response, and he was about to give up and turn back when he heard a faint shuffling from inside. Then, the lock clicked, and then another, and another, and the door creaked open slowly.

Veronica peered out, her face so carefully blank it might as well be a mask. "What do you want?"

He held up his hands. "I just want to talk."

She looked like hell. Her dark hair was wild and unkempt, her eyes red-rimmed and swollen. She wore a baggy sweatshirt and leggings, as if she hadn't bothered to get dressed all day, and the smell of alcohol on her breath was palpable.

"I don't want to see you," she said, trying to slam the door shut again.

But he put his foot in the way, blocking it. "Please, Vee. Talk to me."

"Talk about what? How you used me for inspiration? How you turned my trauma into your next bestseller?"

"That's not what happ—"

She slammed the door, catching his foot before he could remove it. His old hiking boots were sturdy enough to muffle the pain, but it still fucking hurt.

Cursing, he limped back a step. "I'm not leaving until we talk about this. I know I fucked up, but I want to make it right."

"I don't care," came the muffled response from inside. "Just leave me alone."

Connelly sighed, leaning his forehead against the cool wood of the door. He couldn't blame her for hating him—after all, he had used her story as an inspiration for his latest novel.

But he also knew it wasn't just about the book. Their friendship had died the night her life had changed. The night he'd let his own foolish pride keep him away when she most needed him.

He loved Veronica. Always had. He wanted to help her heal, to be there for her. Yeah, it was too little, too late, but he couldn't change the past. All he could do now was help her have a future.

And she couldn't even look at him.

He knocked again, softer this time. "Vee, please. I'm sorry."

The door opened a crack. "Sorry for what?"

"For being a shitty friend. For not being there when you needed me."

She scoffed. "You think you can just come here and make everything better? You think you can just say 'sorry' and everything will be okay?"

"No, of course not. But I want to try."

Veronica studied him through the narrow opening of the door, her eyes filled with skepticism. "What's your plan, then? How do you intend to 'try' and fix everything?"

Connelly paused, looking for the right words. He had to tread carefully. "I don't have all the answers. But I want to be here for you, listen to you, and support you in any way that I can."

A bitter laugh escaped her lips. "Support me? Like you supported me when I was going through hell? You disappeared that night. Left me alone and vulnerable. What kind of so-called friend does that? And then the next time I hear from you, it's that fucking book showing up on my doorstep with a note telling me how sorry you are."

He winced as her words cut like blades. "I was wrong. I was angry and hurt, and then, after what happened, I couldn't look you in the eyes, knowing it was my fault. Knowing I left you with those assholes. It was selfish of me to distance myself because I couldn't handle your pain. I can't change any of that—"

"And you can't change me now. Goodbye, Connelly. Don't come back." She shut the door with a resounding thud, leaving him standing alone on the porch, his heart sinking. He had expected resistance, but he hadn't expected the strong wall of anger and resentment she'd built around herself.

But he couldn't bring himself to walk away just yet. He'd known Veronica long enough to understand her stubbornness, her need for independence, and her fierce self-preservation. Those qualities had attracted him to her in the first place, back when they were kids. But now, it seemed like those very qualities were driving them apart.

Okay.

He'd leave her alone tonight, but he wouldn't let her shut him out completely. He needed to devise a plan, something that would break through that impenetrable wall and show Veronica he was sincere in his efforts to make amends.

He refused to give up on their friendship without a fight.

chapter
four

THE TIRES of Connelly's BMW X7 crunched over gravel, kicking up dust as he pulled off the pothole-filled mountain road and onto the freshly paved drive of Redwood Coast Rescue. Steam Valley, California, was living up to its name this morning, with wisps of mist weaving through the trees like ethereal fingers reaching from beyond the veil. The natural beauty of this place was undeniable, but there was also something haunting about it. The gigantic trees seemed to whisper secrets in an ancient language only the heart could comprehend and cast shadows that danced like phantoms on the forest floor.

Connelly loved it.

What better place for a horror writer to rediscover his creative mojo? If anywhere unlocked the stories buried deep within him, it would be here.

But today was not about his creative problems.

Today was about helping Veronica.

Redwood Coast Rescue had recently reopened after rebuilding from the ashes of a wildfire that ripped through the town last fall. The burn scar still blackened the side of the mountain behind the Rescue, but the land immediately surrounding the new buildings had been replanted. He parked in the lot and took a moment to appreciate the fresh scent of pine that hung in the air. It was a crisp, invigorating aroma that carried a sense of renewal.

That's what this place was—a place for both dogs and humans to heal and find a fresh start. Even before he'd come to Steam Valley, he'd heard about Redwood Coast Rescue's unique approach to rehabilitation, pairing rescue dogs with trauma survivors in a mutually beneficial bond. They'd made headlines before the wildfire, and he remembered being glad that Veronica had found a soft place to land. When Arthur told him where she was, he'd pictured her thriving and making friends and healing.

But then he got here and discovered she wasn't thriving at all.

Connelly adjusted his worn leather jacket, took a deep breath, and approached the main entrance. The air was alive with the sound of excited barks, making him smile.

The Rescue was a handful of buildings laid out in a star pattern, connected by walkways and surrounded by training yards. Each building served a different purpose—a community center, a pet hotel, an adoption center, Dr. Sasha Scott's veterinary clinic, and a headquarters for RWCR, the tactical K9 team led by a former Army Ranger, Zak Hendricks. Zak's wife, Anna, ran the rest of the rescue.

The main building gleamed in the sunlight, its vibrant red exterior bright against the crisp blue sky. Inside, the walls were adorned with colorful paintings and motivational quotes, giving the space a cozy and welcoming vibe. The place was so new it still smelled like fresh paint.

Since he'd called ahead, he was unsurprised to find Zak and Anna waiting at the welcome desk.

"Connelly, good to see you again." Zak extended a calloused hand. Despite the prosthetic leg that replaced the one he'd lost in Afghanistan, Zak exuded a rugged confidence that seemed to draw people toward him.

Connelly accepted the handshake. "Zak." He offered a smile to the redhead beside the man. "Anna."

Anna's returned smile was kind. "Hi, Connelly. How's Veronica? We all miss her around here."

He shook his head. "I wish I had an answer for that. She still won't talk to me. I hope Rylan will have a few free minutes to talk before I leave."

Rylan Cross was the new trauma counselor working with the rescue's Paws for Vets program. In the past, when Connelly had consulted with Rylan, the counselor had suggested that Veronica needed to take things at her own pace. But now he wasn't sure if that was the right approach. Veronica had been doing things at her own pace for years, and nothing had changed. Maybe it was time to push her a bit.

"He's not in yet," Anna said, looking at the clock on the wall behind the desk. "But he should be soon. You're welcome to wait here, but you're more likely to catch him before he gets busy if you wait at the community center since his office is there."

Connelly glanced out the window at the building she'd indicated. The welcome center sat in the middle of the star, and the community center sat at the bottom right point, closest to the parking lot and straight across from the vet clinic.

He shook his head and turned his attention back to Anna. "Actually, I wanted to talk to you both, too. I think Veronica needs a dog."

"I said that months ago." Anna grinned and elbowed her husband, all but bouncing on her toes excitedly. "Didn't I say that?"

Zak chuckled. "Yeah, you did. And I agreed with you then, just like I do now."

Anna kissed him, then gave his cheek an affectionate tap. "Because you are an intelligent man, Zak Hendricks. Most of the time."

Connelly smiled at the playful banter. They seemed genuinely happy together and in sync with each other. He and Veronica used to be like that. Their mutual friends always teased them that they should just get married because they had already acted like an old married couple.

His smile dimmed at the thought.

And now their friendship was barely hanging on by a thread. He couldn't blame her, though. After what she had been through, trust was not an easy thing to give.

He realized Zak was speaking to him and tuned back in.

"...help Veronica," Zak said. "We've seen the power of the human-animal bond, and I think it could be transformative for her."

"So," Anna said, "tell us more about what you're thinking. What kind of dog would be a good fit for Veronica?"

"I'm not exactly sure. I know she loves dogs. Always has. But I want to find one that can handle her anxiety, maybe even help her overcome it."

"Like Alfie," Zak said softly, almost as if talking to himself.

"Alfie? Can I meet him?"

Zak shook his head. "Alfie was Dr. Firestone's therapy dog. She used to bring him to sessions. Veronica adored him."

The silence after that quiet statement was filled with sorrow and pain.

Dr. Amelia Firestone.

The original Paws for Vets therapist had been highly respected and beloved. Veronica had loved her. Trusted her.

And then Dr. Firestone was murdered.

And Veronica retreated to her house.

Antsy, Connelly scooped a hand through his hair, which was getting too long and unruly. He really had to find a barber in town. "Maybe she needs a big dog that will help her feel safe and protected."

Zak sent his wife an unreadable look.

"No," Anna said as if he'd spoken aloud. "I don't think that's a good idea." She turned her attention back to Connelly. "We just had a large influx of dogs from a hoarding situation down south. I haven't finished evaluating them all yet, but a few of them have shown promise as emotional support animals. If you can give me a few more days, I'll have some candidates for you."

Zak leaned against the welcome desk and crossed his arms, a thoughtful expression on his face. "You should talk to Rylan about it, too. He knows the dogs here inside and out. He might have some insight into which would be the best match for Veronica."

Connelly narrowed his eyes at Zak. He sensed the guy wanted to say more, but Zak only lifted his chin toward the door.

"His truck just pulled in. If you hurry, you can catch him before his first session starts."

"Yeah. Thanks." Connelly headed toward the door. Whatever else Zak wanted to say could wait.

Inside the community center, he found Rylan's office down a quiet hallway off the main event space. The door was slightly ajar, and soft rock music drifted out. He knocked lightly before entering.

Rylan looked up from his desk, hazel eyes filled with a mixture of curiosity and kindness. "Hey, Connelly. Good to see you. How can I help you today?"

"Do you have a few minutes to talk? It's... about Veronica."

"Absolutely. Have a seat." He gestured to the comfortable chairs arranged in one corner of the room as he rose from his desk and walked to the coffee bar on the opposite wall. He wore jeans, Nikes, and a US Navy T-shirt that had seen better days. His left arm was covered in bright tattoos from shoulder to wrist. His right arm was missing, replaced with a black and silver prosthesis that looked like something from a sci-fi movie. "Can I get you anything to drink? Coffee, water, soda?"

"No, I'm good. Thanks."

"Okay, give me a minute. I haven't had enough caffeine yet today." He measured out the coffee and started the pot, then grabbed a mug from the cabinet with his prosthetic hand. He moved seamlessly, like he wasn't missing a limb. It was fascinating.

"That's new since I last saw you," Connelly said.

While the coffee brewed, Rylan turned and leaned against the counter. "What, my Terminator arm? It's not actually new. I've had it for a while but only started using it regularly over my plain old plastic prosthesis. There was a bit of a learning curve."

"Is it rude to ask how that works?"

He waved his hand, and the robotic fingers opened and closed. Then he grinned. "It's mind control."

"Really?"

"Well, there's a bit more to it than that, but… yeah. Essentially. It's a myoelectric prosthesis. The residual muscle signals in my arm control it. So I think about the intended movement…" He opened a drawer and picked out a spoon, the robotic fingers pinching the handle with almost the same precision as actual fingers. He held it up. "And my brain sends signals to my stump, which activates the right muscles, and the sensors in the prosthetic translate it into movement in the hand. Pretty cool, huh? Learning to use it effectively took a while, but now I don't even think about it. It's second nature."

Connelly whistled softly. "That's gotta be a pricey piece of equipment."

"It is. This one is the most advanced model available, made by QuenTech Bionics, and costs as much as a new car right now. I was lucky to get in on a beta test because I know a guy who knows a guy who has an in with Tucker Quentin; otherwise, I wouldn't have been able to afford it. And God knows the VA would never spring for one. QuenTech's ultimate goal is to make these babies affordable, but that's still a few years out." He poured himself a cup of coffee, stirred in a spoonful of sugar, and then joined Connelly in the seating area.

"So," he said as he settled into one of the chairs. "How is Veronica?"

Connelly sighed and rubbed a hand over his face. He hadn't shaved in a few days and probably looked as ragged as he felt. "She still won't talk to me. I don't know how to reach her, but I thought a dog might help her feel more secure. She's always loved dogs, and Zak mentioned she deeply connected with Dr. Firestone's therapy dog."

"Mm, yes. Alfie. I've heard a lot about the psychic Papillon. Everyone misses him around here." Rylan took a sip of his coffee, his brow furrowing in thought. "Okay, I need to caveat this by saying I haven't seen Veronica as a patient, so I can't give you specific advice on her condition."

"I understand that. I'm just looking for some kind of guidance with the hope that I can get her to come back to therapy. She was doing well until..."

"Dr. Firestone's murder," Rylan finished for him and nodded. "It's not uncommon for trauma survivors to regress or shut down in the face of triggering events, especially when they lose someone they trusted and relied on. But introducing a therapy dog could be a step in the right direction. Dogs have a unique ability to provide comfort and companionship and can also help regulate emotions and reduce anxiety. They are incredibly intuitive creatures. They sense when someone is hurting, and they often have an uncanny ability to provide exactly what that person needs even before they know they need it. I've seen it time and again since I started working here. What Zak, Anna, and the team are doing is amazing. As far as I'm concerned, they're working miracles here."

"Veronica could use a miracle."

"Ask me; she already has one." When Connelly just stared at him blankly, he nodded. "You."

"What?"

"You cared enough about her to leave your life in Seattle and move here to help her. Not many friends would do that."

"But I don't know how to help her."

"But you're here, trying to figure it out. A lot of people don't have that kind of support behind them, so she's already one step ahead. You may not have all the answers, but your presence alone speaks volumes."

Rylan's words hit Connelly like a punch to the gut, and he sat back in his seat. "And what's it saying?"

"That you love her."

"Shit. Is it that obvious?"

A faint smile tugged at Rylan's lips. "Probably not to her, but, yeah, to anyone else with eyes and a working brain, it's pretty fucking obvious." He leaned back in his chair, his gaze thoughtful as he sipped his coffee. "All right, listen. Supporting someone who has experienced major trauma like Veronica requires patience, understanding, and a willingness to take small steps. It's crucial not to push her too hard, too fast."

Unable to stay seated longer, Connelly popped to his feet and paced the room. "That's the problem. I don't know how far to push her. I'm afraid of making things worse, so maybe I'm not pushing her enough?"

"Could be. While it's important to respect her boundaries and not rush her, gently nudging her out of her comfort zone can also be beneficial. You know her better than anyone. Trust your instincts."

"My instincts say she needs a harder push, something to force her to take that first step, or else she'll just keep retreating from everything until we lose her." His throat closed up at the thought. He couldn't lose her.

"I understand your fear, but remember, it's a delicate balance. Pushing her too hard could trigger her further and do more harm than good. But you're right. Sometimes, a gentle nudge isn't enough." He drained his coffee and set the empty mug on the table between them, then pushed out of the chair and crossed to a bookshelf, running his fingers along the spines until he found the one he was looking for. He pulled it down and returned to his seat, placing the book on the table next to his mug. "You should read that."

Connelly picked it up and read the title. *Embracing Horizons: A Guide to Conquering Agoraphobia and Rediscovering Life.*

"It's a memoir by a woman who lived with agoraphobia for years," Rylan continued. "It might give you some insight into what Veronica is dealing with. It's a complex anxiety disorder. Most people think it's just a fear of open spaces, but it goes beyond that. People with agoraphobia can struggle with a range of situations, from public transportation to crowded places. And some, like Veronica, struggle to leave the house at all."

Connelly set the book down. "But why? She never used to be like this. Even after..." He trailed off, unsure of how much Rylan knew about her past. And, if he was honest with himself, he hated saying the words out loud.

"The sexual assault?" Rylan supplied.

Okay, so he knew it all. That made this conversation easier. "Yeah. She had panic attacks afterward—and who could blame her? Men she thought were her friends abused her, and then the Air Force gaslighted her into thinking it was her fault before sending her packing on some stupid bureaucratic technicality. But, even then, the panic attacks were nothing like this. She could still function in society. Now…" He shook his head. "You should see her, Ry. She's like a ghost haunting that house. A half-finished person. I just… wish I knew why."

Rylan's gaze softened. "The why is hard to pinpoint. Agoraphobia is considered a complication of her original panic disorder. Dr. Firestone's murder was traumatic for everyone, but for Veronica, it destroyed the entire foundation of her recovery. That loss triggered her panic, and now she doesn't feel safe anywhere but at home. But, of course, this is just speculation on my part. Without talking to her, I can't know for sure. You should encourage her to seek professional help—and it doesn't have to be from me. As I mentioned once before, I have a female friend in Portland who does amazing work with sexual trauma survivors."

"She won't do it. I know her. She won't let herself be that vulnerable to anyone again."

"Then you need to support her until she's ready to try. More than anything else right now, she needs to know she's not alone."

"Everything I've tried has backfired so far."

"Agoraphobia is traumatic, overwhelming, and recovery is a gradual process. The best thing you can do is educate yourself." He nodded toward the table. "Read the book. Watch videos online. Then, learn about her triggers and her symptoms. Celebrate small victories together, and don't be disheartened by setbacks. Because setbacks will happen. Don't trivialize her feelings or experiences. It's not about her 'getting over it.' It's about her learning to live with and exist despite the fear. Patience will be crucial."

Connelly winced, which made Rylan smirk. "Patience isn't your strong suit?"

He scratched the back of his neck. "No, not exactly. I've always been more of a jump-in-head-first kind of guy."

"Well, my friend, you'll have to learn the art of taking things slow. But..." Rylan's smirk widened into a full grin as the door opened, and Zak filled the frame. "Give her that push, too. Go get her a dog."

chapter
five

CONNELLY THANKED Rylan and grabbed the book on his way out the door. Zak stepped back to allow him into the hall, then nodded at Rylan before shutting the door.

"Did Anna find a dog?" Connelly asked, tucking the book under his arm.

"So, here's the thing..." Zak hedged, rubbing the back of his neck. "Anna is gonna kill me for telling you this, but we already have the perfect dog for Veronica in our rehabilitation wing."

That did not sound promising at all. "And why is Anna going to kill you for that?"

"Because she doesn't agree. Rebel is... well, she lives up to her name."

Connelly's heart sank. "I was thinking a sweet and gentle dog, something that Veronica could easily bond with. One that could provide comfort and support without over-whelming her."

Zak nodded. "I get where you're coming from. It's the same place Anna is right now, but I know dogs and I know people and I'm telling you, Rebel is what Veronica needs.

She's stubborn as all hell, but she's also incredibly loyal and protective."

"I don't know, man."

"At least come meet her."

Connelly sighed. He had envisioned a calm and gentle companion for Veronica, not a rebellious force of nature, but if Zak believed Rebel was the right fit, then maybe he should consider her.

"All right," he relented. "I'll meet her."

Zak led him out of the community center and across the grounds to another building he hadn't been in before. The sound of barking grew louder, echoing through the hallways, and Connelly's nerves prickled with a mixture of anxiety and curiosity. They entered a bright, open room filled with kennels lining the walls. Dogs of all shapes and sizes paced restlessly inside them. He scanned the room until his gaze landed on a sleek, muscular Doberman standing tall in her enclosure.

Somehow, he knew that had to be Rebel.

Her gaze locked with his, intense and unwavering, as if daring him to look away. There was an undeniable fire in her tawny eyes, a fierceness that seemed to match the name she bore.

Zak approached Rebel's kennel with the ease of a man who was comfortable around even the most intimidating of dogs. And Rebel was the most intimidating dog Connelly had ever seen. Veronica would never have to be afraid of another attack with that beast of an animal at her side.

"Hey, my rebellious girl," Zak called with deep affection in his voice and opened her kennel. "We found someone who needs your kind of spirit."

Rebel's tail wagged.

Okay, she didn't seem so bad. "What's her story?"

"She came from a junkyard," Zak said.

Connelly raised an eyebrow. "A junkyard?"

Zak leaned against the kennel, his gaze fixed on Rebel as he recounted her story. "Yeah, she was abused and abandoned, left to fend for herself. But even in that bleak environment, she never lost her will to live. She fought tooth and nail to survive. I think she'll help remind Veronica of her own strength and resilience." He extended a hand toward Rebel, who nudged it gently with her nose. He smiled. "I've been doing this for a few years now, and it still amazes me how much these animals can teach us about ourselves."

Connelly cautiously approached, keeping a safe distance as he observed Rebel's reaction to his presence. She stood tall and proud, but there was a softness in her eyes that contradicted her intimidating appearance. As he got closer, Rebel emitted a low, rumbling growl, not out of aggression, but almost as if she were testing him.

He stopped in his tracks, unsure of how to proceed.

"She's just sizing you up," Zak said. "Making sure you're worthy. Let her sniff you."

"Okay, but if I lose a hand, you're explaining why I can't write anymore to my agent."

Zak scoffed. "You'll be fine." His grin turned wicked. "Besides, you saw Rylan's Terminator hand. You could easily write with that, no problem. Prosthetics have come a long way."

Connelly eyed the man's metal leg. If anyone knew about prosthetics, it would be Zak. But, still, he wasn't convinced that losing a limb would be worth the potential reward of gaining Rebel's trust.

"Hey there, Rebel," he said in a calm and soothing voice and slowly extended his hand toward her, palm facing up in a non-threatening gesture. "I hope we can be friends."

Rebel sniffed the air, her nostrils flaring as she analyzed his scent. Her growl subsided, and she inched closer, tentatively investigating his hand with her cold nose.

"Holy shit," a deep voice said from the end of the corridor. "Don't tell me Zak conned you into taking that monster."

"Fuck off, Van," Zak said good-naturedly. "She's not a monster."

Donovan Scott approached with his border collie, Spirit, trailing behind him, happily squeaking a ball in her mouth. A former Marine turned dog trainer, Donovan was a big man covered from the neck down in tattoos. A rope of scar tissue cut across his temple, giving him a menacing appearance, and he had the kind of growly voice that made you think twice about crossing him. He was an intimidating guy—at least until you got to know him and discovered he was putty in his dog's paws and crazy in love with his pregnant wife.

"Don't mind him," Zak said. "Van's just bitter because Rebel is better looking than him."

Donovan gave a feral smile. "But at least I got the charm."

"Is that what they call it? I thought the word was 'ugly.'"

"Shut it, Pogo, or I'll use your leg for firewood."

"It's metal, dumbass."

Donovan grinned and turned toward Connelly. "So, you're gonna take the infamous Rebel, huh?"

Connelly looked down at the dog in question, who had moved on from his hand to snuffle at his jacket pocket. "She's for Veronica."

Donovan's smile faded, and he shot a startled look at Zak. "Anna's gonna kill you."

"I know," Zak said, without much concern.

"Uh..." Connelly waved a hand to get their attention. "How exactly is Rebel infamous?"

"She... has a sense of adventure," Zak said.

Donovan scoffed. "Adventure? You mean chaos. Last week, Rebel got into our supply closet and decided to redecorate the SAR office with toilet paper. It was like a snowstorm in there, except the snow was two-ply and came from a roll."

Zak shrugged. "So she has an artistic side. Conn can appreciate that, right?"

Connelly looked from the two of them down to the dog and back. "Uh…"

"Man, Zak. Are you sure about this?" Donovan asked. "I mean, Veronica is—"

"Have I ever been wrong about a human-dog pairing before?" Zak interrupted and stared pointedly down at the border collie at Donovan's side. "You weren't sure about Spirit at one time, and look how that turned out."

Donovan held up his hands in surrender. "Point taken. I just don't want to see our girl get hurt."

"Neither do I, which is why Rebel is perfect for her."

As the two continued to bicker, Connelly knelt down and stared at the dog in question. Veronica needed something or someone to help her break free from the prison of her fears, but was Rebel the right choice? She seemed strong, resilient, and full of spirit, but there was also an unpredictable streak in her that worried him.

As if sensing his uncertainty, Rebel turned her intense gaze toward him. Her eyes bore into his soul, searching for something he didn't know. He swallowed hard and reached out to scratch behind her ears. Rebel leaned into his touch and her leg started thumping the floor. It melted his heart.

"Okay, I trust your judgment," he finally said and stood. "If you believe Rebel is the right fit for Vee, then I'll take her."

Zak clapped him on the back. "You won't regret it."

"But Zak will when his wife finds out," Donovan said.

Connelly frowned. "Is this going to be a problem for you? I don't want to cause a fight."

"Nah," Zak said with a dismissive wave of his hand. "Don't worry about it. Anna's just protective of her people —she's a lot like her pain-in-the-ass brother that way—and as far as she's concerned, Veronica is family. She's worried, which means she's overthinking it. She'll drive herself nuts going through our files, trying to find the perfect dog, which is ridiculous because..." He motioned to Rebel. "The perfect dog is right here. Once she's done being mad, she'll realize that I was right." He smirked. "And then I'll get laid."

"You're a twisted dude," Donovan said with a shake of the head and walked away.

"A twisted dude who is about to get awesome make-up sex." Zak grinned, but once the door shut behind Donovan, he turned back to Connelly and got serious. "In all seriousness, we just want the best for Veronica. She's one of us."

Connelly appreciated the simplicity of that statement and the loyalty and support of this tight-knit group. They were a chosen family, bound together by trauma and love for the dogs they trained. And now, he was becoming a part of that family, too. "Thank you. Vee's lucky to have you all, even if she doesn't realize it."

"She'll come back to us," Zak said without a shred of doubt. "And when she does, we'll be waiting with open arms. Now let's get you and Rebel on the road." He pulled a leash from a line of hooks on the wall and handed it over with a mischievous sparkle in his dark eyes. "Word of warning, keep her on the leash at all times. Rebel has a bad habit of running off."

A cold, misty rain started on the drive back to Veronica's.

Connelly's heart thudded as he stood, rain-soaked, on her porch with Rebel's leash clutched tightly in his hand. The Doberman stood beside him, her muscular frame tense, ears pricked up at attention.

"Here goes nothing," he told the dog and knocked on the door.

"Go away, Conn." Her voice barely reached him through the thick wood, brittle and unwelcoming. "I don't want to see you."

"Please, just hear me out. Just for a minute."

As the door remained shut, he sighed and sat down. Rebel stared at the door a moment longer, then sat down beside him.

"I'm sorry."

No answer. Her stubborn silence only fueled his determination.

"This is Rebel," he said and stroked the dog's head. "She had a rough start. She was abandoned, left to fend for herself until Redwood Coast Rescue found her. They took her in and trained her as a protection K9. I think she'd be good for you. Help you feel more secure."

He paused, listening intently for any sign that Veronica was hearing him, but only silence responded. Drawing in a deep breath, he pressed on.

"Your friends at Redwood Coast Rescue... they miss you, Vee. And there's this new therapist, Rylan Cross, who started working with them recently. He's an ex-SEAL, lost his arm during his last mission. He knows what it's like to face darkness and come out the other side. Maybe better than anyone else. I believe he could help you, too."

Still no response.

Was she even still there?

Connelly leaned his head against the door. "You don't have to face your fears alone, Veronica. Let us in. Let us help you."

Silence stretched on, punctuated only by Rebel's questioning whine and the soft rustling of rain on leaves.

"Remember when we were kids, Vee?"

No answer.

"When we would ride our bikes so fast down the hills in the city, it felt like we could just take off and fly any second. I'd be scared, and you'd look back at me, give me that reckless grin of yours, and say, 'Conn, let's touch the sky.' And some days —on those bikes, with the city blurring by—I really believed we could. You were always the brave one of the two of us. The one who'd charge headfirst into the unknown, daring me to follow. And I did every time because when you're with someone as fearless as you, it's hard not to catch some of that courage."

Was that a sob? Or was he hearing things?

"You were always my protector," he continued. "Those bullies didn't stand a chance against you. I was so small and scrawny back then, but you... you were—" His voice broke, and he cleared his throat. "You are my hero, Veronica."

More silence, heavy and suffocating.

He paused and wiped away a stray droplet that had slid down his cheek, whether from the rain or his own eyes, he couldn't tell. "Let me be your protector now."

Then, finally, barely audible, came a choked response: "Conn, I can't... I can't do this. Please leave. Please."

Fuck. He was making her cry. That was the last thing he wanted to do, and he pushed to his feet.

"All right," he said after a moment. "I'll leave... but so you know, Rebel will stay here for a while. She could use a friend, too."

He glanced down at Rebel. Her head was cocked in question. "I'll be back, girl." Unclipping the leash from her collar, he gave the dog an affectionate pat on the head and ruffled her ears. "Stay."

He walked into the rain without looking back.

But a second later, as he opened his car door, he heard the scrambling of paws on the driveway behind him. He turned and spotted Rebel racing toward him, her tongue out in a happy grin.

Okay. She didn't understand "stay." Good to know.

And, shit. Hadn't Zak warned she liked to run off? He probably shouldn't have expected her to just sit on the porch in an unfamiliar place.

He sighed and clipped her leash back on, then opened the back door of his car to let her in. "Sorry, girl. I'm new to dog ownership. I guess we both have things to work on."

He glanced back at Veronica's house in time to catch her staring out at them with big, haunted eyes from behind the door. The moment she realized he was watching, she slammed the door shut. He was too far away to hear all of those locks clicking, but his imagination filled in the sound with finality. He sighed again and dragged a hand over his face, wiping away the rain.

This was going to be harder than he thought.

chapter
six

HE WAS BACK.

Veronica scowled out the window as Connelly and the massive dog appeared on the path. The Doberman trotted a few paces ahead of him with a stick—no, that was a small tree with the root ball still attached—in her mouth. She looked pleased with herself.

Conn had a leather laptop bag slung over one shoulder and a thermos in his hand. He looked tired. His dark hair was messy, like he'd spent the entire night dragging his hands through it. She could picture him at his computer, frustrated as he struggled to corral the people and images in his head into a story.

How many times had she seen him like that over the years? Countless.

It was the image that always came to mind when she thought of Connelly Davis.

The pang of nostalgia was as sharp as a knife blade. They had been so close once...

But that was before.

Before the assault that had left her broken and afraid.

Before she had shut herself in this house and pushed everyone away.

Before everything changed.

As he drew closer, her heart started galloping in her chest. She wasn't sure if it was because of her anxiety or the way he looked at her with those dark, intense eyes. He had always been able to see right through her, even when she didn't want him to.

He looked so different from the boy she used to know. As a kid, he's been smaller than other kids, scrawny and a little bit nerdy, with his nose always stuck in a book. He'd been bullied mercilessly until puberty hit. Suddenly, he was taller and more muscular than any of the other boys in their class, and he dropped one of his bullies to the ground without breaking a sweat. After that, the guys respected him. The girls flocked to him. And why not? He was handsome and brilliant and, most of all, kind. The whole package. Of course they had adored him. Of course *she* had adored him...

Right up until he stabbed her in the back.

Why the hell was he here?

She didn't want him here.

She didn't want the memories.

Veronica took a deep breath and willed herself to open the door and tell him off. It shouldn't be hard. She just had to walk a few steps, release the locks, grab the knob, and pull.

But if she opened that door, he would come in. He wouldn't give her a choice. And she couldn't let him invade her safe haven. It wouldn't be safe anymore.

She stayed in the window, watching as Conn tossed the stick for the Doberman. He grinned as the dog made a mad dash for it, then turned and walked up the front steps of her porch.

He knocked.

She didn't move.

"Vee?"

She couldn't move.

His heavy sigh carried through the door. "Fine."

She heard him move away, but her exhale of relief caught in her throat when the old rocker on the porch groaned. She looked out the window again. Connelly sat in the rocker and pulled his laptop from his backpack.

He wasn't going anywhere.

After a few more throws of the stick, the dog settled down at his feet, gnawing on her prize. Connelly scratched behind her floppy ear, a small smile crossing his face. He looked so content, so at ease, like this was right where he was meant to be.

How was he able to just sit there, so comfortable in his own skin? Meanwhile, she was trapped inside. Her own mind was a prison.

What was he doing here anyway? Did he think he could magically fix her? Did her father think that too?

She watched as Connelly opened his laptop and began typing.

What was he writing about this time? It was always something macabre with him.

Was he writing about her again? She couldn't stand the thought of it. The last thing she needed was for her trauma to be dissected in another one of his horror stories.

But as she watched, she saw him lean back in the chair and run his hands through his hair. He looked up at the sky, exhaustion and frustration etched on his face. Suddenly, he looked vulnerable, like he needed someone to lean on.

He glanced up, and they made eye contact through the window. She quickly glanced away, feeling exposed and somehow also like a voyeur.

Was he going to sit there all day?

When she worked up the nerve to peek out the window again, she found him typing.

Dammit.

She'd just have to ignore him... which was easier said than done. She tried to keep herself busy. She cleaned even though nothing needed cleaning. She tried to watch TV, but she'd already watched everything she was interested in. She tried to read, and that worked for a little while, but she was still too aware of Connelly's presence on her porch, even when she couldn't hear the old rocker creaking. She closed the book—a highly anticipated romantic comedy sequel—and set it back on the shelf. Her fingers traced over the book spines and stopped at the empty spot where his newest release should have been.

Had she not put it back?

She glanced around, scanning the tables in the room. Nothing. She looked under blankets and pillows but came up empty-handed.

What the hell had she done with it?

She shook her head. It didn't matter. It'd turn up, and she had another copy that Dad had sent her. She found that copy tucked away in a drawer, still in the envelope it had arrived in with Dad's straight-forward handwritten post-it note still stuck to the cover.

Read this, Vee.

She had not read it. She refused to read it, but curiosity pulled at her. She ran her hand over the creepy cover.

The Shadows Within by Connelly Davis.

She had all of Conn's books.

Her favorite was still his first, *Dreadwood Manor,* written when they were just kids. She remembered all the late nights they'd spent on the phone as he talked through his plot problems. All the junk food-fueled critiquing sessions. She'd been so proud of him when he got it published before their freshman year of college was over. He'd dedicated that book to her, calling her his rock and his muse.

He'd also dedicated *Shadows* to her. She was still his muse but for a much different reason.

She opened the book and read the first page.

The moon, a pale and distant voyeur, watched as shadows birthed themselves from the dark tapestry of night in Ravenshade. In this quiet hamlet, where secrets clung to the air with the acrid scent of impending decay, and fears slumbered in every dim-lit corner, Vanessa Vale felt the subtle shift in the night as reality cracked open. She looked up from her typewriter and watched the long, wavering shadows cast by her desk lamp dance across the cluttered room. A half-empty glass of bourbon stood sentinel beside her, its amber contents a feeble attempt to drown out the haunting whispers that lingered in her mind.

She had always been a creature of the night. As a writer, she was most productive when the world was asleep, and the only sounds that filled the air were the creaks of her old house and the clack of her ancient typewriter.

Yet, tonight was different.

Tonight, the four walls that usually comforted her seemed to be closing in, suffocating her.

Tonight, the shadows were alive.

Veronica snapped the book shut and shoved it onto the shelf with the others.

The bastard.

She would never forgive him for writing her into his book like that. Never. No matter how long he sat on her porch.

But as the hours passed, she kept drifting over to the window to watch him. He got up occasionally to stretch and play with the dog, and once, she caught him unzipping near a tree. She glanced away fast and told herself she wouldn't look out the window again.

When the sun began to set, she heard the rocker creak and jumped up from her chair, all but running over to the window. She watched as Conn packed up his laptop and dumped the dregs of his coffee out of his thermos.

He was leaving!

Finally.

But instead of leaving, he walked to the window and tapped on the glass.

She hesitated for a moment before unlocking the window and pushing it open a crack. "What?"

"Hey," he said like she hadn't just snapped at him. "I'm hungry."

"I'm not feeding you."

"Okay." He seemed unperturbed by that fact. "Do you want to go get food in town?"

"No." Veronica looked at the Doberman sitting patiently beside him. Rebel's gaze was sharp and direct and intimidating as hell. "And I'm still not taking the dog, so don't even ask."

"That's fine. I've decided you can't have her. She's my new writing partner."

"Writing partner?"

Conn grinned, showing off those deep dimples under the layer of scruff covering his jaw. "Hell, yeah. She's great at brainstorming."

Veronica scowled. She didn't want to be reminded of those appealing dimples. "Just go away and leave me alone."

He chuckled as he swung his bag over his shoulder. "Don't

worry, I'll be back tomorrow. And maybe then you'll have dinner with me."

She scoffed. "In your dreams, Conn."

He flashed another quick grin at her before jogging down the steps and disappearing into the gathering darkness with Rebel galloping ahead on the path.

Veronica watched him go until she saw a light flick on through the trees. Ugh. Why did he have to rent the old Hendricks place? There were tons of other rental properties in the area that weren't right next door to hers.

And why did she suddenly feel empty with him gone?

She wasn't about to analyze that, but she couldn't deny that there was something about Conn that drew her to him. Maybe it was his easy confidence or the way his eyes sparkled when he talked about writing. She always loved when she saw glimpses of that nerdy boy he used to be.

No.

Wait.

Not love.

Not for Connelly.

Not anymore.

The night stretched out before her like a vast, dark ocean. She took a deep breath and stood up, the familiar weight of the fear settling in her chest. She tried to ignore it, to push it away, but it was like a monster that refused to be silenced.

She would go to the kitchen and pour—

No, she wouldn't think of the fresh bottle of wine that arrived with the groceries Dad had sent. She'd make coffee. She didn't need alcohol to survive the night. She wasn't her mother.

As she walked toward the kitchen, a framed picture on the bookshelf caught her attention. Dad had taken it right after she and Connelly graduated from college and ROTC as newly minted second lieutenants. Conn had been on his way to

Special Tactics Officer Assessment and Selection, taking the next step to becoming a Combat Rescue Officer, and she had just received her first seat assignment on an aircraft.

They were both grinning.

Both so young.

So naive.

The picture was a reminder of everything she had lost, of everything that had been taken away from her.

She turned it facedown and continued on into the kitchen.

Forget coffee.

Wine it was.

That night, asleep in a hazy cloud of alcohol, Veronica dreamed of shadows. They swirled around her, taunting her. She couldn't escape them, no matter how hard she tried. She was trapped in the darkness, and they were closing in, long, icy fingers wrapping around her...

She woke up, gasping for air, covered in sweat. Her heart raced as panic smothered her.

She couldn't breathe.

She reached for her phone and dialed Conn's number before she could think better of it.

"Hello?" he answered, his voice rough with sleep.

Oh, God. What was she doing?

"Vee?"

She hung up and tried to catch her breath. She didn't need him. He wasn't the person she called anymore. He could never be that person again.

She sat up in bed and rubbed her eyes wearily. It was still dark, and the only sound was the gentle rustling of the trees outside her window. She took a deep breath and tried to calm herself down.

She was fine.

She was safe.

That was when she heard it. A faint scratching noise, coming from outside.

Just an animal.

Or a tree branch brushing against the house.

Deep down she knew better.

Someone was out there.

chapter
seven

THE SHRILL RING of a cell phone shattered the silence in the dimly lit cabin. Connelly blinked and came back to the real world. After tossing and turning in bed for an hour, he'd finally made himself a pot of coffee, shuffled out to the computer on the desk in the living room, and, for the first time in months, the words flowed. He'd been lost in the world of his creation, and now reality felt disjointed, dizzy.

The phone rang.

He rubbed his eyes and glanced at the clock in the corner of his computer screen: 2:47 a.m. A call at this hour could only mean trouble.

"Hello?" he answered hesitantly, his voice hoarse from disuse.

A choked sob echoed through the line, and his heart thumped hard against his ribcage. He straightened away from the desk, his back muscles protesting. He'd been hunched over the keyboard for too long.

He rubbed at the pain in his neck and said into the phone, "Vee?"

Dead air answered.

"Veronica?"

No response. He checked the screen. She'd hung up. He tried to call back but got dumped right into voicemail.

"Fuck."

Rebel raised her head from the bed she'd made out of the couch cushions and stared at him with rust-colored eyes that missed nothing.

He exhaled hard and dragged his hands through his hair before shutting the laptop. "We need to go for a walk."

Rebel jumped up, and her tail started a slow wag.

"Yeah, figured you'd like that. Let's go check on Vee." He grabbed a flashlight and his coat on the way out the door. It may be early summer, but Northern California didn't know that. Fog had rolled in off the ocean and twisted around the trees, dampening all sound and leaving a wet chill in the air.

He zipped up his coat and headed out into the night, Rebel bounding ahead of him in the bright white beam of the flashlight.

His phone rang again as they stepped into the woods, and he snapped it up, expecting it to be Veronica.

"Hello?"

"Hey, baby," a familiar voice purred into his ear. "Miss me?"

He stopped walking, and his heart dropped into a freefall, bottoming out somewhere near his knees. It had been months since he'd heard that voice, but he'd know it anywhere.

"Sara?" he breathed.

"That's right, sweetie. Long time no see."

Rebel whined at his feet, sensing his distress. He patted her head reassuringly and tried to keep his voice steady.

"What do you want?"

"I just got into town, and I want to see you."

Connelly drew the phone away from his ear and cursed long and hard. Then he exhaled to calm himself and raised the phone again. "I'm not in Seattle. And if you contact me again, I will call the police and enforce the restraining order."

Sara chuckled on the other end of the line, the sound sending shivers down Connelly's spine. "Oh, come on, baby. You know you want to see me, too."

"I don't want anything to do with you."

Rebel growled low in her throat, her protective instincts kicking in.

Sara's voice turned cold. "You'll regret turning me away, Connelly."

He hung up before she could say anything more, his hand shaking with anger and fear. He thought he'd left her behind when he moved to California, but apparently, she had other plans. Plans that involved stalking him and trying to wiggle her way back into his life.

Goddammit.

Rebel leaned against his leg. He scratched her behind the ear, taking comfort in her warm, steady presence.

"We have to be careful, girl," he murmured. "Sara's not someone we want to mess with."

They continued down the path, Connelly keeping a tight grip on the flashlight as they navigated the foggy darkness. He couldn't shake the feeling that they were being watched, that Sara was lurking somewhere in the shadows, waiting to pounce.

Sara fucking Parker. He hated that she could rattle his usually unflappable nerves.

He picked up his pace and breathed a sigh of relief when Veronica's cabin appeared from the mist. The cabin was dark except for a faint glow coming from one of the windows. He made his way to the front door and knocked softly.

"Vee?"

There was no response, so he tried again, this time

knocking a bit louder. Still nothing. He tried the front door and found it unlocked.

This wasn't right.

She wouldn't leave the door unlocked.

He should call the sheriff.

But what if she was in immediate danger? It would take too much time for Ash or one of his deputies to get here.

He could call Zak. Redwood Coast Rescue was only a few miles away...

But Zak was probably in bed. It would take time for him to get here, too.

Time Veronica might not have.

Mind made up, Connelly peeked inside and shined the light around. The front door led into an open-concept living room and kitchen. He could see straight to the back of the cabin, through the sliding glass doors to the porch and the cliff beyond. It was all empty.

He stepped inside, Rebel following him silently. The dog was suspicious but calm, and he took comfort in that. If someone were hiding in here with ill intent, Rebel would know.

He opened the first door he came to. Bathroom. He shone the flashlight inside but saw nothing out of the ordinary. Just a generic bathroom that could be found in any vacation rental in the country. Toilet, sink, shower stall. All of it was in plain, bland colors that did not suit Veronica.

He kept moving.

The second door was open a crack, and a sliver of light cut across the floor from inside. He knocked but received no response. He looked at the dog in a silent question. She sat down and gave a gentle woof, and he decided to take it as encouragement. He opened the door.

Veronica was huddled under the covers, her eyes wide and

unseeing. Her breathing was shallow and rapid like she couldn't catch her breath after a hard run.

She was in the middle of a panic attack.

Connelly's heart clenched at the sight of his friend in such distress. He approached the bed slowly, his footsteps creaking on the old wood floor, and knelt beside her.

"Vee? It's me, Connelly. You're having a panic attack. It's terrifying, but you're okay."

Veronica didn't seem to hear him. She was lost in her own private nightmare, her body tensed and trembling.

He reached out and brushed a dark lock of hair away from her forehead. Her skin was clammy to the touch, and he could feel her pulse racing beneath his fingertips. "You got this. You just need to breathe through it. Slowly, deeply. In through your nose and out through your mouth."

He demonstrated, and after a few moments, her breathing slowed. Rebel nuzzled between them and pressed her long nose to Veronica's tear-stained cheek.

Connelly stayed right there, crouched beside the bed for what felt like hours, though it was probably only a few minutes. He didn't rush her, didn't try to push her to talk or move. He knew from experience that panic attacks didn't work that way. They had their own timeline, their own rhythm. All he could do was be there for her, a steady presence in the middle of a storm.

Eventually, Veronica's breathing evened out, and she relaxed back into the pillows. She didn't open her eyes, but her grip on the covers loosened. Connelly took that as a good sign.

"There you go. You did it," he said softly. "You made it through."

She didn't respond, but her breathing remained steady.

Connelly stood up, stretching his cramped muscles. Rebel jumped up on the bed and cuddled next to Veronica.

"I'll give you some space," he said. "I'll be right outside the door when you're ready."

He left the door open a crack and made his way to the kitchen to put a kettle on for tea. Veronica had always preferred tea to coffee, and he wasn't surprised to see a wide selection of flavors in the pantry. He was a coffee guy himself. He loved the stuff, loved the bitterness and the buzz of an espresso shot. But the last thing Veronica needed right now was coffee, so he chose a honey lavender tea, mainly because it was labeled "Calm" in a fancy, flowing script.

As he waited for the water to boil, he paced around the kitchen, his thoughts bouncing between anger at Sara and worry for Veronica.

He couldn't shake the feeling that something was off.

It wasn't just Veronica's panic attack, although that was concerning enough. No, it was something deeper, something darker. He couldn't put his finger on it, but he knew it was there, lurking just beneath the surface.

He leaned against the counter and closed his eyes, taking a deep breath. Maybe he was just tired. Maybe he was letting his imagination run wild.

The kettle whistled, interrupting his thoughts. He opened the paper wrapping on the tea bag and put it in a mug, then added the hot water and a spoonful of honey. He stirred it for longer than necessary, trying to calm himself down before he carried the mug back to the bedroom.

Veronica was still lying there, her eyes closed. Rebel had her head on the pillow next to her and was gently licking her hand.

Zak was right. Rebel *was* the perfect dog for Veronica.

He approached the bed slowly so as not to startle her and sat down next to her, holding out the mug.

"Here you go. Some tea to help you relax."

Veronica's eyes fluttered open, and she looked up at him,

her gaze unfocused and distant. He saw the fear in her eyes, the pain of reliving whatever memories had triggered her panic attack.

"Thanks," she whispered, her hands shaking slightly as she wrapped them around the mug. She took a sip and closed her eyes again, savoring the warmth and sweetness of the tea. She wasn't relaxed, but nor was she as tense as she had been when he walked in.

He wanted to reach out and wrap her in a hug, to offer her some form of comfort. But he knew that physical touch wasn't always comforting for someone dealing with trauma, so he remained where he was.

After a few minutes, Veronica spoke again, her voice barely above a whisper. "Why are you here, Connelly?"

He hesitated, not sure how to answer. "I already told you why. Your dad asked me to come. He's worried about you."

Veronica scoffed, her grip on the mug tightening. "My dad. He just wants me to be 'fixed' so he can pretend like nothing ever happened."

Connelly winced at the bitterness in her voice. He knew there was some truth to her words, but he also knew that her father loved her. Arthur just hadn't always been the greatest at showing it when she was younger.

"He loves you," Connelly said.

Veronica shook her head, her hair falling in front of her face. "He loves the idea of me. The perfect daughter, the successful Air Force pilot. But he doesn't know me, not really."

Because you won't let anybody close enough to know you.

But he didn't say that out loud. "Arthur just wants you to be happy. And so do I."

She looked up at him, her eyes searching his face. "Why, though? Why do you care so much?"

Connelly took a deep breath, knowing that this was the

moment of truth. He could tell her the half-truth, the safe answer, or he could tell her the whole truth. The ugly, messy truth that had been simmering inside him for years.

He chose the half-truth. She wasn't ready for the whole one yet.

"Because you're my best friend, Vee. You always have been. " Emotion roughened his voice. "And because...because I feel responsible for what happened to you. I never should have left you at that party—"

"No." Veronica shook her head and set the mug down on the nightstand, her hands trembling. "It doesn't matter. You shouldn't be here. I don't need you or anyone else to help me. I can take care of myself."

Yeah, right. After seeing firsthand how debilitating her panic attacks could be, how they left her shaking and gasping for air, he very much doubted that. He couldn't imagine how she managed to get through them on her own. "But that's the thing. You don't need to. You have friends and family and... me. Please, let me help."

Veronica looked at him, really looked at him for the first time since he arrived. He saw the hesitation in her eyes, the fear mixed with longing. "I don't know if I can be helped, Conn. I don't know if I can ever leave this place."

He wanted to reach out and take her hand. Instead, he folded his into his pockets. "I'm not asking you to leave. You don't have to unless you want to. I'm asking you to let me in."

"You're already in."

"I don't mean your bedroom, Vee," he said dryly.

She scowled, but then her eyes widened in shock. "Wait. How did you get in? Did you break a window?"

"The door was unlocked and open."

Her gaze shot to the bedroom door, and her cheeks drained of color. "I didn't leave it unlocked. I never leave it unlocked."

He'd known as much. "What set off your panic attack?"

She hesitated, her gaze still fastened on the bedroom door as if she expected someone to else to walk through it at any moment. "I had a nightmare, and then... when I woke up, I just sensed someone watching me."

Which jibed with the crawling sensation on the back of his neck. He wasn't a paranoid man by nature, but ever since walking into Veronica's house, he hadn't been able to shake the sensation of eyes on him.

"Okay," he said finally. "I'll sleep on the couch."

"No!" She looked on the verge of panic again.

"If you think I'm leaving you alone, you're fucking wrong."

"I... I'm not alone." She set her hand on the dog. "Rebel can stay with me. You said she's a protection K9. She can keep me safe."

"Veronica—"

"I don't want you here." Her voice came out high and thin as tears brimmed in her eyes.

Connelly's heart sank, but he knew better than to push her. He stood up, his hands still in his pockets, and looked down at her. "Okay. I'll leave, but I'll be back tomorrow. And the day after that. And the day after that. I won't leave you alone, Vee. Not until you let me in."

Veronica didn't say anything, but the tears spilled over, and it broke his heart. He leaned down and kissed her forehead, ignoring her flinch. Then he turned on his heel and left the bedroom, closing the door behind him.

He walked through the living room, and unease settled in the pit of his stomach. Something wasn't right. He didn't know what it was, but he knew that he couldn't leave Veronica alone like this.

Fuck.

He grabbed a blanket from the back of the couch,

wrapped it around his shoulders, and went out onto the porch, making sure the door was firmly locked behind him. He sat down, back pressed to the door, and tugged the blanket tighter around his shoulders.

This was going to be a very uncomfortable night. He should've brought his laptop, but since he didn't, he scanned the dark woods.

Nothing moved.

There were no weird noises.

Nothing was out of place.

And still...

If he'd learned one thing in the military, it was to trust his instincts. And his instincts screamed that someone was out there in those huge, ancient trees, watching.

He flipped them off.

chapter
eight

VERONICA TOUCHED her forehead and swore she could still feel the warm, soft press of Connelly's lips like a brand.

Why the hell had he done that?

She knew Connelly cared about her, but she couldn't understand why he had to make things so complicated. She was damaged, broken beyond repair. She didn't want him to waste his time on her. She was nothing but a burden, a reminder of his mistakes.

The tears kept flowing, and she hugged Rebel closer, burying her face in the dog's fur. She had to get a grip. She couldn't keep falling apart like this. She had to be strong. She had to show Connelly that she didn't need him or anyone else. She was in control, damn it.

But the darkness kept creeping in, suffocating her, and she couldn't shake the feeling that someone was watching her. She knew it was irrational, but she couldn't help it. She'd always been afraid of the dark, even as a grown woman. And now, after what had happened to her, the darkness felt like a living, breathing thing waiting to swallow her whole.

She took a deep breath and forced herself to focus on something else. She tried to remember the dream that had triggered her panic attack, but it had already slipped away like smoke. All she could remember was the sensation of falling, over and over again, with no end in sight.

Rebel whimpered and licked her face, and Veronica realized that she was crying again. She wiped her eyes and took another deep breath. She had to calm down. She had to be strong.

She didn't know how, but she must have fallen asleep because the next time she opened her eyes, sunlight streamed in through her window.

Rebel licked her face and whimpered.

Her eyes popped open wide.

Oh, shit.

She'd been so desperate to get rid of Connelly last night she hadn't thought through this whole keeping-the-dog thing.

Rebel needed to go outside.

And she couldn't go outside.

She looked at the dog, who was staring at her with big, pleading eyes the color of pennies.

"Okay, okay," she muttered, pushing herself up from the bed. "I'll figure something out."

She hesitated at the door to her bedroom, her hand hovering over the handle. She could feel the panic rising again, threatening to choke her. But then she thought of Rebel, and her resolve hardened. She couldn't let the dog suffer because of her fears.

Taking a deep breath, she opened the door and stepped out into the living room. It was quiet, almost too quiet.

She crossed to the front door, and Rebel bounded outside almost before she had it completely open.

Veronica followed, her heart in her throat. Just one step out the door. It was all she could manage. She felt exposed and vulnerable. She dropped her gaze to the porch and frowned at the blanket folded there. She bent over to pick it up and found a note scrawled on the back of a crumpled receipt in Connelly's flowing handwriting.

I'll be back tonight. Keep Rebel close. She'll protect you.

Had he slept out here on the porch all night?

She didn't get the chance to contemplate that because Rebel ran to the edge of the yard, sniffing at the grass along the trees.

"Stay here, please." Her voice was almost swallowed by the sharp wind blowing in off the ocean.

And the dog didn't listen.

Rebel lifted her head, and Veronica swore she grinned before bounding off into the woods.

"No!" She was halfway down the front porch steps before she realized it. Fear froze her in place. "Oh, shit. Oh, shit. Oh, shit."

She couldn't chase after the dog, but she couldn't let her run off into the woods. What if something happened to her? What if she got lost?

Taking a deep breath, she stepped off the porch and into the yard. Her legs shook. She took another step and then another.

And then she couldn't go any farther. She physically could not lift her foot to take another step. She cupped her hands around her mouth.

"Rebel!"

She heard a crash in the woods, but the dog didn't come back.

Panic began to claw at her throat. She called out again, louder this time, but there was no response. The darkness was closing in, threatening to strangle her.

She backtracked to the house. The moment she stepped inside, her lungs opened up, and she drew in a sharp breath.

Veronica slammed the door shut, leaning against it to

catch her breath. She was trembling all over, and her heart was pounding like a jackhammer in her chest.

Rebel was out there, alone and vulnerable, and it was all her fault.

Tears streamed down her face as she tried to come up with a plan. She couldn't go out there, not alone. But she couldn't just sit here and do nothing. She had to do something.

She needed Connelly.

Veronica hesitated for a moment, then went to her bedroom and grabbed her phone off the nightstand. She dialed Connelly's number, her palms sweating as she waited for him to answer.

"Hey, Vee," he said, his voice warm and comforting. "Sorry I had to take off. I had a Zoom meeting with my agent and needed Wi-Fi. How are you feeling? Did you sleep okay?"

"Rebel's gone," she blurted before she could second guess her decision to call him. "I-I don't know where she went. I let her out to pee and she ran off into the woods and—and I can't go after her. Can you please come back and help me find her?"

"I'm in town, but I'm leaving right now. I'll be there in fifteen minutes."

That was the thing about Connelly. He'd always drop everything and race to her side the moment she asked for help. She could always count on him. She'd forgotten that about him.

Veronica hung up and sank down onto the edge of her bed and caught sight of her reflection in the old bureau that had come with the house. Her eyes were too wide, showing too much white. Dark hair hung in limp, greasy strands over her shoulders. Cheekbones too sharp, cheeks too hollow in her pale face.

God, who was that woman? Too weak, too scared to even properly take care of a dog. She didn't recognize herself anymore and hated it.

And then she heard a knock at the door.

She froze. No way it was Connelly already. It had only been a few minutes since they hung up.

Veronica forced herself to stand up. She tiptoed across the living room and peered through the peephole. A man she vaguely recognized stood on the other side, and he had Rebel on a leash. He also had another smaller dog in his arms. A little brown and white dog with long hair and big ears.

Alfie!

And, suddenly, she remembered who this man was—the husband of her former therapist, Dr. Amelia Firestone, who was brutally murdered in her own kitchen a few months ago. Alfie had belonged to Dr. Firestone. A certified therapy dog, he had attended every session and Veronica had loved the comfort he provided. She didn't realize how much she'd missed him until she saw those fluffy ears.

She opened the door a crack. "Hi, Mr. Firestone."

"Please, call me Hank." His smile was gentle and more than a little sad. He'd aged considerably since his wife's murder. His salt and pepper hair had gone completely gray, and the lines fanning out from his eyes were more pronounced.

He patted Rebel's muscular side. "I found this pretty girl down the road. Is she yours?"

"No. Uh, she belongs to a friend. I was just... watching her for him, and she got away from me." She opened the door wider to let Rebel inside. The dog had rolled in something nasty during her walkabout, and the noxious smell wafted in behind her.

Veronica gagged and pinched her nose. "Ugh, that's bad."

Hank gave a rusty-sounding laugh. "You might want to give her a bath."

"Thank you for bringing her back."

"No problem." His smile faded. "It's what Amelia would've done."

"I never had the opportunity to tell you how sorry I am for your loss. Dr. Firestone was a good person. She didn't deserve what happened to her."

"And I'm sorry for yours. I know she was as much yours as mine. She cared about you a great deal, Veronica."

A lump rose in her throat. "I miss her."

"Me, too." After a heavy moment, he exhaled hard and straightened his shoulders.

And Veronica thought that was the end of it. He'd say his goodbye and go about his day.

But instead, he pushed Alfie into her arms. "I can't take care of him. It hurts too much. He reminds me every day that she's not here and— I know Amelia would want you to have him."

"Oh." Startled, she nearly fumbled the small dog and pulled him tight to her chest. Alfie licked her face.

She couldn't believe this was happening. She stared down at Alfie, her heart swelling with emotion. It had been so long since she'd held the dog in her arms, and she had forgotten how much comfort he provided.

"Are you sure?" she asked, tears stinging at the corners of her eyes.

Hank nodded. "I'm positive. Amelia loved you. She'd want you to have him."

Veronica nodded, her throat too tight to speak. She hugged Alfie close to her, enjoying his warmth and his soft fur against her skin.

"Thank you." Her voice cracked on the words. "Thank you so much."

Hank's smile was sad but genuine as he passed her a bag full of Alfie's things. "Take care of him, okay? He's a good boy."

"I will. I'll take the best care of him."

Hank hesitated another beat, almost like he wanted to say something more, but then he turned and walked to the cargo van parked in her driveway. It had "Firestone Electric Solutions" painted on the side next to the cartoon of a surprised-looking electrical outlet holding a plug in its gloved hand.

Veronica closed the door and nuzzled Alfie's soft ears. Warmth spread through her chest as he licked her face again. A tiny spark of joy.

Then the smell hit her.

She looked down at Rebel and drew in a fortifying breath. "All right. Bath time."

chapter
nine

AFTER AN EARLY MEETING with his agent, Connelly packed an overnight bag and then ran into town to hopefully find a sleeping bag. If he was going to be sleeping on Veronica's porch for the foreseeable future, he needed something warmer than the thin quilt from her couch. He froze his balls off last night.

He also wanted a gun.

The process of buying one in California was lengthy, and although his military service helped expedite things, he still wouldn't have it in hand for ten days. He should've brought his gun from home, but he hadn't expected to need a weapon.

Veronica's panicked call came as he was checking out at the sporting goods store.

Rebel's gone.

Dammit, he hadn't left Veronica the leash. Zak had warned him, but Rebel had been so good he'd forgotten about her propensity for running away.

He all but threw his money at the cashier and raced out to his car, throwing the sleeping bag into the back seat. He cursed himself during the entire fifteen-minute drive back to her place. He should've expected it. Of course Rebel wouldn't listen to Veronica. She didn't know her, had only met her yesterday. They didn't have any kind of bond.

He pulled into the driveway and jumped out of the car the second it rocked to a stop. He cupped his hands around his mouth and boomed, "Rebel!"

No response.

Fuck.

Maybe she was at his place, waiting for him to return. He hadn't thought to stop there on the way here. He'd check on Veronica, then jog home and see if he could find the dog.

The door was unlocked, which had his stomach twisting up in knots. Veronica said she never forgot to lock the door, and this was the second time he'd found it unlocked in the last twelve hours.

"Vee?"

He heard a noise from the bathroom.

Was that... a struggle?

And he didn't have a fucking gun.

He called on every second of his many hours of training in the dojo, sinking into an offensive stance as he approached the bathroom door. He took a calming breath and pushed it open...

And froze.

Veronica was in the shower, dressed in her old Air Force PT gear, straddling Rebel. They were both covered head to toe in bubbles, and the floor was flooded with water. A tiny brown and white dog with giant ears sat on the toilet lid, watching the chaos unfold with his front paws crossed in a princely way.

And Veronica was laughing.

Veronica.

Was.

Laughing.

Connelly stared in awe. He hadn't seen her laugh in years.

She had always been beautiful, but at that moment, she was radiant. Her laughter echoed off the tiled walls, filling the room with joy. It was like the sun had come out after a brutal storm, and everything was clean and bright. She looked so free, so happy, with the weight of the world lifted from her shoulders.

Christ, he'd missed her.

This version of her.

The Veronica he remembered.

The Veronica he loved.

He wanted to capture this moment forever, to keep it safe in his heart.

Her eyes met his, and although she stopped laughing, her expression was still soft and filled with joy as she gazed at him.

"Hey," she said softly.

"Hey," he replied, his voice hoarse.

"Found Rebel."

"I see that."

Rebel barked, and Veronica turned back to her, kissing the top of her head. She shut off the water and stepped carefully out of the shower stall, reaching for a towel.

Connelly couldn't take his eyes off of her. Her shorts were tiny, cupping the globes of her ass in a way that made his mouth water. The light gray t-shirt was soaked through, making it clear that she wasn't wearing a bra. He could see the outline of her nipples through the fabric, and suddenly, his jeans were uncomfortably tight. He wanted to strip her out of those wet clothes and lick away every drop of water clinging to her skin. He wanted—

Rebel shook, splattering everything with water, and it was all he needed to snap out of it. He dropped his gaze to the tiled floor.

Fuck. What was he thinking? This was Veronica. He'd known her since they were both on training wheels. And he knew what she'd gone through. He shouldn't be thinking about licking her anywhere.

But he was, and that was a problem he needed to deal with before he scared her away.

He cleared his throat and tried to keep his voice light as he said, "And I see you've found another friend."

Veronica finished toweling off Rebel and grabbed a second towel for herself. She used it to dry off her face, then wrapped it around her hair.

"That's Alfie," she said, reaching for the bathrobe hanging on the back of the door.

Connelly fisted his hands at his sides and waited for her to put her robe on. She was moving too damn slowly, and he wasn't going to be able to process anything she said until she was covered. He wanted to touch her, hold her, kiss her. He wanted to pick her up and carry her to the bed so he could kiss every inch of her body. He wanted...

Everything he couldn't have.

Not with her.

Veronica gave him a curious look. "Are you okay?"

"Yep." Jesus, why did his voice sound so strangled? "I'm fine."

"Because you kind of look like you're constipated. Did you..." She glanced back at Alfie, who was still sitting on the toilet. "Need the bathroom?"

He had to get out of this small room. Because under the scent of wet dog, he could smell her, the clean scent of her skin mixed with the fruity aroma of her shampoo. It was driving him insane.

"I'm good," he forced out, stepping back to let Rebel out of the bathroom. "Just relieved you found Rebel."

At last, Veronica wrapped the robe around herself and tied it closed. "I actually didn't find her. Hank Firestone did, and he brought her home. She stunk, so I gave her a bath."

She picked up the small dog from the toilet and nuzzled his big ears. "And he brought me Alfie. This is—" She stopped short, and her smile faded. "Was. This was Dr. Firestone's dog. He's therapy trained and used to attend all of our sessions. Hank can't take care of him—too many bad memories, I guess—and so he thought Dr. Firestone would want me to have him. I wasn't sure at first, but I think I want to keep him. I've always adored him, and he's... good for me, I think."

Connelly stared at her in shock, his lust forgotten. "Vee..."

She tucked a strand of her wet hair behind her ear. "What?"

"I think that's the most you've said to me since I arrived."

"What?" she said again and gave a nervous little laugh. "That's not true."

"You've mostly just told me to go away and leave you alone."

She hugged Alfie closer to her chest. "I'm sorry."

"No, don't apologize. That's not what—"

But she didn't seem to hear him. "I know I've been terrible. To you. To... everyone. But I... I can't leave this house, and everyone keeps trying to force me and—and I can't."

"I know," he said softly. "And I'm not going to push you. I just... I miss you, Vee. I miss the way we used to be. I miss talking to you, laughing with you, just *being* with you. You're my favorite person."

Veronica's eyes welled up with tears, and he wanted to fix it, make everything better for her. He wanted to take her into his arms and never let her go. But he knew he couldn't. Not yet. Maybe not ever.

He cleared his throat again, shifting from foot to foot. "I'll go check on Rebel and make sure she's not destroying your house."

"Okay." Veronica didn't move. She simply stood there,

hugging the small dog, who seemed perfectly content being in her arms.

Connelly didn't want to go, but he had to. He had to get away from her before he did something stupid. Something he wouldn't be able to take back. Something that would terrify her and destroy this fragile truce they seemed to have reached. He couldn't risk it, so he stepped out of the bathroom...

And was almost knocked on his ass by Rebel as she zoomed by. The dog was still soaked, but she was wagging her tail so hard it was a blur of black and tan.

Connelly chuckled as Rebel raced around the house with wild abandon. He followed her into the living room, where she jumped onto the sofa and shook water everywhere. He grabbed a towel from the freshly washed stack waiting on the dining table to be put away and began to dry off the dog. Rebel barked happily, wagging her whole body under the towel and trying to lick his face.

"You're a menace," he said, ruffling the dog's ears.

He glanced up to find Veronica standing in the doorway, watching them. He expected to see her smiling again at the dog's antics, but instead, she looked... sad.

He straightened and tossed the towel over his shoulder. "What's wrong?"

"It's nothing," she said quickly and stepped into the room. "I'm fine."

"Vee." He moved closer, reaching out to take her hand but stopping short of touching her. He didn't want to scare her away. Not when she was finally opening up to him. "Talk to me. Please."

She stared down at his hand, still outstretched toward her. She didn't bridge the distance between them, but she also didn't take a step backward. He counted that as a good sign.

"It's stupid."

"It's not stupid if it's bothering you."

She shook her head. "It's just... I'm jealous of Rebel."

"Jealous of Rebel?" he repeated slowly, not entirely sure he'd heard her right.

She gave a self-deprecating laugh. "She's so carefree. So happy. She doesn't have any worries or fears. I wish I could be like her."

Connelly's heart ached for her. He finally closed the distance between them, but she flinched away from his touch.

He squashed down the surge of sorrow and anger. He couldn't touch her yet, he reminded himself. He had to wait until she was ready. Until she felt safe with him again. He backed up a step. "But you are like her."

Her eyes widened in surprise. "What do you mean?"

"I mean, you're carefree and happy when you allow yourself to be." He motioned to the bathroom. "I just saw it in there. You have that same spark as Rebel deep down inside of you."

She shook her head, obviously unconvinced. "That was just a—"

He didn't let her finish the thought. "Do you know what she went through before she ended up at the rescue? She was abused and abandoned, and she could've just given up, but she didn't. She's a survivor, and look at her."

They both looked at the dog. Rebel was curled up on the couch, her tail wagging lazily as she basked in the sunlight streaming through the window. Despite her troubled past, she exuded a sense of peace and contentment that was contagious.

"Now she's thriving," Connelly finished. "That's why I chose her. To remind you that happiness and freedom are possible even after going through hell."

Tears welled up in her eyes. "I don't think I can do this anymore."

"Do what?" He knew what she meant, but he needed her to say it out loud.

"This," she said, gesturing around her. "Being stuck in this house. Being afraid to leave. Being afraid to live."

She buried her face in Alfie's fur and let out a long, shuddering breath. Then she looked up, and there—*there* was his Veronica. There was the spark of the fierce, determined woman he'd always loved. He reached out again, this time slowly, giving her the choice to accept or reject his touch.

She hesitated for a moment, then tentatively placed her hand in his. "I'm going to leave the house."

His heart soared as he closed his fingers around hers and gave them a gentle squeeze. "Are you sure?"

"It's time."

Leaving the house proved to be easier said than done. It shouldn't have been that difficult. Her mind was made up, and she was determined to conquer her fears.

But when Connelly held open the door, her feet grew roots. Her mouth went desert dry. Her lungs seized up. The thought of being out in the open, vulnerable to the world...

She couldn't do it.

After a long moment, Conn shut the door. His expression was all sympathetic, but she saw the sorrow in his eyes. He was struggling to understand something that she couldn't explain because she didn't understand it herself.

"It's okay," he murmured. "We'll start slow and work our way up."

She hated the tears burning in her eyes. She hated that he was there to see them. "I think you should leave."

He shook his head. "I'm not going anywhere."

But he had to leave. She couldn't breathe with him here.

Connelly moved toward her. His every step felt like an

assault on her senses. She couldn't take it anymore. She needed him to leave, and she needed him to leave now.

"Please, Conn." Her voice broke on his name. "I can't do this right now."

He stopped in his tracks, his eyes searching hers. She couldn't begin to wonder what he was looking for. The strong, independent woman she used to be? Or maybe the girl who used to stand up to his bullies before he grew enough to fight them off himself? Whatever he hoped to see there, he wouldn't find it. She didn't even know who she was anymore.

She watched as his shoulders slumped, and he let out a sigh full of resignation.

"Okay," he said, taking a step back and holding up his hands. "I won't push you."

The relief was palpable, but she felt guilty for not being able to do what she had promised. "I'm sorry."

"No need to apologize." His tone was gentle and understanding, and somehow that made it all worse. "We'll try again tomorrow."

She dreaded it.

"Is there anything you need? Anything I can do?"

She shook her head and turned her back to him, her hands trembling. "Take the dogs with you."

He hesitated. "Both of them?"

"Yes."

He was silent for a beat. Then she heard him move, and the front door clicked shut.

She pressed her hands over her mouth to muffle her sob as a wave of loneliness washed over her.

Alone again.

Alone with her fears and her nightmares.

She tried to push them away, to focus on something else, but it was no use. Her thoughts kept returning to *that* night. The night that had changed everything...

chapter
ten

Six Years Ago

FOR THE FIRST time in months, she and Connelly were in the same city at the same time, and she couldn't wait to see him. It had been too long since their last meeting— a hastily arranged dinner when they crossed paths at an airport between deployments and training missions.

Veronica kept glancing at her watch, counting the minutes until she was free from her duties. The military and its required protocols were usually a source of comfort for her, their predictability and order appealing to the girl who had grown up with a volatile alcoholic mother and a father who loved his daughter but was away from home working more often than not. But today, those routines felt like shackles.

When she was finally free, she dashed out of the hangar at Lackland Air Force Base, the San Antonio sun burning bright overhead, casting long shadows of her and her fellow officers on the tarmac. A fighter jet roared past, jet wash tingling across her skin. She smelled like oil and sweat and jet fuel and desperately needed a shower. By her calculations, she had just enough time to pop by her on-base housing before meeting Connelly at her favorite coffee shop near the River Walk. He was staying at the Hyatt there, free for a whole seventy-two hours before he had to fly back to rejoin his squadron at Hurlburt Field in Florida. She couldn't wait to share with him this vibrant city she'd fallen in love with. It was so different from Seattle's rainy, hilly streets where they'd grown up.

When she entered her apartment, the air conditioning hit her in a frigid blast that sent chills racing over her skin.

Or maybe that was excitement.

She shed off her uniform on the way to the bathroom and hurried through a shower. She slipped into her swimsuit, a pair of jean shorts, and a tank top that showed off her new tattoo—a delicate, colorful pair of wings just above her left shoulder blade. She'd drawn it herself, and her tattoo artist had done a fantastic job translating her vision into ink. She twisted her hair into a clip and dabbed on some light makeup. She glanced at herself in the mirror before she left. She barely recognized the reflection staring back at her— not Lieutenant Martens, Air Force pilot, but a twenty-something woman who was eager, excited, slightly nervous.

She pressed a hand to her belly to steady the flutter there. God, why was she nervous? It was just Connelly.

Finding parking was a bitch, but even that didn't dampen her mood. She navigated through the familiar streets of San Antonio with an unusual spring in her step as the city pulsed with life around her. Music floated from the open doors of bars and restaurants that lined the vibrant downtown streets. People laughed and talked over their margaritas on terraces. Kids splashed in fountains while their parents sat under the shade of trees, watching them with soft smiles...

And there he was.

Still dressed in his battle uniform with his duffle bag slung over one shoulder, he grinned as he watched the kids play through the water.

The flutter became a rabble of butterflies beating their wings inside her.

"Connelly!"

His head turned in her direction. Their eyes met, and his smile widened. That familiar boyish grin that hadn't changed since their childhood made her heart do an extra little ba-bump. He dropped his duffle bag by a nearby bench and strode over to her, opening his arms for a hug.

"God, Vee." His throat rumbled against the top of her head as he held her tight. "It's been way too fucking long."

"I know."

They stayed like that, just holding each other under the hot Texas sun for several long moments. Finally, he set her back down, his hands lingering on her waist for a fraction of a second longer than necessary.

She took a shaky step back and tugged on the lapel of his uniform shirt. "You haven't even changed."

"Just got in." He looped an arm over her shoulders and snagged his bag. "Walk with me to the hotel. And explain to me again what we're doing today...?"

"Floating the river" was a uniquely Texas pastime she loved the moment she learned about it. It consisted of tubes, beer, and a long stretch of lazily moving water. She explained the concept to him as they strolled toward the hotel.

"I figured we'd grab lunch first, then hit the Guadalupe River. I've already got tubes and a cooler ready to go."

Connelly gave her a skeptical look. "So, let me get this straight. We float down a river... and that's it?"

Veronica laughed at his puzzled expression. "You didn't float when you were at Lackland?"

He shook his head. "The pipeline didn't leave much time for me to explore the neighborhood."

He was talking about the pararescue training pipeline, which started with fifteen weeks of intense special warfare training at Lackland and ended over a year later in a pararescue apprenticeship at Kirtland AFB in New Mexico. She'd seen the new wannabe PJs training on base and knew it was hard as hell. She respected him for getting through it and, in her mind, just proved he deserved to relax.

"Well, floating is fun." She nudged him with her shoulder. "Trust me, you'll love it."

At the hotel, Veronica waited as he checked in, shifting nervously from foot to foot. It was still strange to see Connelly here in her new world, which felt so far removed from their shared past. But his grin was infectious, and she found herself returning it with equal measure as she followed him to the elevator, brushing aside her nerves.

"Wow," she said when he opened the door to his room. It wasn't just a regular hotel room— it was a massive suite, bigger than her apartment, with a vast living room, a dining table that sat eight, a fully stocked bar, and a private balcony.

He turned to shut the door behind them, an embarrassed red flush creeping up the back of his neck. "Too much?"

She laughed. "Oh, definitely."

He looked around the suite with a sheepish grin. "Yeah."

"Well," she said after a beat of awkward silence and swept her arm toward the bedroom. "Go get changed! We have a river to float."

"Oh. Right." He disappeared into the room and quickly changed out of his uniform into swim shorts and a T-shirt.

Then they were off again, leaving San Antonio's charm behind for the more rural outskirts where nature reigned supreme. The city's urban sprawl gave way to vast greenery that stretched out on either side of the road, dotted with trees and sprawling ranches. The sun seemed brighter here, hotter, the sky a vivid, cloudless blue.

They grabbed lunch at a roadside barbecue stand and ate

their brisket sandwiches sitting on a worn picnic table as the scent of mesquite smoke filled the hot air around them.

"Are you still writing?" she asked, taking a swig of her Dr. Pepper.

He finished chewing and washed the bite down with his soda. "When I can. Not much time between training and missions."

"This is new." She reached over the table and thumbed away a bit of barbecue sauce on his chin, covering a thin pink scar that looked freshly healed.

His eyes held hers as her fingers traced his scar. "Yeah, that was a close one." He couldn't entirely hide the hint of gravity in his voice, contradicting his grin. "But nothing to worry about. And I saved a life. That's all that matters."

It was late afternoon by the time they got to the river.

Connelly was shocked at seeing the crowd amassed along its banks. Families, college students, elderly couples—it seemed everyone in Texas had come out to enjoy the river. It was a sea of people lounging on tubes, boisterous and sun-soaked, as they drifted down the winding waterway.

"Holy shit. This really is a thing here, isn't it?"

"Welcome back to Texas, Conn," she said with a laugh as she pulled out their tubes from the back of her pickup truck.

The river was a beautiful translucent green, and the late afternoon sun cast golden rays across the water, making it shimmer and sparkle. Veronica slipped in first, her tube fitting comfortably around her as she kicked off from the riverbank. Connelly followed, a bit more ungainly with his longer limbs. His surprised yelp when he hit the cold water made her laugh out loud.

"How the hell is it so cold? It's a hundred degrees out!" He gasped and pulled himself into his tube. "Jesus. I think my balls shriveled up to raisins."

"Wow. You're a big baby for a badass special operator."

"It's. Cold," he repeated, glowering. "And I have delicate bits you don't have."

Yeah, she didn't want to think about those delicate bits.

Once they were both in their tubes, she hooked her feet on the edge of his to keep them together and settled back.

"Okay, what do we do now?" he asked, bemused.

"We just relax and enjoy."

It took a while—longer than she expected—but she finally saw the tension leave his shoulders.

"There you go." She opened the cooler and tossed him a beer. "Now you're getting the hang of it."

She watched him as they floated. Marveled at how the sunlight gilded his dark hair with gold. Admired all that lean, hard muscle under bronzed skin. His dark eyes were softer now, and he closed them as he leaned back against the tube. One arm lazily trailed in the cool water, fingers skimming through it, causing little ripples.

Damn. He looked good.

She'd missed him. Not Lieutenant Davis, combat rescue officer, but Connelly, her childhood best friend whose laugh was as familiar to her as her own heartbeat.

A slow smile spread across his face. "What?" he asked without opening his eyes.

She realized she'd been staring, and her cheeks flushed hot. She told herself it was just the sun. "What?"

"You're staring."

"I'm just... glad you're here."

He cracked an eye open and smiled at her. "Me, too."

They floated for hours, alternating between animated conversation and a comfortable silence as they soaked up the sun. Now and then, they would pass under a bridge or an overpass where groups of people stood waving and cheering at the river-goers.

Connelly eventually surrendered to the lull of the sun and

water. He fell asleep with his head tipped back against the tube, mouth slightly open in a picture of perfect relaxation that made Veronica chuckle as she snapped a photo with her phone.

That was prime blackmail material right there, which she'd definitely be showing to his next girlfriend.

A quick, sharp pain speared through her chest at the thought of him having a girlfriend. She blinked, surprised at the sudden sting of jealousy. Where the hell had that come from? She'd never thought of Connelly as anything more than her friend.

Her best friend.

Nothing more.

So she just had to banish all of these other weird thoughts about him out of her head.

As the sun began to dip below the horizon, painting the sky with hues of orange and purple, Veronica nudged his tube gently with her foot. He woke with a start, tipping himself into the water and splashing her. He lunged for the tube before it could escape, then hung on the side and rubbed a hand over his face to wipe away the water.

"What the...?" he mumbled. "Did I doze off?"

"Yeah, you did." She nodded toward the riverbank, where everyone was pulling their tubes ashore. "And this is our stop."

Disappointment flickered over his face. "Ah, damn. I'm not ready for it to end."

She wasn't either. She hated the thought of parting ways with him and returning to her quiet apartment alone, and she brooded on the thought as they packed the tubes and cooler back into her truck.

"Hey, Martens!"

She looked up at the familiar voice and smiled at the three men approaching them. Captain Blake Edwards had become a good friend since she was stationed at Lackland. He always traveled with his entourage—Lieutenant Mason Foster and Lieutenant Tyler Bennett. She didn't know them as well, but she did consider them friends, too, and thought it unfair that people on base called them The Three Stooges behind their backs.

She waved them over, intent on introducing Connelly. "Hey, guys! Get a float in today?"

"Sure did. Wait. Jesus, is that Draft Dodger Davis?" Mason grinned and reached out to clap his palm to Connelly's. "Hey, man. Haven't seen you in years."

Connelly laughed and greeted each man with more hand slaps. "Edwards, Foster, Bennett. You guys haven't changed a bit."

"I'd say you look like hell, Drafty, but that wouldn't be giving hell enough credit," Tyler said, earning him a playful shove from Connelly.

The men laughed.

Veronica stared at the four of them in surprise. "Wait. You guys know each other?"

"Hell, yeah, we do," Mason said. "We trained with Drafty... when was that? 2016?"

"Sounds about right," Connelly confirmed.

Blake wagged a finger in the air between them. "How do you two know each other?"

"Childhood friends," they said simultaneously, and then, "Jinx," also at the same time, just like when they were kids.

Blake glanced back and forth between them, and his smile dimmed just a little. "Huh. Small fucking world, isn't it?"

"This is awesome," Tyler said, looping an arm around her shoulders and then Connelly's. "Our favorite PJ and our favorite pilot. We're headed back to the city to hit the clubs. You guys wanna join?"

She looked at Connelly. He stared back at her, an unreadable expression on his face. Was he hoping she said yes?

"Okay," she said. "Yeah, sure."

If she wasn't mistaken, disappointment flickered in his gaze before he hid it behind a smile. "Sounds fun."

And it was fun. She danced with Connelly and Blake, with Tyler and Mason, and a few other guys she knew from the base. She drank margaritas and did shots with the guys. By the time the club closed, she was buzzing and giggling, the world spinning a little too much as they stumbled onto the sidewalk.

Connelly's fingers wrapped tightly around hers, grounding her when she felt she could float away. For a moment, just a brief moment, his thumb caressed the back of her hand. The simple contact sent a jolt of something warm up her arm, all the way to her heart. It was so fleeting, almost accidental. Yet, she found herself wishing for more.

"Party at Drafty's!" Blake declared, and the other men let up a cheer.

Connelly dropped her hand and sighed.

At the Hyatt, Blake beelined across Connelly's suite for the bar.

"Putting those royalty checks to use," Blake said, pouring himself a large glass of gin that he topped with only the tiniest bit of tonic. "No way a second lieutenant could afford the presidential suite. Shit, I could barely afford this with my captain's salary."

"I forgot Drafty got them dolla dolla bills." Tyler flopped down on the couch, cracking up like he'd made the funniest joke ever.

Veronica suddenly had a headache. She turned to Connelly, and the movement threw off her balance. He wrapped an arm around her waist to steady her.

"I need to get out of this swimsuit," she muttered.

"Okay. I'll help."

The Three Stooges whooped and cat-called.

Connelly sent them a deadly glare. "Get a grip. She's drunk, assholes."

He was drunk, too. She could tell, but he was handling it better than she was.

In his bedroom, she broke away from him, swaying a bit before she flopped down on the bed. She stripped off her tank top. "Why do they call you Draft Dodger? You weren't alive for the draft."

Connelly pinched the bridge of his nose like he also had a pounding headache. "Blake came up with it when he found out I was a published author. Play on words. You know, because I'm dodging writing my next draft by being in the military."

"Ah," she said without much humor. "Funny."

"Not really." He glared at the door as laughter burst from the other side. "Assholes."

"People on base call them The Three Stooges." She stood and worked her shorts off her hips, struggling when the denim got caught on her sandal. "I thought it was mean, but... it kinda fits them, right?"

He didn't answer. She glanced over her shoulder at him and found him watching her with an intensity that made a shiver run down her spine. He looked away quickly, a flush creeping up his neck.

"Yeah," he finally answered, his voice rougher than usual. "It fits them."

She managed to get the shorts off and turned her attention to the tiny knot that held together her bikini top. She fumbled with it, too drunk to work out how to untie it. Noticing her struggle, Connelly moved toward her. She felt his body heat before she saw him standing directly behind her. She looked up and saw their reflection in the mirror over the en suite bathroom sink.

"Here." He undid the knot, then stayed there for a

moment too long, his fingers lightly brushing the curve of her spine.

She held the top to her breasts. "Thank you."

What was she doing?

She should go into the bathroom and finish changing. She had no clothes with her, but he'd lend her something to sleep in. She knew it. All she had to do was ask. Then they could go back to... what? The Three Stooges? The idea of rejoining the trio was highly unappealing.

Their gazes met in the mirror.

She let the bikini top fall to the floor.

His breath caught on a sharp inhale.

In that silence, she felt something shift between them, a line that blurred and smudged with increasing uncertainty with each passing second. The familiar dynamic of their friendship seemed to dissolve into thin air.

The ache in Connelly's eyes mirrored the one blooming low in her belly. She turned around to face him, her hands resting against his chest. She could feel his heart pounding beneath her touch.

"Don't say anything," she whispered.

His eyes darted to her lips, then back to meet her gaze. "Vee, I—"

"No." She knew what he would say and didn't want to hear it. If he said it, everything changed between them.

She was too drunk to realize that everything had already changed.

She closed the distance between them to muffle his words with a kiss. Their bodies collided, and she found herself being pushed back against the bed as he kissed her with a fierce, pent-up need she hadn't expected. He groaned low in his throat as she slid her fingers through his hair, pulling him down on top of her.

His hands were on her waist, sliding up and down her

exposed skin as if he'd done it a million times before... as if touching her like this was second nature to him. He tasted like the margaritas they'd been drinking all night, sweet and sour and totally intoxicating. She tilted her head back to catch her breath, but he wouldn't let her, his lips skimming down her throat to her breasts. He sucked a nipple into his mouth, and, oh God, she was arching into him instinctively, gasping his name, needing more of him, wanting all of him.

Connelly's control seemed to be teetering on the edge, his breaths coming out in ragged pants against her neck. But then suddenly, he stilled.

"Vee," he choked out. He pulled back just enough to look at her, his gaze searching her face for something she couldn't quite decipher. "You need to be sure."

"I'm sure." She threaded her fingers into his short hair and tried to pull him back in for another kiss, but he stopped her.

"No. You need to be absolutely, one hundred percent sure. I-I can't do this... not with you... if you're going to have regrets in the morning. It'll break my heart."

The confession hit her like a bucket of ice-cold water, sobering her immediately. She sat up and scooted out from under him, grabbing a pillow to cover her chest. "What... what are you saying?" Her voice sounded slightly hysterical even to her own ears.

His face was a mask of vulnerability and uncertainty as he sat back. The swim shorts did nothing to hide the ridge of his erection. "I'm saying that..." He trailed off, took a deep breath, and blurted, "I've been in love with you for a long time, Veronica."

Her heart stuttered. "W-what?"

He got off the bed and began pacing the room, his hands locked behind his neck. "I'm sorry. I didn't intend for it to go down like this, but I was going to tell you this weekend. It's why I booked this stupid suite. I thought it was romantic or some shit. Jesus, I'm an idiot."

She stared at him, barely comprehending the words falling from his mouth. "W-what?" she said again.

He stopped pacing and spun to face her. "I don't want to ruin our friendship, but when you kissed me... I can't just be your friend anymore. I want more."

She felt like she was free-falling. Her plane had just stalled out, and she couldn't regain control. She was going to crash.

"No," she whispered, and his face drained of color. She shook her head. "No. You can't be in love with me. That's stupid. Oh my God, that's the stupidest thing I've ever heard. We're drunk. We're just... drunk. And you're not in love with me. Not really."

He took a step toward her, then another, until he was close enough to touch. But he didn't. He just looked at her, his eyes full of hurt and confusion.

"Do you think this is easy for me?" His voice broke on the last word. "I've been hiding these feelings for years, Vee. But I can't do it anymore."

And there it was. The crash. She swore her heart stopped at that moment. "Do... what?"

"This." He waved a hand between them. "Us."

"But... we're friends," she said desperately. "You're my best friend."

"We *were* friends," he corrected. "But it's not enough for me, and if you don't want more, you need to tell me now so I can step away. I need to figure out how to move on without you. Because this... being close to you like this and knowing you don't feel the same... it's too hard, Vee. It's killing me."

His words hung between them like ice, freezing the moment, freezing her. She wanted to deny it and laugh it off as some sort of weird joke. But the earnestness in Connelly's eyes was impossible to ignore, impossible to refute.

When she didn't respond, he ran a hand over his head. "Fuck."

He looked as lost and broken as she felt. She had always known him to be steady, unruffled even in the toughest situations. Seeing him like this, so exposed and raw, shattered something inside her. She had done this to him. She had pushed him to this edge without ever realizing it.

"I think I'll go back to Florida tonight," he said finally and went to the closet, pulling out his duffle. He crossed to the bathroom and grabbed his toiletry kit. "Feel free to stay here. It's all paid for the weekend, and you shouldn't drive until you sober up."

"But—"

"I'm sorry," he said quietly, his eyes full of sadness, and walked out of the room.

"Wait!" She grabbed her tank top, pulling it back on over her bare breasts as she chased him out.

But he was already gone.

"Whoa," Tyler said from the couch. "What's his problem?"

She looked over at the three men. She'd forgotten they were there. She swiped at her eyes in frustration, hating that they were seeing her cry. "I should go."

"Hang on." Blake popped to his feet and draped an arm around her. He pushed a glass full of alcohol into her hand. "Forget about him. He's always been a pretentious asshole. You don't need him. You can hang with us. "

She stared down into the clear liquid that smelled like lighter fluid. It made her stomach turn, but when he tipped the glass toward her mouth, she drank.

And she drank.

And the night blurred...

Present Day

Veronica squeezed her eyes shut, trying to block out the memories. But they were too strong. Too vivid. She could feel their hands on her again and the cold press of the gun against her temple when she tried to fight them off. Could hear their laughter in her ears. Could taste the bile rising in her throat—

A wet nose pressed against her hand, and she opened her eyes, staring down at the two dogs in shock. Rebel's eyes were direct and intense. Alfie's were soft and sad.

Connelly hadn't taken them with him.

Damn him.

She stroked a hand over Rebel's blunt wedge of a head, then scooped Alfie up and buried her face in his soft fur.

Rebel whined and nosed her hand again as if sensing her distress. Alfie squirmed in her arms, nuzzling against her neck.

She held them close, taking comfort in their warmth. They were the only living beings she trusted. The only ones who didn't make her feel like she was losing her mind.

She wondered how long it would be before even they couldn't stand being cooped up with her anymore. Rebel had already run away from her once. How long before Alfie abandoned her, too? And how long before Connelly gave up and let her push him away for good?

Or maybe he already had.

The thought made her heart ache.

She didn't want to be alone anymore, but she didn't know how to be around people without hyperventilating.

Veronica spent the rest of the day in bed with the dogs. She barely moved, swamped with memories of what she had lost. The sun began to set, casting a warm orange light on the walls. She realized she hadn't eaten anything all day, and her stomach grumbled. She sat up, gently pushing the dogs aside, and made her way to the kitchen. She opened the fridge door and was greeted with an unappetizing array of leftovers. She sighed and closed the door. She didn't feel like eating anything.

But she should probably feed the dogs. She rummaged through the dog supplies Connelly had brought with him and the ones Hank Firestone had left for Alfie.

She dumped kibble into each dog's bowl and watched Rebel devour hers in big, gulping bites while Alfie nibbled at his. She let them outside, praying that neither one ran off. They didn't. While they both did their business, she glanced over at the spot where Connelly had slept last night, half-expecting to see him there again.

He wasn't.

Of course he wasn't.

She'd told him to leave.

The dogs came back inside and followed her to bed. She curled around Rebel's muscular body while Alfie nuzzled into the crook of her legs behind her knees. She closed her eyes, hoping to drift off to sleep. But her mind wouldn't let her. It was too occupied with thoughts of Connelly. She knew he cared for her, but she couldn't let him in. Not after what had happened to her. And not after what he did. He'd just use anything she told him as fodder for his next novel. How could he ever expect her to trust him again?

She heard a noise outside her bedroom window and bolted upright, heart racing. Rebel's ears pricked up, listening to the same noise that had caught her attention. Alfie was oblivious, still sleeping soundly.

Veronica held her breath and listened for it again, but all she heard was the sound of the wind rustling through the trees. She hesitated, then got up and walked over to the window, peering out through the slits in the blind. The sun had set, and she couldn't see anything other than the vague dark shapes of the forest, but still, the hair on the back of her neck stood up.

She shut the blinds and crawled back into bed, pulling Rebel close.

She never should've sent Connelly away.

chapter
eleven

SO THIS WAS THE WRITER.

Connelly Davis.

Coming here every night, sleeping on the porch.

Ruining everything.

He stared down at the man, his lip curling in disgust as he cataloged each of the writer's features. Dark hair. Straight nose. Strong jaw. Evenly spaced features. Long eyelashes. Just like the photo still crumpled in his jacket pocket.

Did his muse find the writer handsome?

The thought made his blood boil.

It would be so easy to slide a blade under that stubbled jaw and open him up, watch him bleed out. It would be messy as hell but so very satisfying.

He took out his knife and knelt over the sleeping man, leaning close enough that he could feel each warm exhale.

So easy...

But as he hovered the sharp edge over the writer's throat, something inside him held back. Was it fear? No, he was never afraid. It was something else. Something he couldn't quite put his finger on.

Maybe curiosity?

He'd never had a rival before. His past muses never had anyone protecting them. This could be an exhilarating challenge. The next logical step of his evolution.

He sheathed his knife and eased off the porch, careful not to make any sound. He knew he should leave before the writer woke up, but he needed to see her.

His beautiful, broken Veronica.

Just a glimpse.

He slipped around the side of the house to her bedroom window. The blinds had been drawn, but the slats were cracked just enough that he could see her on the bed. He pressed his gloved hand to the glass.

Soon, he promised silently. Soon he'd set her free.

She sat up and looked right at the window. The big black and brown dog next to her also lifted its head and seemed to zero in on him with scarily intelligent eyes.

Shit, he'd forgotten about the dog.

Time to go.

As he faded back into the shadows, he thought of the book. He still had it. Had read it cover-to-cover, studied every sentence, analyzed every gory detail.

The writer's mind was as twisted as his.

A new plan took shape in his mind.

He was tired of watching. It was time to play.

But for now, he would let the writer live.

Let them both live.

Just for a bit longer.

Connelly jolted awake and sat up on his elbow, scanning the dark forest. Nothing moved except for the fog rolling in from the ocean, curling around the trees.

So why did it feel like he wasn't alone? He could've sworn someone was just right here, standing over him.

Had he been dreaming?

But it had felt so real.

Had Veronica come outside?

He glanced toward the silent house. He hadn't heard a peep from inside since he came back around midnight and spread his sleeping bag out on the porch.

No, the presence he'd felt hadn't been her.

He rubbed a hand over his face and sat up, pushing the sleeping bag down around his waist. The early morning air had a bite, but he welcomed it. He'd just do a walk around the property to reassure his overactive imagination that everything was okay.

He slipped on his boots and grabbed a flashlight, then set off into the murky forest, wishing he had Rebel at his side. The mist was thick, making it difficult to see more than a few feet ahead. Trees loomed like ominous shadows, and the underbrush was a tangle of vines and thorns.

Monsters lurked in these woods, or so said local legend. The stories went back for centuries. Stories that had inspired his last book.

In shadows so deep, the Stalker hides...

A twig snapped beneath his boot, and he jumped at the unexpected crack of sound.

Fear his presence, where moonlight dies...

Fuck. He was scaring himself.

Connelly shook his head, trying to stop the ominous nursery rhyme from playing on a loop in his mind. He focused on his surroundings— the damp smell of the forest, the crunch of leaves underfoot, and the soft hoot of an owl in the distance.

As he walked, he kept his flashlight trained on the ground, looking for any signs of footprints. Nothing. It was as if he were the only one in the forest.

Okay. So he was just paranoid.

He took a deep breath, reminding himself that he was a grown man and a former pararescue officer. He was no stranger to danger or fear. Hell, he made a living off fear. So he needed to get a grip.

He turned back to the house and did one more circuit around the perimeter to make sure everything was fine. He made it to Veronica's bedroom window, and his blood ran cold as his flashlight beam glinted off the glass.

There, in the condensation, was a hand print. A large, human print, as if someone had pressed a gloved hand to the glass.

He grabbed his phone and tried to get a picture of it, but it was too dark without using the flash, and the flash caused too much of a glare. He watched helplessly as it faded before his eyes, then scanned the trees again.

He wasn't paranoid.

It wasn't his imagination.

Someone was out there.

chapter
twelve

"NOT DOING MUCH TYPING TODAY."

Connelly looked up from his laptop and blinked at Rose Rawlings as she set a mug of coffee in front of him. "I didn't order this."

"On the house. You look like you can use it." She slid into the booth across from him. "Not getting much sleep?"

He thought of the night on Veronica's porch and waking up to the sensation of someone standing over him, the chill of immediate danger raising the hair on the back of his neck. He felt the chill now, even though Rose always kept the Mad Dog Pub warm and cozy.

He reached for the coffee. "No. Not really."

Rose propped her chin on her hand, and her new wedding ring glinted in the light. She was a beautiful woman with long black hair, bright blue eyes, and a body built for male fantasy. For a short time, when he first arrived in town, he'd considered asking her out but quickly realized the sheriff was madly in love with her and backed off. He had no interest in getting on Ash Rawlings' bad side.

Now, he considered Rose a friend. Her pub, a quintessential rustic dive, had been his choice of office space more often than not since moving to Steam Valley. He loved the place and usually enjoyed the company, but today, he wished she'd leave him alone.

"Book not going well?" she asked.

He exhaled a short laugh. "It's not going at all." And the long nights on Veronica's porch weren't helping. He'd have to sleep in his own bed tonight, though he loathed the thought of leaving her alone. If he were exhausted from lack of sleep, he wouldn't be able to protect her—but was there even anything to protect her from? He wasn't sure, but he needed to be functioning at one hundred percent, just in case.

He took a long sip of his coffee, savoring the bitter taste and letting it warm him down to his bones. Maybe the caffeine would kick-start his brain.

He lifted the mug to Rose in a toast. "Thanks for this. What do I owe you?"

She waved a dismissive hand. "It's on the house."

He expected her to go back to tending the bar, but she stayed put.

He raised a brow at her. "Don't you have work to do?"

She motioned to the redheaded man washing glasses behind the bar. "I have Jeremy now. I can take a break."

The man— or kid? He looked young enough to be fresh out of high school and was of average height and build with a shock of orange-red hair. Other than his hair, he wasn't particularly noticeable, but something about his face looked familiar.

As if reading his mind, Rose leaned in. "That's Jeremy Firestone. I heard he and his Dad were struggling without Dr. Firestone's paycheck, and Ash had been on me to hire some more help, so here he is. He's shy but otherwise a good worker."

Ah. That was why he looked so familiar. He was a younger

version of Hank Firestone, who was a regular at The Mad Dog.

"He looks just like his father." Connelly watched Jeremy disappear into the back room with a bus tub full of dirty dishes. "How's he doing?"

"How do you think? He lost his mom," Rose said flatly. "Which is not an easy thing at any age."

And she'd know since her mom had been murdered when she was only thirteen.

"Fair point." Which reminded Connelly he hadn't spoken to his mom since last week. He should call her.

"So..." Rose waved away the sad topic and tilted her head, studying him. "I heard a rumor you've been sleeping on Veronica's porch."

He stared at her in shock. "Who the hell told you that?"

"Just a rumor." She lifted a shoulder. "Small town. Nothing stays secret around here."

Connelly rubbed a hand over his face. "She won't let me in."

They both knew he meant more than into the house.

Rose nodded and slid from the booth as the bell over the door sounded. "Have you spoken to Rylan about it?"

Before he could answer, Ash Rawlings stomped into the pub, his usual scowl firmly in place. He strode over to Connelly's booth, pausing briefly to give his wife a quick kiss.

"Do you mind closing for a bit? I need to talk to Connelly, and I feel safer doing it here where we're less likely to be overheard."

Rose stared up into her husband's eyes, and her brow furrowed with concern. "I'll lock up. It's been slow anyway."

"Thanks." He dropped a thick manila envelope on the table and slid into the spot Rose had vacated.

"Is this about the lurker at Veronica's place?" Connelly asked.

Ash scowled. "What lurker?"

"I found evidence of someone hanging out under her bedroom window last night. There was a handprint in the condensation on the glass. I called the non-emergency number and reported it to your department this morning."

Ash's scowl deepened. "Why am I now just hearing about it?"

So the deputy hadn't taken him seriously. He'd wondered. Had the man even filed a report? Probably not.

"Who did you speak to?" Ash demanded.

He thought back to the conversation and shook his head. "I didn't catch his name."

Ash growled softly. "I'll find out and handle it. Next time something like that happens, call 9-1-1 so there's a record that my dumb-ass deputies can't sweep under the rug."

"Okay," Connelly said, his gaze flicking between Ash and the envelope. "So if you're not here about that, what's this about?"

"I was hoping you'd tell me."

Apprehension curdled the coffee in his stomach as he reached for the envelope. He'd seen crime scene photos before and, having been trained by the Air Force to treat the worst kinds of wounds under the worst kinds of conditions, he wasn't usually squeamish.

But this...

This was different.

Because this was a scene directly from his twisted imagination— a woman, her body mangled and broken, lay in a pool of blood. Her face was a mask of terror, her eyes wide and staring. The next few photos were just as graphic. Bile rose into his throat, and his hand shook.

"What the hell is this?"

"That..." Ash leaned forward, his eyes intent. "Is your victim."

Connelly looked up. "I didn't do this."

"No, but you wrote it," Ash said grimly and pulled out a copy of *The Shadows Within*. Connelly recognized it as the one he'd signed for Rose a few months back, but now it was tabbed with sticky notes and marked up with highlighter.

"Chapter Three. The first death." Ash opened the book and slid it toward him.

He didn't have to read it. He knew the scene. Remembered agonizing over each word as he worked late into the night to meet his deadline. It was that first inkling in the book of *something's not right here*, a reader's first shiver of fear. It was one of the last scenes he'd written before sending it to his editor because he'd felt like he needed to know the rest of the story before he could do it justice. He'd wanted it to be quietly gruesome. He'd wanted his main characters—and his readers—to be unsure whether the death was a freak accident or something more sinister.

The whole book played with fear. The Shadow Stalker—his fictional version, not the legendary one that supposedly hunted in the mountains around town—fed off fear and attacked people struggling with phobias. His first victim, Caroline Harris, was acrophobic, afraid of heights, and died from a fall off a cliff because she thought someone was chasing her.

Connelly looked at the crime scene photos. The similarities were eerie. The twisted limbs, the shattered bones, the blood-soaked ground. The fear etched into the victim's face. Even the color of the victim's hair and her red coat. Like she was cosplaying as the book character.

But this was real.

This was someone's daughter, someone's sister, someone's loved one. Some sick fuck had taken his words and brought them to life in the most horrifying way possible.

He looked back up at Ash and found he had to clear his throat before he could speak. "Did the fall kill her?"

"No. She was shot. We believe she was dead before she went over the cliff. There were also signs of sexual assault."

"That's not like my book."

"So I discovered when Rose gave me her copy to read this morning." He tapped the open book. "But the killer left your book behind with this scene highlighted. He wanted us to make the connection."

"Jesus. What the fuck?" Connelly dragged his hands through his hair and stared down at the highlighted passage. "What was her name?"

"May-Lynn Tapia. She was twenty-six and taught kindergarten over at the elementary school." Ash leaned back in his seat and studied him for a long moment. "Listen, Connelly. Whoever did this to May-Lynn is clearly fixated on your book, and if I were a betting man, I'd lay down money on the probability of their obsession shifting to the book's writer. You. So you need to be careful until we catch this guy. That means no more sleeping on Veronica's porch."

"How does every-fucking-body know about that?"

"It's a small town. People talk."

He was starting to prefer the anonymity of Seattle, where he knew the neighbors in his high rise by sight and not name. "I can't leave her alone, and she won't let me in."

"Do you have reason to be worried about her safety?"

"No," he said a little too quickly, mostly trying to convince himself.

Ash just stared at him with narrowed eyes.

"All right, maybe," he relented after a moment. "It's just... a weird feeling I've been getting lately, like I'm being watched. But it only happens at her place."

"And you mentioned an intruder?"

"Not an intruder. A lurker. Or..." He shook his head. The

more he thought about it, the more he wondered if he'd dreamed the whole thing. "Honestly, Ash, I'm not even sure I saw what I thought I saw. I was tired. It was dark. The photos I took of the window showed nothing. So... I don't know. I could've been imagining it."

"But it spooked you enough to call the police," Ash pointed out. "And I read your book. You're not the kind of guy to spook easily."

"Yeah, not usually."

Ash nodded. "Then I'll station a deputy at her door as well as yours."

Oh, she was going to love that. "She can't see them."

Ash grunted noncommittally.

"I mean it. Right now, her house is her sanctuary. It's the only place she feels safe. If she loses that... I don't even want to think about what it would do to her."

Ash's expression softened. "I'll tell them to be discreet."

Connelly slapped a hand down on his laptop to close the lid, then scrubbed at his face. "This is so fucked. Did May-Lynn have family? I feel like I should do something for them."

"I'd prefer it if you didn't contact them. We're not releasing the information about the connection to your book to the general public."

"It'll get out," Connelly said. "Small town."

Ash scowled. "I'm aware, but I plan to have this guy in handcuffs before it does."

"I'll do anything I can to help."

"Good." He pulled a battered green leather notebook from his pocket and flipped to a clean page, then held out a pen. "Start by making a list of anyone you've ever pissed off."

Connelly stared down at the blank page for a beat, then accepted the pen. "You're going to need a bigger notebook for that."

Ash smirked. "That long, huh?"

"Let's just say I wasn't a popular guy when I left the Air Force."

"Okay, what about your readers? Have you received any weird fan mail recently?"

Connelly froze with the pen posed over the paper. He looked up, and his expression must have given him away.

"Fuck," Ash said, drawing the word out. "You have."

"Not fan mail, but..." He slowly set the pen down. "I do have a restraining order on a woman in Seattle named Sara Parker. I met her at a writer's conference. She said she was an aspiring author, and we became friends. Then more than friends, but things started getting weird, and I ended it."

"Weird, how?"

"She doxxed a critic who panned one of my books, and she would rip into anyone who gave my books less than five stars. It got uncomfortable, so I ended our professional relationship."

"What about your personal relationship?"

"It wasn't exactly a relationship. It was a fling. When it ended, I thought she seemed okay with just being friends and colleagues. Writing is a lonely gig, and it's nice to have someone to vent to who understands it. She was a talented writer on her own. She would send me some of her work to critique, but over time, I started to notice her writing was more and more like mine, like she was stealing my voice. That was when I cut her off professionally, and that was also when things escalated. She started showing up wherever I was. Conferences, book signings. I took my parents to Hawaii last summer for their anniversary, and she was there, but I didn't realize it until another reader pointed out her Instagram to me. She had posted all kinds of pictures of me, and almost all of them were taken without my knowledge. Some were... uh, personal. She must have taken them while I was sleeping."

"She was stalking you?"

He nodded. "So I got the restraining order."

"Have you heard from her since?"

Connelly's heart pitched into his stomach, like that first gravity-defying second of stepping out of a plane with nothing but a parachute strapped to your back. He used to love that feeling. Now, not so much.

"Yeah," he admitted. "She called me a few days ago. I told her I'd report her to the police if she contacted me again."

Ash scowled. "You should've contacted me right away."

"What were you going to do? She's in Seattle." He motioned to the crime scene photos. "And she didn't do this."

Ash leaned forward in his chair, his eyes boring into Connelly's. "You don't know that. She could have hired someone to do it for her, or she could have traveled here to commit the crime herself."

"But you said May-Lynn was sexually assaulted..."

"Women are capable of sexually assaulting other women. It's rare but not unheard of."

Jesus. He had never considered that possibility, but now that Ash had said it out loud, it made a sick kind of sense. Sara's obsession with him had always been intense, and she had shown a willingness to cross lines in the past.

"What do you need me to do?"

Ash collected his notebook and pen as he stood. "Stay vigilant. Anything out of the ordinary happens, you call me, day or night. If, for whatever reason, you can't get in touch with me, call Zak or Donovan or anyone at RWCR."

"You don't want me to call your office?"

Ash's lips thinned into a grim line. "My department is a mess. I can't trust half of my deputies. I've been working on cleaning house, but it's been a slow process. You're better off contacting me directly."

"That doesn't make me feel very safe, Sheriff."

"Good. I don't want you to feel safe. People let their guard down when they feel safe, and I cannot lose anyone else on my watch." At that moment, he looked like he had the weight of the world on his shoulders. "There's been too much death around here lately."

"Hey, Ash? Don't worry about me. I may be a nerd, but I know how to take care of myself."

Ash studied him for a long moment, then nodded and knocked his fist lightly on the tabletop. "Counting on that. I'll be in touch."

chapter
thirteen

VERONICA AWOKE with a start as the first rays of the sun broke through the blinds. She squinted, blinking away the remnants of her nightmare-fueled sleep, and took in the room through half-lidded eyes. Dark shadows still clung to the walls, the dim light of the morning not yet strong enough to chase them away. Her sheets were a jumble of knots, and her pillow was damp with sweat from hours spent tossing and turning.

Rebel lifted her head from her spot at the foot of the bed and let out a soft woof that puffed out her jowls. At the noise, Alfie poked his head up from under the blankets, where he'd burrowed at some point during the night. He had a serious case of bedhead, his fluffy ears sticking up at all angles.

Veronica laughed softly and soothed a hand over his head. He gave an excited full-body wiggle, turning in several circles.

"All right, dogs," she murmured. "I suppose you have to go outside?"

Rebel all but melted off the bed and stretched lazily, first her front paws and then her back. Alfie was a lot less graceful and took a flying leap off the bed, his ears flaring out like wings.

The dogs were ready to go.

She was not.

She looked toward the window, and the paranoia from the night before flooded her mind. She wanted to huddle back under her covers and disappear from the world, but she couldn't. The dogs needed to go outside. They needed food. She couldn't ignore them just because she was feeling like shit.

Besides, feeling like shit was par for the course nowadays. When was the last time she hadn't woken up in a tangle of sheets soaked with fear sweat?

So long ago, she couldn't remember.

She clenched her fists until her nails dug into her palms and forced herself to stand up. The hardwood floor was cold on her bare feet, but she welcomed the sensation. It grounded her in the present.

She shuffled to the closet and grabbed a robe, wrapping it tightly around herself as she walked out of her bedroom to the front door.

"Okay, Reb," she said to the bigger dog, her palms slick with anxiety on the door knob. "Please be good again like you were last night. Don't run away."

The dog sat and eyed her, then the door, and then her again. Almost like she was saying, *Are you gonna open it or what?*

Veronica drew a deep breath and held it. *Here goes nothing.* She opened the door just wide enough for Rebel and Alfie to slip through. Alfie went right to the yard to lift his leg on an overgrown bush, but Rebel... didn't.

Once on the porch, Rebel glanced back with a doggie grin and a naughty glint in her eyes.

"Rebel! No! Don't you even think about—"

It was too late. The Doberman vaulted off the porch and disappeared into the woods. Alfie watched her go, then looked back at Veronica with a question in his sweet eyes.

"Alfie, come back inside," she pleaded, close to tears. She couldn't let him run off, too. At least Rebel was muscular and powerful and could handle herself if she ran into any dangerous wildlife, but Alfie was only eight pounds, and most of that was fluff. He was tiny and fragile and used to being pampered. Dr. Firestone had always treated him like a prince, putting charming bowties on him and carrying him around in her tote bag.

If he went into the woods, he'd be lost. Veronica would never see him again.

She grabbed a freeze-dried chicken treat from the bag Hank Firestone had left and held it out to him. "C'mon. Be a good boy. Come inside with me."

Alfie sat and stared at her, head cocked.

Dammit, she should just walk out there and scoop him up. He was ten feet away. She could go ten fucking feet.

Just as she was psyching herself up to take her first step outside in months, Alfie stood and trotted toward the woods.

"Alfie!" Her voice came out too high with panic. "Stay!"

The tiny dog didn't listen and dove into the underbrush.

Oh, God. She couldn't breathe. It was like the air had turned to water. No matter how much of it she sucked into her lungs, she was still drowning. Her head buzzed with static, and the world spun around her.

She had to get Alfie back. She couldn't let anything happen to him. Not after everything else she had lost.

With shaking hands, she grabbed Alfie's leash and stuffed her feet into tennis shoes she hadn't worn in months. Back at the door, she hesitated.

She could do this.

She had to do this.

She took a deep breath and stepped out onto the porch. The fresh morning air hit her like a punch to the face, and she stumbled back, gasping as her lungs constricted again.

She gripped the porch railing until her knuckles turned white.

She couldn't do this.

She *couldn't*.

But she had to.

Alfie was out there.

Alone.

In danger.

She sucked in another deep, hitching breath and forced herself to take a step forward. And then another. And another, her movements slow and hesitant, like a newborn deer discovering its legs for the first time. The grass was wet with dew and soaked through her shoes. But as she followed Alfie's tiny paw prints into the woods, each step became a little easier.

She *could* do this.

The forest was alive with the sound of birds and insects. The sun was just barely over the horizon, casting long, golden rays through the trees.

It was... beautiful.

She slowed and stared up at the towering trees. Their branches formed a natural canopy, creating a sacred space where time seemed to stand still. She watched in wonder as shafts of sunlight played through the leaves, casting a kaleidoscope of greens that ranged from the deepest emerald to the most delicate mint. She'd never seen so much green in her life. It was in the ferns blanketing the forest floor, the moss coating the tree trunks.

It was quiet here, and for the first time in months, her mind quieted, too.

But, no. The longer she stood there, the more she realized the forest wasn't actually quiet at all. The foliage rustled in a soothing, rhythmic symphony with all the other hushed sounds of wildlife, replacing the familiar hum of the sheltered world she had left behind.

And then she heard it.

A high-pitched bark that could only belong to Alfie. She followed the sound, pushing through the ferns until she saw him. He was perched on a rock, his little tail wagging like crazy.

Rebel sat beside him, looking pleased with herself.

"What are you two doing? You're supposed to listen to me. Bad dogs!"

Alfie's tail stopped wagging, and his ears drooped, but Rebel was unrepentant. She gave a huff and turned, trotting away again.

"No! Come back!" Veronica hurried forward and scooped Alfie into her arms, nuzzling his head as she clipped on his leash. "Oh, your big sister is in so much trouble."

She followed Rebel's trail and spotted the dog strolling leisurely along a path, occasionally stopping to sniff an interesting rock or pee next to a bush. Rebel wasn't in a hurry. She wasn't chasing anything. She was literally just out for a nice walk.

And, Veronica realized, so was she.

Holy shit.

She was out of the house, taking a walk with her dogs, and she wasn't hyperventilating. Her heart wasn't pounding out of her chest. Her palms weren't sweating.

She was calm.

She couldn't remember the last time she had felt this way. It was as if the woods had a magical power over her, erasing all of her fears and worries with every step she took.

Rebel led her to a clearing. The sun was rising higher in the sky, casting a warm glow over the open space. Flowers of every color dotted the ground, and a small stream bubbled nearby. A hidden paradise, untouched by the cruelty of the world.

Veronica sank to the ground with Alfie still snuggled in

her arms. Rebel trotted over and lay down beside them, her big wedge head resting on Veronica's bare thigh.

She closed her eyes and breathed in the scents of the forest, feeling the warmth of the sun on her skin, savoring the moment. She was sitting in the middle of a field, surrounded by nature, and she felt alive. It was as if a weight had been lifted off her shoulders, and for the first time in years, she felt a glimmer of hope.

Maybe, just maybe, she could overcome her fears and start living again.

A long time later, as morning stretched into afternoon, Rebel stirred and rose to her feet, shaking the dew off her coat. Veronica realized she had lost track of time. It was getting late, and she still had to make it back to the house.

Reluctantly, she turned back, retracing her steps through the woods. But this time, it wasn't as hard. Her pace quickened, her movements surer, as if she was rediscovering an old skill. As she emerged from the woods and into the clearing, she spotted Connelly's car parked outside her house.

No. She wasn't ready to face anyone yet. She wasn't ready to let anyone in.

But then, she saw Connelly's face, and something inside her shifted. He was smiling at her, that boyish grin of his that had never failed to make her feel better when they were kids.

"You're outside," he said, his voice tinged with awe. Then his gaze skimmed down her body. "In... your pajamas."

Heat rushed into her cheeks. "Rebel ran away again."

Those dark eyes of his shifted to the dog. "She doesn't look lost."

Veronica glanced down at Rebel. Once again, she wore that cocky, self-satisfied expression. "I think she did it on purpose. I think... she was taking me for a walk."

Connelly chuckled, and a warm flush spread through her body at the sound of his laughter. It had been so long since she had heard him laugh like that, and it made strange, fluttery things happen in her chest.

"Well, I'm glad she brought you back safe and sound." He stepped closer, his eyes flickering over her face. "How do you feel?"

It was a loaded question. He had always been able to read her like a book, even when she didn't want him to. She hesitated, unsure of what to say.

Rebel barked and bounded off toward the house, breaking her from her uncertainty. She took a deep breath and turned to him.

"I feel... alive." She looked up at him, really looked at him, for the first time in years. He had changed since they last saw each other— his hair was longer, his face more lined— but the essence of him was the same. He was still her Connelly. Her best friend. "Thanks for being here, Conn."

"Nowhere else I'd rather be," he said, holding out a hand. "C'mon. You gotta be freezing. Let's get you inside. I brought lunch."

She didn't take his hand, and she saw the quick flash of hurt in his eyes before he turned back toward his car and grabbed a bag out of the front seat. It was from the Mad Dog Pub, and her stomach rumbled as the scent of fried food drifted toward her as she trailed him into the house. She'd always enjoyed the Mad Dog's food and suddenly realized how much she'd missed eating there.

As they ate together in companionable silence, she marveled at how easy it was to be with him. Like they were still kids, back in Seattle, playing by the lake with Rainier looming in the distance. They'd dreamed of climbing that mountain. They'd made up stories of all the amazing adventures they'd have once they were adults.

And now here they were, in the shadow of another mountain, decades older. They never did have any of those adventures they'd dreamed of. At least not together. That was partly her fault. She'd pushed him away after the assault because being close to any man—even her father—had sent her into a panic attack.

But it was his fault, too, for writing that damn book. It didn't matter that he'd changed her name and some details; she knew it was her story. He'd taken her trauma and turned it into entertainment. It didn't matter that the book had been a success and had helped other survivors. It didn't matter that he'd dedicated it to her. It still felt like a betrayal, and she wasn't sure she'd ever be able to forgive him for it.

But maybe she could move past it.

She put down her sandwich and stared at him, noticing for the first time the bags under his eyes and the way his hands shook slightly as he reached for his drink. He looked like he hadn't slept in days.

Her heart sank into her stomach. He was keeping something from her. "What aren't you telling me?"

He set down his barely touched sandwich and reached for a napkin. "It's nothing you need to worry about. I want you to focus on healing." He wrapped up his sandwich and got up to put it in the fridge.

When he turned back, his smile was a bit too bright and strained around the edges. "How do you feel about trying a car ride? We could drive up to the Rescue, and you could talk to—"

"No."

His smile faded. "You managed a walk."

That didn't mean she was ready for more. And Redwood Coast Rescue was the very last place she wanted to go. "I'm not going back to the therapy group. Or talking to that new counselor."

"Why not?"

Because he's not Dr. Firestone. But she didn't say that out loud.

"Because I don't need therapy. I'm doing just fine," she lied.

Connelly's eyes narrowed, and she knew he saw right through her. "You don't have to keep pretending with me, Vee. I know you're struggling."

Veronica bristled at the use of her childhood nickname. It was a name only Connelly had ever called her, and she hated the way it made her feel vulnerable. "I'm not pretending. I'm fine."

Connelly leaned forward, his eyes blazing with intensity. "No, you're not. You're a mess, and you need help. You need to talk about what happened to you, and you need to deal with it."

"I don't want to talk about it. And I don't want to deal with it."

"Then what do you want?"

She didn't know the answer to that. All she knew was that she wanted to feel something other than fear and shame. But telling him that seemed too intimate, so she kept her mouth shut and put entirely too much focus on picking up the remains of their lunch.

Connelly growled with frustration. "You are so goddamn stubborn."

Veronica glared at him, her eyes flashing with anger. "And you're so goddamn pushy. Why can't you just let me be?"

"Because I care about you, damn it," he said, his voice rising. "I've always cared about you, even when you were pushing me away. And I'm not going to stop caring about you now just because you don't want to deal with your shit."

Anger surged at his words. She was tired of people telling her what she needed to do, of people who thought they knew what was best for her. She slammed the paper bag into the trash can, then turned back to face Connelly.

"You know what? Maybe I am stubborn. Maybe I don't want to talk about it. Maybe I don't want to deal with it. But that's my choice, and you need to respect that."

She watched as his expression shifted from frustration to something else entirely. But before she could decipher what it was, he closed the distance between them and grabbed her wrists, pinning them above her head against the wall.

Fear and arousal blended in a confusing mix. She tried to pull away, but he held her firmly in place.

"You can't keep hiding forever," he said, his voice low and rough. "You're stronger than this."

Her breath hitched as he leaned in, his lips brushing against her ear. "Let me help you."

She should have fought him off, should have screamed for him to stop. But something inside her craved this kind of attention. It had been so long since anyone had touched her like this. Not since before the attack.

Her body responded before she could even process the thought, arching into his touch. He pulled back slightly, his eyes locked on hers as he searched for any sign of resistance. When he found none, he lowered his head and kissed her.

It was a bruising, desperate kiss, filled with all the pent-up emotions they'd both been holding back. Her body melted into his, her hands tangling in his hair as she slanted her mouth against his, wanting more.

But then he gave more, kissing her fiercely, crowding her against the counter, and the familiar wave of panic washed over her.

She pushed him away. "No. Stop." Her voice cracked on the word. "I can't do this."

Connelly drew back instantly, his eyes dark with desire

and regret. "Fuck," he said, his voice hoarse. "I shouldn't have done that."

She slipped past him and retreated to the living room, needing to put as much distance between them as her little cabin would allow. "You need to go."

"Vee—"

He reached for her, and she flinched. "Go! I don't want you here."

He stared at her for a long moment, then swore under his breath. "I'm sorry," he murmured and walked out of the house.

Veronica didn't move until she heard the front door shut, then rushed to it to make sure all the locks were engaged. She leaned her forehead against the wood and exhaled a sob.

Why had he done that?

And why had it turned her on before the panic took control?

This was *Connelly*. She grew up an only child, but he was around for so much of her childhood he was like an honorary brother. She'd never seen him as anything else.

Until that night in San Antonio.

Until now, and that all-consuming kiss.

And, for a split second, she had wanted all of him.

Now, their friendship was irrevocably changed. They could never go back to the way things had been before.

She touched her lips and sank down the door until her butt hit the floor. The dogs came rushing over. Rebel licked at her tears. Alfie jumped into her lap. She pulled them both in for a hug. "I think I just lost him for good."

chapter
fourteen

AS ASH HAD PROMISED, a deputy car sat in front of Veronica's house, just out of sight of her front door. That made Connelly feel better about leaving her, even if it meant he was about to catch hell from the sheriff for continuing to sleep there.

After she'd kicked him out for the kiss—he still couldn't fucking believe he'd done that—he'd walked home to retrieve his sleeping bag, then waited until he was sure she was asleep before planting himself on her porch for the night. He hadn't slept much. The creeping feeling of being watched was worse. And he still had at least a week before he was able to pick up his gun.

At least she had the deputies watching out for her.

And he needed to talk to Rylan again about how to handle that idiotic kiss without scaring her away.

At Rylan's office, he raised his hand to knock, but the door swung open before his fist made contact with the wood.

"Hey." Rylan was in the process of pulling on a jacket. "I was just heading out."

"Sorry. If you're busy, I can come back."

"Nah. I'm going over to the RWCR office. They're gearing up for a search. It's my first official mission as the team's trauma counselor." He shut and locked his door, then lifted his chin toward the building's front. "Walk with me. What's up? Is this about Veronica?"

"Yeah. I did something boneheaded yesterday and made things worse." Embarrassment burned up the back of his neck at the memory as he fell into step beside Rylan.

"What'd you do?"

"I kissed her."

Rylan stopped walking like he hit a wall. He blinked a couple of times. Opened his mouth, then snapped it closed again. "Yeah, that was boneheaded," he said finally, his slight southern accent more pronounced with the words.

"I know," Connelly muttered. "It was stupid. I don't know what I was thinking. She was sexually assaulted, and I—I never should've—I was frustrated and—that's no excuse. I shouldn't have touched her. Jesus." He dragged a hand over his face. His eyes felt gritty from lack of sleep, and his stubble had grown past a five o'clock shadow two days ago. "I wish I could take it back."

"Okay, let's unpack it." Rylan started walking again. "Was it a power move? You said you were frustrated. Were you trying to dominate her or... What exactly were you trying to accomplish?"

"I don't know."

"I think you do."

"I just... wanted her back. My Veronica. I miss her. I love her." It was strange to say it out loud. Had he ever? He didn't think so, and the words felt as foreign as another language. "I've always loved her, but she put me solidly in the friend zone when we were kids, and I respected that. I was happy to be with her any way she'd have me."

"Have you asked her how she feels about the kiss?"

"No. But she kicked me out of the house."

"That was her spur-of-the-moment reaction to something that probably startled her. That was her self-preservation kicking it. But now that she's had time to process it, how does she feel about it?"

"I don't know. I haven't spoken to her since. I slept on her porch and left before she woke up."

Rylan's mouth ticked up in a smile. "You're gonna catch hell from Ash for that."

"I'm expecting it, but I'm going to keep doing it until she lets me in, or I know she's safe. If Ash has a problem with it, he can kiss my ass."

Rylan laughed and stopped just outside the door to the RWCR command center. Inside, the office buzzed with activity as the team geared up for the search.

"Okay, listen," Rylan said. "If you're serious about helping Veronica, communication is key."

"I know. I want her to feel safe talking to me."

"Then you need to open up and talk to her first. You need to tell her how you feel and encourage her to share her feelings. A lack of communication is the biggest relationship ender, and we men are especially bad at talking about feelings because we were taught from birth to be strong and unemotional."

Connelly winced. He wasn't good with feelings unless they belonged to a fictional character. Talk about his real feelings? To Veronica? Jesus. He'd rather face a pack of rabid wolves with nothing but a butter knife for a weapon.

"Believe me, man, I get it," Rylan said with a soft chuckle. "After I lost my arm and my Navy career—something I had worked for most of my life—the last thing I wanted was to talk about my fucking feelings. And keeping all that inside almost killed me. Once I finally let myself feel and talk about it, I came to understand that strength isn't about hiding your pain or pretending you're okay when you're not. It's about acknowledging that you're hurt and still going on. It's about opening up and letting yourself be vulnerable to the people you love. That's real strength."

Rylan was right, and Connelly knew it. He needed to go to Veronica and lay bare his feelings and intentions, even if the prospect felt as dangerous as baring his chest to those rabid wolves and inviting them to claw his heart out.

"All right. I'll talk to her."

Rylan clapped him on the shoulder. "Good man."

Just then, the door opened, and Ash's big body filled the frame. His expression was a storm cloud when he spotted Connelly. He was on the phone but covered the receiver with one of his massive hands. "Hey, dumbass. What the fuck did I tell you about sleeping on her porch?"

Rylan snickered and pulled open the other side of the double doors.

Connelly ignored Ash and followed Rylan inside to where Zak, Donovan, and Pierce St. James were leaning over a map. "Jesus. Ash is grumpier than usual today. What's going on?"

"Missing woman," Zak said and marked off a section of the map. "She went for a run this morning and hasn't been seen since. RWCR is mobilizing with the sheriff's department to assist with the search."

Connelly's heart dropped into his gut. If Ash was this wound up, he likely suspected this woman was the next victim. And if the killer continued to follow the pattern of the deaths from *The Shadows Within*, then the next one would be death by claustrophobia.

The character, Rebecca Thompson, was buried alive.

Jesus.

He set down his laptop bag and pulled off his jacket. "What can I do to help?"

Zak didn't look away from the map and marked off

another section that Pierce pointed to. "What do you know about search and rescue?"

"K9 search and rescue? Not much," he admitted. "But I took part in more than a few rescue ops in the military. Put me to work."

Zak studied him for a moment, then finally nodded toward the blond man in a backward USMC baseball cap sitting at a bank of computers in the corner of the room. "All right. Hook up with Sawyer. He's our guy in the chair. You can help him coordinate the search effort." He folded the map and grabbed a bright red windbreaker with RWCR K9 Search & Rescue printed in white on the back. "Sawyer, we're headed out to the search grid."

Sawyer waved a hand in acknowledgment but didn't turn away from the computers. "Radio when you get there."

Connelly watched them go, then walked over to Sawyer. A chocolate lab lay under his desk, snoozing with her head resting on his foot. She opened her eyes and watched his approach, but Sawyer didn't seem to notice.

Did he tap the guy on the shoulder? Clear his throat?

He decided on the latter. "Hey, I—"

"Jesus!" Sawyer jumped in his seat and pulled off his headset. When he turned, his pale blue eyes stared past Connelly's shoulder. "Warn a guy next time."

"Sorry. I didn't realize you…" Flustered, Connelly trailed off and looked up at the monitors. They showed colored maps, search team rosters, and a profile of the missing woman. "How do you…?" Again, he trailed off, unsure of the etiquette. Was it rude to ask a blind person how they did something a seeing person didn't think twice about?

Sawyer's scowl softened into a grin. "Nah, it's okay, man. I'm used to people sneaking up on me. You were gonna ask how I use the computer, right?" He tapped his headphones. "Screenreader. And I'm not completely blind. I can see movement. It's complicated." He spoke in rapid-fire sentences as he went back to typing out commands on a brail keyboard. "You're Veronica's friend, the author, right? Connelly Davis? I've listened to some of your books. Creepy stuff."

"Uh, yeah. Zak sent me over to help."

"You got any search management experience?"

"I was a Combat Rescue Officer in the Air Force."

"Chair Force, huh? Meh. I guess that'll do."

"I spent more time jumping into hostile environments than in a chair. I have the knees of an eighty-year-old to prove it." Connelly chuckled and pulled up a chair. "You were a Marine?"

Sawyer grinned again. "What do you mean, were? Once a Marine, always a Marine. But, yeah, I'm medically retired, thanks to the sniper's bullet that blinded me. Are you up to speed?"

"All I know is there's a missing woman."

Sawyer typed something, and the woman's profile came up on the main screen. "Her name is Lucy Harper. Thirty-two years old, five-eight, around a hundred thirty pounds. Brunette with heterochromia—one blue eye and one brown. She has no kids or a significant other and works as a park ranger in the Redwoods National Park."

"So this isn't just a case of a hiker who took a wrong turn."

"Nope. Lucy Harper knows her way around the woods. She lives in the next town over but habitually drives to the state park here for her morning run on her way to work." Sawyer put another map on the main screen next to Lucy's profile. "She was last seen arriving at the Canyon Ridge Trailhead at six-thirty this morning. At nine, she didn't show up to work, which, according to her boss, is unlike her. He called the sheriff's office, and a deputy found the car at the trailhead with blood on the door."

Sawyer pulled up a photo of the Subaru Outback and the spatter of blood across the pearly white paint of the driver's side door.

"Looks like someone took her by surprise and hit her over the head."

"That's the going theory," Sawyer confirmed.

Just like in his book. Fucking hell. "Did he put her in a vehicle?"

"We're not sure. There was a van in the parking area shortly before she arrived, and it left shortly after, but we have no idea if it's involved or if it just belonged to another runner. It's a popular running trail. Ash put out a BOLO for the van's description, but there were also drag marks from her car into the woods, so it's more likely he—we're assuming the assailant is a man—just dragged her off somewhere. We'll know more when the dogs get there. If she was dragged anywhere, they'll find her trail."

But if the killer were smart, and if he was actually recreating the deaths from *Shadows*, then he'd know how to hide his trail. Connelly groaned softly and scrubbed his hands over his face.

Sawyer stopped typing and turned. "What?"

"Nothing."

Those pale eyes narrowed. "I may be blind, but I can hear just fine, and that groan was tinged with guilt. What did you do?"

"Ash told me not to say anything."

"Yeah, well, Ash can be a myopic son of a bitch. Every bit of information is crucial in a case like this. If you have something to contribute, spit it out. We don't have time for secrets."

Connelly sighed, realizing that Sawyer wasn't going to let it go. "In my last book, there's an entity that feeds on fear.

Yesterday, Ash showed me images of a recent murder that copied the method of death of the first victim in my book."

Sawyer's eyebrows shot up in surprise. "You're telling me this is some sick copycat shit?"

"Ash thinks so. And after seeing pictures of the first crime scene, I have to agree. It was..." He exhaled softly and shut his eyes but opened them again because the image of May-Lynn Tapia's mangled body seemed to be permanently burned into the backs of his eyelids. "It was like the killer had reached into my imagination and pulled out the exact scene."

Sawyer was silent for a solid five seconds. "Well, that's fucking creepy." He turned back to his computer, and after a moment of typing, an e-book of *The Shadows Within* appeared on screen. He didn't speak again for a long time as his screenreader scanned through the book.

Connelly watched as the familiar pages flew by.

Finally, it stopped on the first death scene, and Sawyer sucked in a sharp breath. "Wait. May-Lynn was murdered? Word around town is she fell off the cliff. Does Ash think she was pushed?"

"No. She was dead before she went over the edge."

"Jesus. That poor girl." The screen flew through the pages again until Sawyer found the second death scene. "Claustrophobia. Buried alive in a cemetery. Holy fuck, man. Your brain is a scary place."

"Tell me about it."

"Okay." He cracked his knuckles and pulled up the maps on the screen again. "This could be a good thing. If he's following the book, she's not dead yet. He wants her to suffocate, which means we have time. Not a lot of time, but still. We need to shift the search focus to cemeteries near the abduction site. Get on the radio and tell the team what we're thinking."

Connelly grabbed a radio. "Not just cemeteries. We need to search anywhere someone could potentially be buried."

"Which isn't on the bluffs along the running trail. Too rocky."

"Wait." Something on one of the maps caught Connelly's eye. He set the radio back down and moved closer to the screen to get a better look. "What's that?"

"Describe it," Sawyer said.

Sawyer was so good with the computers it was easy to forget he couldn't see. "Uh... grid number G10. There's a big blank spot in the middle of it. What's there?"

Sawyer turned back to his keyboard and typed something, then pressed a hand over his headphones to listen to the response. "It's a cave."

Adrenaline poured into Connelly's blood. "That's it. She's there."

"How do you know?"

"I just do." Every cell in his being knew it. There was no way the killer could bury a victim in a cemetery in the middle of the day, but nobody would notice him in a cave in the middle of the woods. He crossed the room in long strides and snapped up his coat. "Send the teams there."

Sawyer spun in his chair, tracking his movement to the door. "Where are you going?"

"To the cave."

"Ash is already pissed at you. Sure you want to add yourself to Zak's shitlist, too?"

"We sent them in the wrong direction. They're too far away. I can get there faster, and Lucy doesn't have much time." Images from his book flashed through his mind — the claustrophobic darkness of the cemetery, the description of Rebecca's terror as she suffocated, the unfathomable evil that lurked within the pages. Then he pictured Lucy Harper living out that horrifying fiction in real-time, and he couldn't bear the thought of another innocent life being snuffed out because of his twisted imagination. He had to get to her.

Sawyer's voice cut through his thoughts. "Wait."

He paused, his hand gripping the doorknob tightly. "What?" He turned to face Sawyer, anticipation and anxiety sweeping through him like wildfire.

Sawyer's blind eyes seemed to bore into his soul. "I'm coming with you."

"No."

"You need someone to watch your six."

He hesitated, unsure how to respond. Sawyer was a smart man and brilliant on a computer, but he had to know his lack of sight was a significant disadvantage in a dangerous situation like this. "Sawyer, man, I'm sorry, but how are you going to watch my six?"

"Not me." He pushed away from the computer. The moment he moved, his dog stood and stretched, then sat and waited for her next task. "Zelda. She'll watch both of our backs. Besides, we go hiking in that area all the time." He tapped a finger to his temple. "I have it all mapped out."

Connelly stared at him. "I don't want anyone else to get hurt because of a fucking book I wrote."

Sawyer's expression hardened. "Look, Connelly, I understand your concern, but I've managed to navigate these woods just fine since losing my sight. Plus, Zelda here has been trained as a guide dog, and she's one of the best in the business." He patted Zelda's head affectionately.

Connelly glanced at the lab. Intelligence gleamed in her brown eyes. She could be a valuable asset in navigating the treacherous terrain around the cave, and Sawyer's familiarity with the area would significantly increase their chances of finding Lucy before it was too late.

Reluctantly, he nodded. "All right. But we stick together,

and we don't take any unnecessary risks. No heroics, understood?"

"Deal." Sawyer grinned, and there was a surprising hint of meanness in it. "Don't worry, we'll find her. We won't let that sick fuck get away with this."

chapter
fifteen

THE DRIVE to the state park felt both endless and fleeting at the same time. The road twisted and turned through the dense forest, the hum of the engine filling the tense silence inside the car.

Time was running out. Each passing second was another second closer to Lucy's suffocation, and Connelly couldn't bear the weight of that responsibility.

He gripped the steering wheel so tightly that the leather creaked.

"Ease up," Sawyer said. "Keep doing that, and you're gonna rip the wheel right off the steering column."

He glanced over. Sawyer sat calmly in the passenger seat with Zelda behind him, her head resting on his shoulder. The dog was alert but calm—a steady, reassuring presence. Despite Connelly's initial reservations, there was relief in knowing he wasn't going into this alone.

He exhaled and made himself loosen his grip on the wheel. "Yeah, sorry. I'm worried."

Sawyer's lips quirked. "I can hear that."

"If Lucy is buried, she's running out of oxygen, and we're running out of time. How long is the hike to the cave?"

"About forty-five minutes from the trailhead."

Too long. They were cutting it too close.

He parked near the trailhead, out of sight of prying eyes. He opened the car door and was immediately greeted by the crisp scent of pine and the distant sound of birdsong. The forest was alive, vibrant with the energy of life, but Connelly couldn't shake off the heaviness that hung in the air. Adrenaline buzzed in his veins as he hopped out of the car and hurried to the trunk. He grabbed the backpack he'd filled with supplies before leaving the rescue.

"Let's go."

Sawyer swung his cane out of the car and tapped it on the ground, expertly maneuvering through the uneven terrain. Connelly followed closely behind, the weight of the backpack digging uncomfortably into his shoulders. He used to be able to carry heavier rucksacks through hostile terrain without breaking a sweat, but that was a lifetime ago. Now, his body groaned with every step, reminding him of the toll that age and countless missions had taken on him.

The three of them set off into the woods, their footsteps muffled by the carpet of fallen leaves. The path ahead was dappled with sunlight, casting shadows that danced and shifted with every gust of wind.

The hike to the cave was grueling. Every step seemed to test Connelly's resolve, the weight of the backpack growing heavier with each passing minute. Sawyer and Zelda moved effortlessly ahead, the dog and his cane guiding him with unwavering precision. He walked like he was sighted, but once in a while, he stopped moving and clicked his tongue, then tilted his head like a dog as he listened for the echo.

The terrain shifted gradually, the path leading them up a steep incline, the silence of the woods broken by the sound of their heavy breathing. The shadows grew longer as the sun began to set, casting an eerie glow over the forest.

"We need to pick up the pace," Connelly said the next time they paused for a water break. "We're losing daylight."

Sawyer took a drink from his water bottle and wiped his mouth with the back of his hand. "Describe our surroundings."

Connelly looked around. "Tall trees, mostly redwood and pine. Some underbrush, but not too dense. The ground is rocky in places, and there's a small stream off to our left with a fallen tree over it like a bridge."

"Is there a boulder shaped like a giant chess piece up ahead on our right?" He indicated the direction with his cane. And sure enough, there was the boulder.

"Yeah, it's there."

Sawyer nodded. "Good. That means the cave is right around here somewhere."

"You don't know where?"

Sawyer gave him a dry look as he capped his water. "I don't do much spelunking."

"Right. Sorry."

As they continued pushing ahead on the barely-there trail, the air felt heavy with an unspoken tension, as if the trees themselves were holding their breath in anticipation. There was something sinister here. The shadows seemed to linger just a little too long.

A chill crawled up Connelly's spine, his senses on high alert. He felt the weight of eyes on the back of his head and turned but saw nothing behind them except the empty trail.

Was the killer still here?

It made sense. The guy wouldn't just leave Lucy to suffocate. He'd want to see his handiwork.

Connelly quickened his pace, the backpack bouncing heavily against his back as he caught up with Sawyer.

"Sawyer," Connelly whispered.

Zelda suddenly stopped moving and pressed close to

Sawyer's side. Her hackles raised, she sniffed at the air, her nose twitching as if catching a scent that sent warning signals to her primal instincts.

Sawyer knelt and placed a hand on Zelda's head to calm her. "Yeah, I know. I hear him behind us. But he's not going to come out." He kept his voice calm as he continued stroking his dog's head. "That's not his style. He attacks vulnerable women, people he perceives as weaker than him. We intimidate him, which is why he's skulking behind us, watching us instead of attacking."

"What do we do?"

Sawyer straightened and pushed his cane out in front of him again. "No unnecessary risks. No heroics, remember?"

Dammit, he hated having his own words thrown back at him. He glanced behind them but again saw nothing out of the ordinary. He hurried to catch up with Sawyer. "We can't let him get away. He'll kill again."

"Right now, our focus has to be finding Lucy Harper, or else he'll have another victim."

Sawyer was right.

Connelly knew it, but it still needled at him. He wanted to make the killer pay for what he'd done, but if they didn't find Lucy in time, he'd be the one to blame.

"Tell me about the victim in your book," Sawyer said, breaking the silence. "What exactly happens to her?"

"I told you already. She's buried alive in a graveyard."

"But how did the killer do it?"

"I don't fucking know."

That smirk was back on Sawyer's face. "You wrote the book."

"Yeah, but... he's a supernatural being that feeds on fear. He can just..." He snapped his fingers. "And open up a grave."

"Obviously, our guy didn't do that. But there was something about this place that reminded you of the scene enough to drag your ass all the way out here. What was it? What made you so certain Lucy is here?"

Connelly paused, his brow furrowing as he tried to pinpoint exactly what it was about this place that had struck a chord within him. He took a deep breath, the scent of pine and damp earth filling his nostrils. "It's hard to explain. He couldn't do it in a cemetery—not in broad daylight. So I looked at it like if I were writing this killer trying to imitate the book, what was the next best option? And my mind skipped from graveyard to crypt to cave."

"The darkness. The confined space. It echoes the fear of being buried alive. He wants to recreate that terror." Sawyer shook his head. "Said it before, but I gotta say it again, man. You have a twisted as fuck imagination."

Connelly chuckled grimly. "Comes with the territory, I guess. But it's not just the darkness and the confined space that made me think of a cave. It's something else. Something deeper." He paused and tried to wrangle his gut instinct into words. "In my book, the graveyard where the victim is buried is surrounded by a dense forest. The trees loom over her, casting long shadows that seem to whisper the secrets of the dead. It creates this suffocating atmosphere, a feeling of being trapped not just physically, but mentally as well."

Sawyer nodded in understanding. "So you think this killer chose this particular cave because it mirrors the psychological torment he wants his victims to experience?"

"Exactly. He's trying to recreate that same sense of being buried alive, of being utterly helpless and at his mercy. But he still needs it to be close enough to my book that it's recognizable. He wants the fear to seep into the minds of those who discover his handiwork. It's a twisted homage, a sick form of artistry. It's his way of taunting me, showing me that he's studied my work and knows how to manipulate my fears."

"You're afraid of being buried alive?"

"Isn't everybody?"

"Solid point."

"Yes, I write about my fears. And yours. And humanity's. It's why my books do so well. It's why people connect with them. But this... this is something else entirely. It's like staring into a mirror and seeing a distorted version of myself. And I don't like what I'm seeing."

"You're nothing like this guy," Sawyer said without a shred of doubt.

Connelly appreciated Sawyer's confidence, but deep down, he couldn't shake the unsettling feeling that there was a sliver of truth in his own words. He had built his career on exploring the darkest corners of the human psyche, but now he found himself confronted with a tangible manifestation of those very fears.

Zelda suddenly froze and gave a guttural bark of warning.

Sawyer tightened his grip on the leash, his fingers white from the pressure. "Shh, Zelda. It's okay."

Connelly strained his ears, trying to identify the source of Zelda's agitation.

It came in whispers carried on the wind, faint but unmistakable. Words that echoed with dread. "Help me... please... somebody..."

Connelly's blood ran cold. A woman's voice. It was faint, barely audible above the rustling leaves and creaking branches, but it was there.

Zelda strained at her leash, her instincts honing in on the source of the desperate pleas. The echoes of the woman's voice grew louder, guiding them deeper into the heart of the forest.

As they approached the source of the sound, the dense foliage gave way to an opening in the ground—a gaping maw leading into the depths of the earth. It was a cave entrance, obscured by overgrown vegetation and hidden from prying eyes.

"She's down there."

Sawyer grabbed his arm. "Wait. We need to call the team and—"

"There isn't time." Connelly shucked his backpack and pulled a flashlight from the side pocket. He clicked it on, casting a narrow beam of light into the darkness of the cave. "You call the team. I'm going in."

"Aw, fuck," Sawyer muttered and grabbed his radio. Zelda whined anxiously at his side, her tail tucked between her legs. He patted her head reassuringly. "All right, go. But be careful, Conn. I won't be able to find you if you get hurt down there."

Taking a deep breath, Connelly steeled himself for what he might find, then lowered himself into the mouth of the cave. The damp air enveloped him, its earthy scent mingling with a sense of foreboding. He couldn't help but feel like he was descending into the belly of a beast.

The beam of his flashlight wavered, revealing ancient rock formations and glistening stalactites that seemed to stretch out like skeletal fingers. Deeper he went, each step echoing off the walls as if the cave itself was alive, whispering secrets kept hidden for centuries. The darkness seemed to cling to him, suffocating and disorienting. Panic threatened, fueled by his own words on the page. But he pushed it down, reminding himself that this was reality, not fiction. There was no monster down here, hiding in the shadows, feeding off his fear.

The pleas for help grew softer like she was losing strength.

Connelly pushed deeper into a narrow tunnel, trying to follow the echo. "Lucy! Can you hear me? We're here to help!"

The darkness swallowed his words, leaving only silence in its wake. He pressed on, heart pounding wildly as he navigated through narrow passages and crawled past low-hanging ceilings.

Jesus, he hated tight spaces. He couldn't breathe, and every inch of progress felt like an eternity, the air growing thicker with each step he took, gagging him with its stagnant scent.

"Lucy?"

His voice reverberated through the cave, the desperation and urgency in it bouncing off the walls and filling the oppressive silence. But there was no response, only the eerie echo of his own words lingering in the air. His heart sank as he pressed forward, his flashlight casting long shadows that danced ominously across the rough, damp walls.

And then, like a whisper in the wind, he heard it—a faint sob. It was barely audible, but it sent a surge of adrenaline coursing through his veins. He quickened his pace, following the sound as it grew louder and more desperate. With each step, the walls closed in around him until he had to walk in a crouch. Was he even going in the right direction? The tunnel dead-ended, but the sobs echoed all around him.

"Lucy?" he called out again.

The sobbing grew louder, mingling with muffled cries for help.

"Hold on! I'm coming!" He backtracked and found another, narrower passage forking off to the left. Her voice came from the other side, but his shoulders were too broad to fit.

"Connelly?"

He jumped at Sawyer's voice and swung his flashlight beam around to illuminate the man and his dog.

"Jesus. What are you doing in here?" Stunned, he shone his light a few feet over at the gaping crack in the rock he'd jumped coming in, then swung it back at Sawyer. "How did you get in without falling?"

Sawyer snorted. "Hear that, Zelda? He doesn't think you're very good at your job."

Zelda huffed as if to say, *Jerk.*

"She would never let me fall. Hell, for that matter, I'd

never let me fall. I can tell when there's a drop in front of me. The air's different."

Shame burned up the back of Connelly's neck. "Sorry. I don't mean to underestimate you."

Sawyer waved the apology away. "Hey, no worries. A few years ago, I didn't think I could do anything either. I thought my life was over, but I got Zelda and realized that wasn't true. I can still do everything I did before. I just have to go about it differently now. I came down to let you know the calvary's on the way with gear to extract her. I shouted, but you didn't hear me."

"What's their ETA?"

"Fifteen minutes."

"Is our stalker still up there?"

"Nah. When Ash radioed, I heard him beat feet out of there. We got him running scared."

Not for long, Connelly thought but he didn't bother saying it out loud. They both knew it. This guy wasn't done with his sick game yet.

Sawyer cocked his head, listening, and his pale blue eyes narrowed. "Is that Lucy? Jesus, she sounds terrified."

"Yeah. I'm pretty sure she's on the other side of this wall, but she can't hear us."

"Can we get to her?"

"There's a tunnel, but it's narrow as hell. I can't get through." He eyed Sawyer and then the passage consideringly. Sawyer was built like a runner, all long, lean muscle. "But maybe you can."

Sawyer nodded. "Let's do it. Point me in the right direction."

chapter
sixteen

SAWYER LISTENED as Connelly gave detailed instructions on how to maneuver through the tight space and thought, *This is a bad fucking idea.*

"If you get in there and find her," Connelly added and dropped a rescue glow stick in his hand, "crack this to pinpoint her location, then calm her down until help arrives. Give her some water if you can. She's probably dehydrated. Try to find out if she's injured and where. That knowledge will help with the extraction process."

Sawyer nodded, his heart pounding with a mix of fear and determination. He took a deep breath, steadying himself before he began the arduous task of squeezing through the narrow passageway. Zelda whined anxiously behind him, sensing his unease. He wanted to pet her, but his arms were already pinned at his sides by the walls.

"It's okay, girl. I have to do this. Conn, keep her out here with you. I don't want her to get hurt."

With Connelly's voice as his guide, he inched forward, relying on his heightened senses to navigate the claustrophobic space. The jagged rocks scraped against his back and skinned his arms as he maneuvered deeper into the darkness.

This was what he'd thought blindness would be like when he woke up in the hospital in Germany after taking a sniper's bullet to the brain. When they told him he'd never see again, he'd imagined a life of absolute darkness, and the idea of it was terrifying. Suffocating. If this had been how his blindness manifested, he wouldn't have survived it. He didn't know how anyone could. Humans weren't meant to live in the dark.

The walls pressed in on him like a vice, squeezing his body with unrelenting force as he walked and then crawled forward. The earth resisted his progress, making it feel like he was trying to move through quicksand. The air thickened and became suffocating, causing sweat to pour down his face and soak into his T-shirt. He inhaled musty dirt and each breath left a dry, gritty feeling in his mouth.

Every inch forward was a battle of will and determination, each movement bringing him closer to Lucy but further from the safety and comfort of open space. The jagged rocks tore at his skin, leaving angry welts in their wake, but he pressed on, driven by the haunting sobs of a woman he'd never met. The noise surrounded him, bouncing off the walls, mixing with his own labored breaths and grunts of effort. He could sense her fear and pain, the raw emotions resonating within him like an electric current.

He knew what that kind of terror felt like.

Finally, after what felt like an eternity, his hand brushed against something cold and clammy and soft. Not rock. And he hoped to God, not an animal. He reached out further and realized he had found a pair of trembling hands bound by rope.

"Lucy?" he whispered, his voice filled with both relief and concern.

She recoiled as much as she could in the same space. "Who's there?"

"My name is Sawyer Murphy. I'm here to help."

Lucy's breathing hitched, her voice catching in her throat. "Oh God, thank you. I didn't think anyone was coming. Are you with the police?"

"Ah, no. Not exactly. I'm with Redwood Coast Rescue, and so is my friend Connelly who is waiting just on the other side of this wall with my dog, Zelda. But the sheriff is on his way with equipment to get you out." As he spoke, he felt around until he found the glow stick. When he cracked it, the glow filled his field of vision with the smattering of light and shadows he'd grown used to.

But then Lucy moved closer, and his brain kicked into gear, remembering that he had once been able to see. And for an instant, he saw a blurry image of her face, scraped up and tear-stained, her bi-colored eyes showing too much white. Even caked in mud and blood, she was stunning. Her description didn't do her justice.

Then she stopped moving and disappeared into the blurry white noise again.

Dammit, he wanted to see her.

Which wasn't what he should be worrying about now.

He cleared his throat. "Are you injured?"

"Yes. He—he shot me and pushed me into a hole. I-I tried to climb out, but I got stuck here."

"Where did he shoot you?"

"My leg. I used my shirt as a tourniquet."

His heart ached for her. He could only imagine the pain she was in, both physically and emotionally. "Good. Smart. I'm going to touch you, okay? I want to check your leg."

With a steady hand, he reached out and gently touched her leg, his fingers tracing the makeshift tourniquet. He felt the warmth of blood and the irregularity of fractured bone beneath her skin. The touch elicited a sharp intake of breath from Lucy, and there was a tremor in her voice when she spoke again.

"I thought I was going to die down here."

"Nope. I'm not gonna let that happen. Help is on the way, and we'll get you out of here. Just hold on a little longer." His fingertips lingered over a soggy mass of fabric that was wrapped around her thigh. The tourniquet was still tight, so he left it in place and rummaged through his pockets until he found the cool metal of the water bottle. He unscrewed the cap and held it out in her direction. "Here. Drink it slowly."

Lucy took the water bottle from Sawyer's outstretched hand, her fingers trembling as they made contact. "Thank you."

As she drank, Sawyer could hear desperation and relief in each gulp. But she was drinking too fast, so he reached out and gently pulled the canteen away from her. "Whoa, take it easy. Let's see how that settles, then you can have some more."

She caught his hand before he could pull away and held it tightly as if afraid to let it go. "Please don't leave me."

His heart cracked right open and he squeezed her hand back. "I'm not going anywhere, Lucy."

chapter
seventeen

HE REALLY WASN'T COMING BACK.

Yes, she'd told Connelly to stay away, but she never in a million years thought he'd actually, you know, stay away. It wasn't like the stubbornly persistent man she knew.

Veronica drew a fortifying breath and stepped out onto her porch as the dogs did their morning business in the yard. She looked toward the old Hendricks place. On a clear day, she could only see the slope of the roof and the glow of his living room light. Today had dawned damp and foggy, and she couldn't see a damn thing.

She should go over there and make sure he was okay.

But could she walk over there?

Her recent walk through the woods with Rebel had been a huge step in the right direction, but it hadn't been planned. She'd only done it out of fear for the dogs' safety, and she wasn't sure she could convince herself to consciously step off the porch and walk down the road to visit someone's house.

Veronica clutched the doorframe, her knuckles turning white as she debated with herself. The familiar tendrils of anxiety began to weave their way through her thoughts, constricting her chest and making it difficult to breathe.

Rebel and Alfie finished their business and trotted back toward her, tails wagging eagerly. Their playful energy was infectious, reminding her of the things she loved about life beyond these four walls. She couldn't let fear dictate her actions any longer.

Rebel nudged against her leg as if urging her to make a decision. Fear coiled in her chest, threatening to paralyze her—

No.

Dammit.

She could do this.

She sucked in a deep breath, forcing her lungs to open and accept the cool, damp air. Then she scooped up Alfie and, hugging him close, took a small step forward. The familiar creak of the porch boards echoed in the silence, breaking through the fog that clouded her mind.

It was just a short walk down the road.

She could do this.

She focused on the rhythmic thump of her heartbeat, using it as a metronome to keep her pace steady. With each step, she willed her body to defy the flight instinct. Inside was safer. She should run back and—

NO.

She was so tired of being afraid all the time.

She hugged Alfie tight, and he laid his head on her shoulder as if hugging her back. His fluffy ear tickled her chin, and a smile tugged at the corners of her lips.

Alfie, the psychic dog.

That was what the guys had called him in therapy because he always seemed to know who needed him the most each session.

A weird tug in her chest made her stop moving. Was that... longing? Did she actually miss the guys?

Yes.

Holy shit, yes, she missed them.

She missed Zak with his brash confidence and snarky comments. She missed Pierce with his calm demeanor and unwavering support. She missed Donovan's booming laugh and Sawyer's infectious enthusiasm for life. All of them had become like a second family to her, and in their absence, she felt a void that not even her four-legged friends could fill.

And she especially missed Connelly. Her best friend, who had always been there for her, even in her darkest moments. Connelly, who had dropped his life in Seattle to come here and help her. Connelly, who had slept on her porch every night until she forced him to leave.

She never should have sent him away.

Veronica took a moment to steady herself, leaning against a nearby tree as her emotions threatened to overwhelm her. The weight of her past traumas pressed down on her, threatening to crush any progress she had made. But then she felt something warm and wet against her hand. Rebel nudged her palm with her snout, her rust-colored eyes full of concern. She knelt and pressed her forehead to Rebel's.

"You're a good girl, Reby. The best girl." She smiled through her tears and kissed the top of Rebel's head.

Rebel wagged her tail, then bounded down the trail toward Connelly's house.

"Okay. Let's go." Gathering her strength, Veronica stood up straight and wiped away her tears. She took a deep breath, letting the fresh scent of blossoming flowers fill her lungs. The sun bathed the world in warm, golden light, casting a gentle glow on everything it touched. It was the type of day that whispered of new beginnings and endless possibilities.

She followed Rebel's lead to Connelly's house. Each step was a monumental victory she couldn't wait to share with him. He was going to be so shocked. And, she hoped, pleased. She laughed, imagining his expression. Her heart raced with anticipation. She couldn't deny the growing ache deep inside her, the need to reconnect with the person who had always understood her, even when she couldn't understand herself.

Rebel bounded ahead, tail wagging furiously as if sensing the nervous energy buzzing around Veronica. The old wooden porch creaked beneath Veronica's weight as she stepped onto it, and memories flooded her mind. She could picture Connelly sitting here, his strong frame sprawled in the Adirondack chair as he typed on his laptop, frantically trying to get the story out of his head as fast as possible.

She reached out and turned the doorknob, praying that it wasn't locked. The door swung open effortlessly as if welcoming her back into Connelly's world. She took a deep breath, inhaling the familiar scent of him. It was a mixture of books, coffee, and something uniquely him— a scent that felt like comfort and homecoming all at once.

She stepped inside. "Conn?"

There was no response, only the faint sound of Rebel's paws clicking against the hardwood floor as she explored the familiar space.

Panic began to well up inside Veronica once more, threatening to extinguish the flickering flame of hope that had brought her here. She clenched her fists, determined not to let despair consume her.

Taking a deep breath, she moved further into the house. The living room was filled with remnants of Connelly's presence—stacks of unfinished manuscripts, dog-eared books strewn across the coffee table, and scattered sheets of paper filled with his messy handwriting. There was a mug of cold coffee sitting on a coaster beside his laptop.

He'd had another late night of writing.

A creak from the back of the house had her jumping out of her skin, and her anxiety only ratcheted up when Rebel let out a low growl of warning. She swung toward the noise.

There, standing in the dimly lit hallway, was a man.

Not Connelly.

He was tall and lean, with sharp cheekbones and shadowed eyes, a silhouette carved against the vague light filtering in from the window at the end of the hall. A sense of danger oozed from him as if it were a part of his poorly lit frame.

Suddenly, it felt like she was trapped in one of Connelly's horror stories, and she was the victim, not the heroine. This was not real; it couldn't be. She shook her head fiercely, willing herself to wake up from this terrible nightmare.

She wanted to run. She wanted to sic Rebel on him and race back to the safety of her home.

But what if Connelly was in danger?

"Who are you?" Her voice came out steadier than she felt, and she was glad for it. It was important not to show fear, not to give him that power over her.

Instead of responding, the man continued to stare at her, his face unreadable in the dim light of Connelly's home. The silence stretched on until it felt unbearable. The tick-tock of the wall clock in the living room echoed through the house like a countdown timer.

"Where's Connelly?"

The stranger didn't move. There was a cold stillness about him that made her skin prickle. The fear that she had tried so hard to push away seeped back in, chilling her from the inside. She held Alfie tighter and wished she had his uncanny ability to sense people's intentions.

"Where is he?" she repeated, her voice rising higher as the panic started to win out.

Again, silence was her only answer.

Frustration bubbled up inside her, mixing with the fear and transforming it into something more potent—anger. Anger at herself for being scared, anger at Connelly for not being here when she needed him... and anger at this silent stranger who dared to invade the sanctuary of Connelly's home.

The man took a step forward, and fear lanced through her, but instead of freezing her, it spurred her into action. "Rebel!"

The dog didn't need more prompting. With a deep growl, she launched at the man and clamped onto his outstretched arm. She was a whirlwind of teeth and snarls, fearless and unforgiving. The stranger tried to shake her off, but she held firm with her teeth buried deep in his flesh.

Then he punched her.

Veronica saw red at Rebel's yelp of pain, the anger burning away all of her fear. She gently set Alfie down, and with adrenaline surging through her veins, she launched herself at the man, using all her weight to knock him off balance. They tumbled to the floor, and for one terrifying moment, she found herself face-to-face with the intruder. He was wearing a mask. That was why she could only make out vague features.

But his eyes...

Those dark eyes were dead inside, without a spark of humanity. This man was dangerous. Deadly. And furious.

She clenched her fists and punched him as hard as she could.

For several heartbeats, he just blinked at her, stunned, as if he hadn't expected her to fight back.

Yeah, don't like it much, do you, asshole?

She pulled her fist back again. "Who are you? Where's Connelly?"

He shoved her. His lanky body hid deceptive strength, and she hit the wall hard, knocking her head against a small table. She saw stars, but her feisty Doberman had shaken off the blow and launched back into the fight. Rebel lunged for his leg. He stumbled against the opposite wall, knocking frames askew and smearing blood across the wood paneling.

"Good girl," Veronica croaked out in between breathless

gasps. She staggered to her feet, head spinning, as the man struggled to disentangle himself from the dog. His shirt ripped, and she thought she saw some kind of tattoo or birthmark low on his stomach before he managed to shove Rebel away.

He ran for the door, shoving past Veronica. She wasn't steady on her feet, but anger fueled her to give chase. Rebel easily took the lead, snapping at his retreating figure until he disappeared into the golden glow of morning, his silhouette swallowed up by daylight.

She burst out of the house behind him, gulping in the cool, fresh spring air as if she'd been underwater for too long. The bright sun was momentarily blinding, and she skidded to a stop on the porch steps, watching as the intruder disappeared into the forest.

Rebel stood beside her, chest heaving, a low growl still rumbling from her bloodstained muzzle.

"It's okay," she told the dog, though she didn't fully believe it herself. She patted Rebel's muscular side, and the contact was soothing. "We're okay. We're okay now."

She pulled Rebel back inside and shut the door. Her heart was like a wild thing trying to escape its cage, and she leaned against the door for a moment to catch her breath. She wanted to curl up and cry, but there was no time for that.

Connelly's life might be in danger.

She groped in her pocket for her phone and dialed his number. Straight to voicemail.

She cursed, her hands shaking as she ended the call. She tried again, praying he would pick up this time. The ringing seemed to echo in the quiet house, making the silence all the more oppressive. Again, it went to voicemail.

"No." She would not lose Connelly. Not now. Her fingers trembled as she dialed 911, the digits blurring together on the screen.

"911, what is your emergency?" The voice on the other end sounded calm and collected, in sharp contrast to the chaos of a few moments ago.

"Some... someone broke into my friend's house. I-I think he might be in danger. The intruder ran off into the woods when I arrived. But he was... he wasn't supposed to be here. And Connelly's not here." Her lips felt numb, her tongue clumsy.

Was she even making sense?

Alfie pressed against her leg, offering all the comfort in his little eight-pound body. She scooped him up and held him close.

The operator asked for more information—Connelly's address, what the intruder looked like, and if Veronica had been harmed. The questions were a blur, and she answered them mechanically, all while her gaze never strayed from the blood smeared on the wall.

The operator assured her they'd send someone over right away. She hung up, slid down against the door, and buried her face in Alfie's soft fur.

The adrenaline was wearing off, and reality was sinking in. She was alone in a house that wasn't hers, a house that now echoed with violence. Every small sound seemed amplified, from the steady tick-tick-tick of the clock to the low hum of the refrigerator. Her heart was still racing, and she felt cold despite the warmth flooding in from the windows. She held onto Alfie tighter. His soft fur was a comforting balm against the icy fear slowly seeping back into her veins.

She thought about Connelly, his smile that could light up even the darkest corners of her mind, and his way of always making her feel safe. Now he was missing, possibly in danger or... or...

The door moved at her back and she jumped up with a yelp of fear. The intruder was back! Maybe this time with a gun. She should run, but she looked around the living room in panic and realized her legs were too shaky to move. As the doorknob began to turn, she tightened her grip on Alfie, bracing herself for what was about to come.

But instead of the ominous figure she expected to see, in walked a shell-shocked Connelly. He was covered head-to-toe in mud and smelled like a musty dungeon, but she'd never seen any man look so beautiful.

He was alive.

She threw herself into his arms. He caught her without question and held her tight. He'd always catch her. She hated herself for forgetting that.

"Vee?" After several long moments, he drew away. "What are you doing here?" He looked at her and then at the blood stains on the wall. "Jesus. What happened?"

Without his support, she was shivering so hard she struggled to remain upright. She stuttered, attempting to explain everything that had happened while he was gone, but the words wouldn't come.

A siren cut through the air outside as a deputy vehicle skidded into the driveway.

"What the hell?" Connelly muttered.

Their arrival only amplified the fear clawing at her chest, but she took a shaky step back from him. "I called them. I didn't know where you were, and the intruder... he... he got away."

"Intruder?"

"I don't know who he was," she whispered. "He didn't say anything... but I think he was looking for you."

He stared at her, concern and confusion warring on his face. Then his gaze flicked back to the blood on the wall, and realization widened his eyes. He scrubbed a hand through his mud-caked hair. "Fuck. The stalker. He must've left the cave and come right here."

"Cave?" Momentarily distracted from the fear, she eyed the mud coating him. "Why were you in a cave?"

Before he could respond, there was a knock on the door, and two uniformed officers stepped inside, their stern expressions giving way to surprise as they took in the disarray of the living room—the skewed frames, the blood on the wall, and the two disheveled individuals staring back at them.

"We got a call about a break-in and a potential assault." The older of the officers, a burly man with salt-and-pepper hair, spoke first. His tone was mildly irritated as he gave Veronica an impassive once-over. "Are you all right, ma'am?"

She nodded weakly and took a step closer to Connelly, needing his strength. He was her anchor in this storm. Without him, she'd be blown away.

The younger officer, a woman with steel grey eyes and a stern expression, studied their surroundings critically. "I'm Deputy Delgado, and this is my partner, Deputy Turney. Could you tell us what happened here?"

Connelly spoke up then. "I was out on a rescue all day with RWCR and the sheriff. I came back and found all this. Where the hell were you guys? Ash promised to have someone sitting on Veronica's house."

"This isn't Veronica's house," Turney pointed out with a faint sneer. "We were exactly where we were supposed to be. How do you think we got here so fast?"

"It wasn't fast enough," Connelly snapped, running a hand through his hair, the mud flaking off onto the hardwood floor. "This guy's dangerous. He's killed once and nearly succeeded in taking a second victim today. And he was here, in my house, fighting with Veronica, but you didn't notice?"

"Our job was to sit on Veronica Martens' house," Turney replied, biting off each word. "The sheriff said nothing about watching your place, too. We can't be everywhere at once."

Delgado sent her partner a look of barely concealed contempt before smoothing her face into an unreadable mask.

Veronica knew that feeling well. She'd once been a woman in a male-dominated profession. She knew what it was like to have to defer to men who thought they knew more than she did solely because of the different equipment between their legs.

Connelly gave the older deputy a hard stare but said nothing. Turney probably didn't notice, but Veronica knew him to his core and could see the threadbare patience in his gaze. He didn't have a hot temper... until he did. Then watch out.

She needed to diffuse the situation and put a hand on his arm. "I'm okay."

He looked down at her, and his eyes softened. "Vee, are you sure?"

"I'm fine," she muttered, even though she knew she was far from it.

Connelly scowled. He looked like he wanted to argue, but the female officer spoke up again.

"You said the intruder ran into the woods?"

Veronica nodded.

Delgado reached for her radio. "I'll call in backup to search for him and the forensics team to dust for prints, take samples of that blood."

Turney grumbled something under his breath and stepped out onto the porch.

Delgado ignored him and stayed focused on Veronica, her gaze sympathetic. "In the meantime, you should go to the hospital—"

"No." The suggestion had her throat closing up with panic. "No, I can't."

Connelly put a soothing hand on her back. "I was a medic in the Air Force. I'll make sure she's okay, and if she's not, I'll drive her to the hospital myself."

Delgado eyed him, then gave a curt nod. "I'm afraid you won't be able to stay here until after the forensics team is finished."

"We'll be over at Veronica's," Connelly said. "Would it be okay if I grabbed some fresh clothes from the bedroom closet?"

Delgado hesitated for a moment, glancing toward the hallway that led to the bedrooms. "Just a minute," she said, then reached for her radio again, murmuring something into it. A moment later, she nodded at Connelly. "All right, make it quick."

Connelly disappeared down the hallway, sidestepping the streaks of blood. Veronica watched him go and found herself grabbing onto Alfie for support. The little dog whined anxiously and pressed up against her, obviously distraught by the lingering tension in the room.

While he was gone, Deputy Delgado snapped some photos of Rebel's bloodied muzzle. "Looks like this good girl took a chunk out of the guy."

Veronica nodded and tried to speak but found her throat had seized up. She cleared it and tried again. "She bit his arm and his leg."

"Good girl," Delgado said again and stoked an admiring hand over Rebel's head. Rebel's tail thunked against the floor, and she gave the deputy a sloppy doggie smile. "That should help us identify him."

Connelly returned a few moments later with a duffel bag slung over one shoulder and exchanged a few murmured words with the deputy. He showed her what was in his bag, and she nodded.

"Okay," she said. "We'll get this sorted out as fast as we can, but I recommend you two find somewhere else to stay for the night."

Staying anywhere but at home was out of the question.

Thankfully, Connelly already knew that and said, "We'll be staying at Veronica's."

"If you insist, I'll personally make sure the sheriff assigns someone more..." She trailed off and glanced toward her partner on the porch, then lowered her voice. "*Competent* to the protection detail."

"Thank you." Connelly nodded and turned to Veronica. "Ready?"

chapter
eighteen

VERONICA DIDN'T SAY a word during the walk back to her cabin. She walked with single-minded purpose, eyes focused on the path ahead like a horse with blinders on.

Connelly let her have the silence until the door shut behind them. He opened his mouth to say... he didn't know what. But he didn't get the chance to utter a sound. She held up a hand, stopping him, and went into her bedroom. Alfie trotted after her without a backward glance. The bedroom door shut behind them.

Rebel, still bloodstained, sat down next to him and stared up, a look of confusion in her eyes.

He met the dog's gaze until she looked toward the bedroom.

"I know. I don't like being shut out either." He rubbed her soft ear. "Let's get cleaned up and give her some time. Alfie will take care of her for us."

In the bathroom, he took a moment to dial Ash. The sheriff needed to know what happened at his place, and he didn't trust the deputies to do it.

When he finished explaining, Ash sighed. "I'm sorry about

that. Delgado is still green, but she's one of the good ones. Turney… is not."

"Then why not get rid of him?"

"It's on my to-do list." His tone said that the to-do list was about as long as a redwood was tall.

"Any word on Lucy's condition?" Connelly asked. The rescue had taken hours, and Lucy had lost consciousness before they managed to free her.

"She's very dehydrated and has lost a lot of blood. She slipped into a coma, but the doctors are still optimistic about her chances. Sawyer's staying with her."

Connelly smirked. "Yeah?"

"Yeah, I don't know. Said he promised her or some shit. I still can't believe you sent the blind man into a cave."

"Worked, didn't it? He found her and kept her calm until the calvary arrived."

Ash grunted. "If you want updates on her, he'd be the one to contact. I'm headed to your place now to meet the forensics unit."

"If you need me, I'm at Veronica's." Though, this place was nothing like how he pictured Veronica's home. He picked up the hand towel hanging beside the sink and shook his head at the rooster printed on it. Farmhouse chic. Veronica almost certainly didn't buy that. It must have come with the rental, like everything else. There was nothing of the vibrant woman he'd known here, and he could hardly picture the once fiercely independent Veronica living amidst these rooster-printed hand towels and dainty floral motifs. The Veronica he knew had loved sharp colors and bold artwork that made a statement. Her old apartment had been an eclectic mix of pop art and abstract paintings that seemed to shout out their existence at anyone who entered, each piece selected for its vibrancy and ability to stir emotions.

Now, Connelly stood amidst the neutral tones of this

quaint country cabin, a place as calming as a cup of chamomile tea on a quiet morning, and heavy sadness filled his chest. He ran his fingers over the coarse fabric, picturing Veronica's smiling face from the days of their reckless youth. Those bright, wild eyes that dared the world to hold her back.

"I'll need to talk to her," Ash said, drawing him back to the conversation.

He sighed and set the towel down. "I know. I'll prepare her for it."

There was a lot of shuffling on the other end, and then Ash came back to the line. "How is she?"

Connelly looked at the closed bathroom door. "Not sure yet."

"I need to catch this fucking asshole," Ash muttered. "Don't let Veronica out of your sight until I do."

"Wasn't planning on it. Hey, Ash?" he added before Ash could end the call. "I need a gun. I bought one the other day, but the waiting period... I can't wait any longer."

"No, you can't. I'll get you one."

"Thanks," he said, but Ash was already gone. He set the phone on the counter and scrubbed his hands through his hair. Crusted mud fell to the floor at his feet.

"Okay. Shower," he said to Rebel, who was sitting next to the door, watching him suspiciously. "Then it's your turn."

Her ears flattened, and she crouched down, making herself as small as possible.

"That's not going to save you, girl."

He washed off the mud, then pulled Rebel into the stall with him and scrubbed the blood off her. It amused him when he scratched under her ears, and both of her legs thumped on the tile floor.

"You're a good girl." He kissed her long nose. "Thanks for protecting our Vee today. You're getting all the treats with dinner."

At the T-word, Rebel's ears perked, and she turned a tight circle in the small room, nearly knocking him off his feet.

"Okay. Okay!" He laughed and opened the bathroom door, intending to let her out while he dressed. She had other ideas. She ripped his towel off and burst through the door, prancing right past a wide-eyed Veronica, the towel flying behind her like a white flag.

Veronica stared at him, her eyes going even wider as her gaze slid down the front of him.

"Shit. Sorry." He reached blindly for the first thing he could find to cover himself—the hand towel.

To his shock, Veronica burst out laughing.

He looked down and saw the cock covering his cock, and his ears burned with embarrassment. He pushed the door shut with his foot, threw the stupid rooster towel in the trash can, and quickly dressed. He wasn't usually self-conscious about his body, but this was Veronica. She'd never seen him naked before, and he'd always hoped if she ever did, it would be under sexier circumstances. Not because a dog stole his towel.

Jesus.

He waited until his face stopped burning before opening the door.

Veronica wasn't in the living room anymore. He peeked into her room, but she wasn't there either. Nor was she in the kitchen, though there was a freshly opened bottle of wine on the counter next to an empty, unused glass. A cool, salted breeze swept across the kitchen, and he looked toward the back door, his heart jumping into his throat when he saw it open.

She wouldn't have gone out there willingly, would she?

"Veronica?"

He found her sitting on the deck chair with Alfie on her lap, staring out over the restless Pacific. Her eyes were closed, and her fingers were buried in Alfie's fur. Instead of wine, she had a glass of water on the table beside her.

"What are you doing out here?" He settled into the seat next to her.

Rebel padded over, still dragging the towel, and dropped it at his feet before resting her head on Veronica's knee.

"Thanks, monster," he muttered. "But I don't need that anymore."

A smile flitted over Veronica's mouth, but she still didn't open her eyes. "You should've seen your face."

His ears burned again. "Can we pretend that never happened?"

The twitch of a smile widened. "Not a chance in hell, buddy."

This was his Vee. The one he remembered. For just this instant, she was here with him, and it made his throat close up. It took several seconds before he trusted himself to speak without his voice breaking.

"What are you doing out here?" he asked again.

"I challenged myself to sit here for ten minutes."

"How long has it been?"

"Not long enough."

He watched her. The longer she sat there, the more she relaxed, the easier her breathing. "I think you'll make it."

Finally, she exhaled and opened her eyes. "I was scared today."

He wanted to reach for her, to squeeze her hand but stayed still. "I know. I'm sorry I wasn't there."

"But I didn't freeze. I didn't let the fear win."

A silence settled between them, broken only by the lapping of the waves and the distant cries of seagulls. Connelly took a deep breath, tasting the salt in the air, but she spoke again before he settled on what to say.

"I'm tired of letting fear win, Conn."

"Then don't."

"It's not that easy."

"You did it today."

"That was different. That was a tangible threat I had to deal with. But the daily fear? The fear that keeps me locked in the house? It's not tangible. It's not logical. I know it's not, but knowing that doesn't stop it." Tears squeezed from the corners of her eyes, and she shook her head hard as if to fling them away. "If I could just decide to stop being scared, don't you think I would've done it by now? I'm exhausted. I don't even know myself anymore. If I could've woken up one day and just decided to be normal again, I would have done it ages ago."

"Normal's overrated."

She didn't seem to hear him. Or, if she did, she ignored him. "It's not a voluntary reaction. It's not controllable. I walk outside, and every nerve in my body screams for me to run back inside, to lock the doors, to hide. I don't know why. I don't know how to stop it."

Connelly studied her profile in the fading light, taking note of the lines of exhaustion etched into her face. The Veronica he knew was a fighter; she had always been a fighter. But now, that fight seemed to have ebbed away, leaving only a hollowed-out husk of the woman she once was.

"But you're sitting outside now," he pointed out.

Her arms tightened around Alfie. The dog licked her cheek before burrowing under her chin. "It's taking everything I have to stay put and not run inside and drown myself in that bottle of wine."

So the fight hadn't completely disappeared from her, after all. "That's still a victory. And you faced down a killer today. Most *normal* people wouldn't have been able to do that. Another victory. A huge one. You can conquer this."

"How?"

"You could start by talking to Rylan Cross."

"No."

"Or go back to group therapy. The guys there miss you."

She turned toward him, her eyes huge and full of a desperation he had never seen before. The sight sent a pang of guilt through him.

"You think I can just go back? Walk into that room full of men and just... trust them?"

"Yes, because they're your friends."

"Friends?" She scoffed as more tears slid from her eyes. "I was raped, Connelly. I was raped by three men I thought were my friends. And when I told them no, tried to fight them off, they pulled a gun on me."

He flinched at the reminder. What she'd gone through that night... it was unthinkable. Unbearable. "They were never your friends."

If she heard him, she didn't acknowledge it. "How can I ever trust anyone again?"

"Do you trust me?"

She pressed her lips into a thin line and turned to stare at the sunset.

It hurt, and the hurt rankled. He clenched his jaw, swallowing down the bitter taste of regret. "Do you blame me for leaving you alone in the hotel that night? Leaving you with those men?"

"You couldn't have known," she whispered. "You thought they were your friends, too."

"But you blame me anyway."

The silence between them stretched out, filled only by the soft rustle of the wind through the spring leaves and Rebel's soft snore from where she lay curled up with the towel at Veronica's feet. Twilight encased them in its cool embrace.

"I'm sorry," he said at last, breaking the silence. "I know

that doesn't make up for anything, but I'll be sorry for losing my temper and leaving you there until the day I die."

"No. I shouldn't have made a big deal about..." She trailed off and took a breath. "About what happened between us that night. About that kiss and where we seemed to be headed with it. It scared me because you're... you. And I never saw you as more than a friend until suddenly, that night, I did."

"I've always wanted more than friendship with you." He said it suddenly, almost too candidly, and the words seemed to hang in the air between them, the ghost of a truth he had long kept secret. In the thick silence that followed, he could hear his own heartbeat too loudly in his ears.

Veronica turned and stared at him, her teary eyes wide in surprise, her mouth opening slightly as if to speak. But no words came out.

He shifted uncomfortably, feeling more naked now than he had in the bathroom with nothing but that ugly hand towel. "I probably shouldn't have said that."

"No, you should have. I..." Her voice trailed off. "I need to go back inside."

He didn't move as she set Alfie down and stood. Didn't move as she passed by him close enough that he could smell the familiar scent of her favorite lotion—warm vanilla and dark cherry. Didn't move as her fingers brushed the back of his hand in a light touch. A kind of peace offering. He longed to reach out, to pull her into his arms and convince her to stay.

But he didn't.

As she reached the door, her slender fingers lingered on the pull of the sliding door. She didn't look back at him, but he could see her shoulders tense. "I don't blame you for what happened to me, Connelly. I blame you for using it for fodder for one of your books."

That finally got him moving. He burst out of the chair, hating that he made her flinch. "It wasn't like that."

"It was a betrayal I can never forgive." She opened the door and stepped inside, shutting the door with a firm thump in his face.

He pulled it open and followed her. "No. You're not walking away from this conversation. Not again." He crossed to the bookcase in the living room and pulled his book off the shelf. "Did you even read the whole thing?"

Temper sparked in her eyes as she poured wine into the waiting glass. "Fuck, no. Why would I?"

"Because I didn't write it *about* you, Veronica. I wrote it *for* you. To remind you how strong you are. To remind you that you can conquer any-fucking-thing." He slapped the book down on the island beside her glass. "Even fear."

chapter
nineteen

"READ IT. And if you still think I betrayed you, I'll deserve all of your hatred and more." Connelly went to the front door and whistled to the dogs. They charged in from the back deck, tails wagging. "We'll be out front. And I'm staying tonight, but I'm not sleeping on the porch again. I'll take the couch."

He stepped through the door and disappeared outside. She hated him for that, for the ease with which he could leave if he wanted.

Veronica downed the glass of wine without taking a breath, then stared at the book like it was a vile creature.

The Shadows Within.

She traced the embossed letters on the cover with a trembling hand. She didn't want to read it. She was afraid it might reveal more about her than she was ready to face.

But she faced a killer today. She went for a walk and sat on her deck. After all that, she wasn't about to back down from this simple challenge.

She could read a damn book.

The dogs' playful barks echoed from outside, reminding her that she was not alone.

Drawing a deep breath, she took the book to her bedroom,

opened the cover, and began to read. As the world Connelly had written unfolded before her, it was like walking through a mirror image of her own fears, magnified and darkened. It was gruesome, violent. It was terrifying... and intoxicating, like the heady rush of a roller coaster's first drop. With each page, she was unwillingly pulled deeper into the town of Ravenshade.

Hours passed. Her wine glass stood empty. Connelly let the dogs into the bedroom, and they curled up on either side of her, Rebel against her legs and Alfie under the blanket at her hip. At one point, she heard the sheriff in the living room talking to Connelly, but she ignored them. She was too engrossed to break away from the hold the book had on her. The tale was all-consuming, a window into her own struggles wrapped in a veil of fiction.

Connelly's writing skill pulled every emotion from her with an intensity that left her raw and unsettled. She saw all the obvious pieces of herself in Vanessa Vale: the physical description, the stubbornness, the overwhelming fear that kept her trapped inside her home. But underneath it all ran a current of resilience. Despite the mounting threats, Vanessa never surrendered. She stumbled and fumbled—yes. She was terrified—yes. But she didn't give up. And she prevailed.

When Veronica finally set the book down, her eyes stung from staring at the pages for so long, but she couldn't deny the truth. Connelly hadn't betrayed her. He had used her painful past to craft a story of fear and triumph, and he'd dedicated it to her.

She flipped to the front of the book and read the dedication again:

For Vee, the strongest person I know.

She traced the words, and tears welled in her eyes. Connelly had taken something so private and intimate, something that had scarred her so deeply, and turned it into a story of hope and fortitude.

In the book's protagonist, she didn't see the broken woman she saw when she looked in the mirror. Instead, she saw a warrior. A survivor. A woman who refused to be broken by the darkness that threatened to engulf her.

Was that how Connelly saw her?

She climbed off the bed and found him asleep on the couch, his laptop open on his lap, the blue glow of the screen illuminating his face. His head was tipped back, his mouth slightly open. He looked peaceful, the lines of worry that usually furrowed his brow smoothed out in sleep.

In an instant, she was thrown back to San Antonio and that day on the river when he fell asleep on his tube. She still had that picture of him, and looked at it more often than she cared to admit.

She hesitated for a moment, then quietly approached him. The living room felt empty and quiet now, the only sounds being the soft hum of the laptop fan and Connelly's steady breathing.

She stopped by the couch, looking down at her childhood friend. The man who used her pain to create a horror masterpiece. A story that mirrored her own life and yet gave her a sense of hope she hadn't felt in a long time. She wanted to hate him for it, for making her confront her demons through the pages of his book. But she couldn't. Not anymore.

She reached out and gently closed his laptop, setting it aside on the coffee table. He stirred but didn't wake up. She unfolded the quilt from the back of the couch and draped it over him.

Tomorrow.

She'd tell him what the book meant to her tomorrow.

She returned to her room, carrying *The Shadows Within* with her. But this time, she didn't open it to read. She clutched it against her chest like a cherished amulet as she lay down in bed and snuggled the dogs.

Veronica bolted awake as the scream tore from her throat, and less than a heartbeat later, her bedroom door flew open. Connelly was there, gun in hand, sweeping the room like the professional badass he was.

Rebel growled, her hackles rising until she realized who it was. She settled at the foot of the bed again, but she was tense, alert, ready to spring into action at a moment's notice. Alfie poked up from under the blankets and yawned. Somehow, the sight of him calmed Veronica more than the tough, muscular dog sitting guard over her feet. She scooped him up and buried her face in his soft fur.

"Are you okay?" Connelly asked, his voice soothing even as he continued to scan the room for threats.

She gasped for air and looked around the room, her eyes darting from one corner to the next. It was dark and quiet, but she couldn't shake the feeling that something was watching her.

Connelly stepped closer, his gun still at the ready. "Don't worry. You have nothing to be afraid of, Vee. I've got you. You're safe here."

She nodded and forced herself to draw deep, even breaths until her heartbeat slowed from a gallop to a trot. "Okay," she managed after a moment. "Okay," she repeated and loosened her death grip on Alfie. She set him back down on the bed and watched as he snuggled under the blankets.

Connelly set the gun within easy reach on the nightstand and sat on the edge of the bed, his gaze never leaving her. "Do you want to talk about it?"

She shook her head and hugged her knees to her chest. "It was just a nightmare."

"I know how hard it can be to shake those off." He

reached out and brushed a strand of hair from her face. "I'll be right out in the living room if you decide you want to talk."

She leaned into his touch, grateful for the warmth and comfort he provided. "Stay with me. Please." The words were out of her before she could think better of them.

If Connelly was shocked, he did a good job hiding it. Without a word, he crawled onto the bed beside her, staying on top of the blankets. He didn't touch her but scooted close enough that their foreheads nearly pressed together.

"Was it my book?" he asked softly.

Moisture gathered in her eyes. She pinched them shut, willing herself not to cry, and shook her head. No, it hadn't been his book. It hadn't even been the asshole who attacked her yesterday. It was the same nightmare she always had, three blurred faces leaning over her, laughing, grunting... faces of friends twisted into demons. A tear squeezed out despite her efforts, and he caught it on his thumb.

"I hate seeing you cry, Vee. I wish I could trade places with you, take all of your fear into me just to give you a moment's peace."

She sniffled, wiping away the tears with the back of her hand. "But you can't. No one can. It's just something I have to deal with."

Connelly's eyes darkened with concern. "But that's the problem. You're not dealing with it."

"I know." It stung to admit, but he was right and she was so tired.

Tired of the fear.

Tired of not feeling like herself.

Tired of... everything.

She didn't know how much longer she could live like this.

She scooted forward until her forehead pressed against his, and she felt the warmth of his breath on her skin. It was a comfort, an anchor in the storm of her thoughts and feelings.

And for the moment, she wasn't scared. She could never be afraid of him.

"Can you... hold me?"

Connelly's arms slid around her waist and pulled her close. There were still blankets between them, but she liked the solid weight of his body against hers, the strength of his muscles beneath his t-shirt, and found herself relaxing into his embrace. He was a protector, a defender, and she felt safer with him than she had with anyone in a very long time.

"Where did you get the gun?" she asked, her voice muffled against his neck.

"Ash came by. He wanted to question you, but I told him you needed time."

"Thank you."

He rested his chin on top of her head. "You never did tell me why you were at my house earlier."

"And you never told me about why you were in a cave."

His soft chuckle made his throat hum against her cheek. "I helped RWCR with a rescue. I helped save a woman today."

Something in his voice—exhilaration with a note of... was it longing?—had her pulling back to look at him. "You loved it."

He breathed in deeply and exhaled in a rush. "I did. I forgot how good it feels to help someone during the worst moments of their life. I've missed it. Don't get me wrong, I love writing. I've always wanted to write—you know that. But I think I need to help people, too. I think that's why I haven't been able to write for a while now."

She pushed herself up on her elbow. "Are you going to join the team?"

"I'm considering it."

"You should." The words gave her a pang of envy. She wished she could be like him, finding a balance between the past and the present. But her past was a gaping hole, sucking up any possibility of moving forward.

Reaching out, she traced the faint scar on his chin. That scar represented everything Connelly Davis was. A fierce protector. A capable healer. A supportive ally even in the worst moments.

"You should," she said again. "I'm sure the team could use a medic."

Connelly caught her hand and kissed her knuckles gently. "Vee," he said in that soft voice of his, full of compassion. "Why does that make you sad?"

"I..." She wanted to be happy for him that he'd found his place again, found a purpose, and she hated that he'd picked up on the note of sadness in her voice. "I wish I could be like you."

"What do you mean?"

"You have... life." The last word came out choked, causing Rebel to whine softly, her ears perking up in concern. Alfie squirmed to get closer. She gave them both reassuring pats and settled into Connelly's waiting arms.

"You have it, too," he whispered into her hair, holding her closer. "You're full of life. Always have been. You've just lost your way a bit, is all. You're so much stronger than you think."

"But what if I'm so broken I can't ever be fixed?" she whispered against his shoulder. It was her greatest fear, one she'd never before spoken out loud, and she held her breath for several long seconds until he responded.

"No one's completely broken." His hand cupped her head, fingers threading through her hair in a comforting rhythm. "Sometimes we just need to find a new way of being. It's like that big mosaic you used to have on your apartment's wall. The one you found at that flea market in San Antonio? That was just a bunch of broken pieces of glass glued together, but nobody would have ever looked at it and called it broken.

It was beautiful, and, in that new form, the glass pieces were stronger than they used to be."

His words sunk deep into her heart, spreading like roots through the barren places she'd been too afraid to explore. She nestled herself deeper into his arms, craving the warmth and safety he provided as his fingers continued their calming stroke through her hair.

"You always know what to say."

"Not always," Connelly admitted with a sad chuckle against her temple. "After what happened to you, I had no idea what to say. It's why I wrote the book. I never meant for it to hurt you."

"No, I should've read it instead of just assuming it was a cash grab at my expense. I know you better than that. I'm sorry I held it against you. I was just too hurt and confused and didn't want to see the truth."

He gave her a squeeze. "You don't need to apologize, Vee. I was confused, too. And hurt. And angry—so fucking angry. At those shitheads for hurting you. At myself for leaving you there. At the Air Force for brushing it all under the rug because Blake-fucking-Edwards was a general's son. You know I punched him after I found out what he did? Broke his jaw. That's why I had to leave the PJs. He got his dad to say I was reckless and dangerous, and eventually, they made up some bullshit excuse to push me out, too."

"My dad told me. I'm so sorry. I know it must've hurt after all the work you did to get into pararescue."

"Yeah." His lips curved into a smirk. "Worth it."

Silence fell between them, filled with the soft sounds of their breathing and the occasional snore from Rebel. She closed her eyes, a strange kind of peace settling over her.

"Did it help?" she asked in a faint whisper.

"What, punching the bastard?"

"Writing the book." She felt his fingers pause in her hair before resuming their soothing strokes.

"It did," he admitted after a moment.

Veronica allowed another silence to stretch between them, her thoughts wandering to the past. Before the rape. Before the Air Force. Back when they were kids playing around in his backyard in the summertime, the dry grass crunchy under bare feet and carefree laughter ringing through the air. There had been something wonderfully simple about those days. She wished they could go back.

"You made me brave," she said. "In the book."

"You *are* brave."

"I don't feel it."

"Because bravery isn't about not being scared. It's about being scared and doing it anyway. Like you did today." Connelly's lips brushed her temple. "So, are you going to tell me why you went to my place today?"

She hesitated. "Because you weren't here."

"You told me to stay away."

"I didn't mean it."

"I'm here now."

"I know. I'm glad for it." She breathed in, taking his scent deep into her head and lungs. "Can we just... stay like this for a while?"

"We can stay like this forever if that's what you want."

She didn't know how long they lay there together, wrapped in the cocoon of the bed and each other's arms. But eventually, the tension drained from her body.

Forever, she thought as she drifted to sleep. She liked the sound of it.

chapter
twenty

CONNELLY WOKE to find Veronica's side of the bed empty, and he could hear her talking to the dogs in the other room. After spending so many nights sleeping on the hard wood of her front porch, he'd slept like a rock in her bed. He smiled a little at the memory of holding her as she drifted to sleep, and his heart seemed to expand, filling his whole chest.

He stretched, every single one of his muscles protesting after yesterday's cave rescue. But it was a good ache. He felt alive, purposeful. He felt like a piece of his soul had slotted back into place, a piece he'd not even realized was missing.

He would join RWCR, he decided, and swung his legs out of the bed. The wood floor was cold under his bare feet as he padded into the kitchen, drawn by the scent of fresh coffee and the comforting sound of Veronica's voice as she animatedly babbled to Rebel and Alfie. He leaned in the doorway for a moment to watch them. Veronica was wearing a faded band shirt and flannel pajama bottoms, her dark hair piled into a messy bun atop her head. She moved around the kitchen with ease, adding dog food into two bowls while speaking in a high-pitched tone that made Rebel's ears perk up and Alfie scamper around excitedly.

She looked good. Relaxed. Peaceful. Happy, even.

A wave of tenderness washed over him. He wanted to hug her, just wrap his arms around her, bury his face in all that dark hair, and breathe her in. He hesitated, debating until he finally decided, *fuck it*. They'd already crossed that line last night. If she didn't want him touching her in the light of day, she'd tell him, but he wouldn't know until he tried. He went to her, wrapping his arms around her as she straightened from setting the dog dishes on the floor.

"Morning," he said against her temple.

To his surprise, she didn't startle at the unexpected touch. She leaned back against him, relaxing into his arms.

"Good morning," she replied with a lightness that made his heart do strange things.

"Any more nightmares?"

She shook her head. "Not even a dream. I slept better than I have in years."

Typically, the last thing an author wanted to hear was that he was a cure for insomnia, but this time, Connelly welcomed the news. He tightened his arms around her. "Maybe it was the company."

"Hm. Maybe." She turned around, her dark eyes meeting his, and there was a warmth in them that he hadn't seen in a long time. "The dogs *are* good company."

When he opened his mouth to protest, she laughed softly and reached out to smooth her thumb over the crease between his brows. "You, too. Maybe I should keep you around."

He caught her hand and brought it to his lips. "Maybe I'd like that."

She moistened her lips. "I think... I'd like that, too."

He didn't miss the subtle shift of her body closer toward his, and he found himself closing the gap between them, drawn by the warmth of her skin, the twinkle in her eyes, the vanilla and cherry scent of her. Before he knew what he was doing, he tilted his head down, his lips brushing against hers. Veronica stiffened for a moment before melting into the kiss, her arms winding around his neck as she pressed herself closer.

He tasted coffee on her lips, and it was more intoxicating than any drink he'd ever sipped. Her hands found their way to his morning stubble, grazing it lightly before threading into his hair. His senses were overwhelmed—all thoughts of caution tossed aside as he deepened the kiss, earning a sigh from Veronica that sent a shiver down his spine.

Connelly heard Rebel growl somewhere in the background but chose to ignore it for now. Untangling himself from Veronica was going to be an uphill battle, and he had every intention of dragging this moment out as long as possible.

But eventually, he had to draw back for air and rested his forehead against hers, eyes shut tight. They were swaying together in the quiet kitchen as they both caught their breaths.

He finally opened his eyes to find her watching him, her gaze soft and filled with a tender affection that made his pulse quicken.

He gave her a small smile, tucking a loose strand of her hair behind her ear. "Are you okay with this? With us... being more than friends? Because I still want to be more than friends, Vee."

She hummed an affirmative.

"You sure? I don't want to push you into anything you're not ready for." He wanted her—God, how he wanted her—but not at the expense of her comfort.

Determination flashed in her eyes as she flattened her hand against his chest. The gesture was both intimate and comforting, a silent reassurance that this was okay, that she was okay. "I'd tell you if I wasn't."

"Or if it gets to be too much?"

"I'll tell you. Promise."

Taking a deep breath, he wrapped his arms around her again, pulling her tight against him. His lips found hers once more in a slow, sweet, lingering kiss. He could feel her smile against his lips, which only encouraged him further.

Rebel let out a series of deep barks and ran into the living room. Alfie joined in, yapping wildly as he scampered behind her toward the front door.

Someone knocked.

Veronica broke from the kiss, and her entire body tensed.

"Shh." He rubbed a soothing hand over her back. "It's okay. It's probably Ash. I'm sure he's impatient to get your statement. You know him."

The knock came again, louder this time. All the warmth and peace that had filled the room a moment ago seemed to evaporate.

"I'm not ready," she whispered and buried her face in his shirt.

"Want me to tell him to get lost?"

"No." She sighed and stepped out of his arms, and he instantly missed the warmth of her body against his. He could see the anxiety in her eyes as she glanced toward the door. "No. Let's get it over with."

"How about you stay in here and brew a fresh pot of coffee for us? I'll go let him in. Give you some time to steady those nerves."

"Okay. Coffee." She straightened her spine. "Yeah, I can do that."

He watched her for a moment longer, his gaze taking in the determined set of her shoulders and the way she was nervously biting her lower lip.

"Just remember to breathe, Vee." He leaned forward and pressed a quick kiss to her forehead before moving toward the door. "Rebel. Alfie. Come on. Away from the door."

The dogs instantly obeyed, but not without whines of protest.

He opened the door to find Ash standing on the other side, his clothes rumpled like he'd slept in them—if he'd slept at all. Judging by the shadows of exhaustion around his eyes, he hadn't. His expression was always serious, but today, it was grave.

"Ash," he greeted, stepping aside to let him in. "You look like you've been dragged through a hedge backward. Long night?"

The sheriff gave him a curt nod as he stepped over the threshold. "You could say that. How's Veronica?"

"Honestly, she's better than I expected. She's making coffee." He closed and locked the door, then led Ash into the kitchen.

Veronica looked up at their entrance, her eyes wide, but her hands were steady as she pulled mugs down from the cupboard. "Morning, Sheriff. Do you want coffee?"

"I won't turn down caffeine." He sat heavily in one of the chairs at the table, dragging a hand over his reddish-brown beard. "You wouldn't happen to have an IV bag lying around so I can mainline it?"

Veronica's shoulders relaxed, and she even gave a soft laugh. "Sorry, you'll have to drink it the old-fashioned way. Black?"

"Yes, thank you."

She poured mugs for the three of them—black for Ash and Connelly, cream and sugar for her—and carried them over to the table. When she sat, Connelly pulled his chair close enough to hers that their legs touched under the table.

The sheriff eyed them over the rim of his mug, and a smile flitted over his hard lips before he took a testing sip. "How are you two holding up after yesterday?"

Connelly started to answer but closed his mouth and

looked at Veronica. She was the one who had faced down a killer yesterday, and he didn't want to put words into her mouth.

She took her time in answering, drinking her coffee in silence for several long seconds. "I'm okay. I think... it put some things into perspective for me." She looked at Connelly with a soft smile, then over the table at Ash. "Did you find him?"

"No." Ash's eyes hardened. "And I'm afraid I have bad news."

"Shit," Connelly said and set his mug down. "Lucy?"

"No, no. She's still in the hospital, still fighting. Getting stronger and angrier every minute, according to Sawyer."

Dread curdled the coffee in his stomach. "Then who?"

"We don't know. Haven't ID'd the body. It was..." Ash swallowed, and the color left his face. "Horrific."

"Which scene was it?"

"I believe he was trying to reenact the aichmophobia scene."

"Fear of sharp objects." Connelly shut his eyes and took a moment to breathe through the flood of anger and regret. He never should've written that scene. "Fuck. That's a bad one."

"It was the worst thing I've ever seen in my life," Ash said. "But other than the knives, it was nothing like the scene in your book. We saved Lucy, then Veronica and Rebel got the better of him, and it pissed him off. He lost control."

Veronica's gaze ping-ponged back and forth between them. "Wait. What do you mean it wasn't like the scene in his book? Why the hell would it be like the book?"

Ash sat back in his seat. "Jesus, Davis. You haven't told her?"

Connelly winced.

Ash sighed heavily and met Veronica's gaze over the table.

"This killer—the guy you and Rebel scared off yesterday—is obsessed with his books."

"So that's why the deputies were sitting in front of my house?" she asked.

"Yes. Given that the heroine of the book is loosely based on you, we thought it best to provide protection."

Connelly turned toward her. "I'm sorry I didn't tell you sooner. I was afraid it would trigger your anxiety."

She sat back in her chair, her eyes wide and staring as though seeing him for the first time. "So this guy... the guy from yesterday... he's... he's a fan?"

"It appears that way," Ash answered. "We have people going through every fan letter, email, and social media DM that Connelly's ever received. We're also looking into the former girlfriend, Sara Parker."

"Girlfriend?" Veronica echoed faintly.

Connelly reached out to touch her hand, but she pulled away, wrapping her arms around herself.

He let his hand fall back onto his lap. "She wasn't a girlfriend. She was a mistake. An obsessed reader I stupidly slept with—*one time*—before I realized how absolutely crazy she was."

"We haven't found her," Ash said. "Seattle police say she left the city, and a traffic cam caught her three weeks ago at a rest stop off I-5 in Oregon, headed south."

"You think she's here?" Connelly asked.

"I do, yes."

"And you still think she's involved?"

Veronica shook her head. "The intruder at Connelly's was definitely a man."

"We're not ruling out any possibilities until we find her," Ash said evenly. "And anything you remember about the man from yesterday can help." He pulled a notebook from his pocket and flipped open the battered green leather cover. "So, can you walk me through the whole thing, starting from when you got to the house?"

Veronica's hands clenched around her mug, all the color draining from her face. Connelly watched the changing emotions in her eyes— fear, shock, anger. She sucked in a shaky breath and blew it out slowly.

"Okay," she said finally, her voice a bare whisper. "Okay. I hadn't seen Conn yet that day, and I was worried, so I walked over..."

Connelly listened as she recounted every detail, from how she'd noticed the front door was unlocked to how the man had attacked her and Rebel had intervened. His heart raced with each graphic detail, a knot of guilt and worry twisting in his gut.

She could've ended up in the hospital, fighting for her life like Lucy Harper. Or worse, dead like May-Lynn Tapia and the unnamed victim from last night.

His books were meant to thrill and entertain, not inspire real-life horrors. He had never imagined that someone would take his words this far.

Occasionally, Ash interrupted with questions, which Veronica answered as best as she could. When he asked her to describe the man, she shook her head.

"It was dark in the hallway, and he was backlit by the window in Connelly's bedroom. I mostly just saw his silhouette. But—" She stopped. "He was young. Maybe mid-to-late twenties. I think he had dark hair... but maybe that was just a hat. The hair on his arms was light, so it was probably a hat. I'm just not sure."

"Did you notice any identifying marks?" Ash asked. "Tattoos? Scars? Birthmarks?"

"No, I—" She stopped again, considered. "Actually, when Rebel bit him, she ripped his shirt, and I think I saw a mark low on his stomach." She motioned to her pelvis. "Or maybe on his hip? It was just a split-second glimpse, but it looked big. Like one of those red birthmarks babies sometimes have… what do you call them?"

"Port wine stain?" Connelly suggested.

She nodded. "Yeah, that's it. But I'm not even sure if that's what I saw. It could've just been blood."

"Okay," Ash said, and after a second complete run-through of the events, he closed his notebook. He pinched the bridge of his nose like he had a headache and then looked at the two of them for a long moment. "Okay," he said again. "Listen. We have his DNA and blood now. He's devolving and getting sloppy. It's only a matter of time until we catch him, but until we do, I want both of you to take every precaution. I'd feel better if I could move you to a safe house…"

Veronica shook her head.

"Yeah, didn't think so, but I had to try. So, here's the deal. I'll still have my deputies stationed on the road, and I'll hand-pick every one of them so you don't end up with another one like Turney. Zak has also agreed to rotate his men and dogs through bodyguard shifts each night. They'll camp in your front yard."

When Veronica opened her mouth, no doubt to argue, he held up a hand. "This is non-negotiable." He turned to Connelly. "I assume you'll be staying here with her every night?"

"I'm not leaving her side."

"Good."

Veronica shoved out of her chair. "Do I have any say in this?"

"No," Ash said unequivocally.

"Not in this," Connelly added in a gentler tone. "We want you safe."

She stared at him, defiance flaming in her eyes and her jaw set. But he could see the fear lurking beneath the anger.

"Fine," she conceded after a moment. "But this is my house. My rules. They're not allowed inside unless I invite them."

"Or if you're in danger. That's also non-negotiable."

"I can live with that."

"I'll have Zak arrange the first shift tonight." Ash finished his coffee and set his mug down on the table, his expression softening with genuine concern. "You two... just be careful. I'll be in touch with any updates."

Ash let himself out, leaving behind a silence that buzzed with tension.

Connelly finally broke it, pushing back his chair and standing to bridge the distance between them. "I know you're pissed at me. You have every right to be. I should've told you all of this before now, but I was afraid you'd withdraw. I was afraid I'd lose you."

"I need to think," she said curtly and walked through the sliding glass doors to stand on the deck and stare out over the ocean.

He watched her, his gaze tracing the rigid line of her back and shoulders. Tension vibrated off her in palpable waves. The last thing he wanted was for her to push him away out of anger or fear.

He moved to her, stopping just a breath away. He wanted to reach for her, to reassure her with his touch, but he held back, respecting her need for distance. "Talk to me, Vee."

The silence lingered between them as she continued to stare out at the ocean. The waves crashing against the cliff below echoed around them.

After what felt like an eternity, Veronica gave a slight nod and turned around. "You're right I'm angry. At you." She motioned toward the front of the house. "At Ash. For thinking I'm some fragile flower that can't handle the truth."

"Vee..."

"And I'm mad at myself because, dammit, you were both right to think that." Her eyes were bright with unshed tears, but there was determination behind the tears. Her hands curled into fists at her sides. "I'm done being afraid. I'm done with being so weak that you didn't think you could trust me with all of this. I want control over my life again. I want to learn to defend myself."

He set his hands on her shoulders and rubbed down her arms. She was covered in goosebumps even though the morning was warm. "That's the Veronica I remember," he said softly. "The fearless pilot who wouldn't back down from any challenge."

A weak smile tugged at the corners of her mouth as she looked up at him. "Well, she's been gone for a while. But I think it's about time I brought her back."

He grinned, released her shoulders, and held out his hand in invitation. "Want to start now?"

chapter
twenty-one

CONNELLY PUSHED ALL of her furniture to the edges of the living room, then went out to his car parked in the driveway behind her poor Hyundai, which hadn't been driven in months.

She followed him as far as the front porch. "When did you get your car?"

He popped the trunk and pulled out a gym bag and a folded mat. "I asked Ash to bring it over when he stopped by last night."

He returned to the house and unfolded the mat. It was bigger than she expected, covering most of the living room floor. The dogs hopped up on the couch and watched them with curiosity—Rebel with her front paws crossed regally and Alfie sitting on her back like a little prince surveying his kingdom from his mount.

"Come here." Connelly beckoned her over, all masculine confidence. "I'll show you some basic Judo throws."

"I don't know..." She eyed the mat. "Judo?"

"I am a black belt. Fully qualified to teach."

"But you barely survived our playground tussles."

"That was before special forces training and years of dedicated mat time." He stretched his arms over his head to loosen his muscles, and she found her gaze wandering down as his T-shirt rode up, exposing his flat stomach. His sweatpants hung low on his hips, and the gray fabric didn't leave much to the imagination.

An ache bloomed in her belly, catching her by surprise. Was that... desire? She hadn't wanted anyone for a very long time. In fact, the last person she'd wanted was...

Him.

At that party.

Right before her life became a living hell.

He caught her staring and grinned. "Like what you see?"

Dammit. She flushed and looked away, wrapping her arms around herself. She hated that he caught her. Hated it more that she was staring in the first place.

This was Connelly.

She shouldn't feel anything but the warm affection of friendship toward him, but the emotions swirling inside her went way beyond friendship.

"Hey," he said softly and extended a hand. "No pressure, Vee. You set the pace."

She blew out a long breath and looked at his open palm, then back up into those deep brown eyes so full of understanding.

This was Connelly.

There was no man in the world she trusted more.

She placed her hand in his, allowing him to lead her onto the mat. His fingers closed gently around hers, warm and solid.

"First lesson," he began as they stood face-to-face, "is balance. You want to be grounded but flexible enough to evade attacks."

She swallowed hard as he moved behind her and placed his

hands on her shoulders. Her body was tense, every muscle coiled like a spring ready to snap.

"Relax," he murmured in her ear. "I'm here with you. You're safe."

She took a deep breath and forced her body to loosen.

"There you go. Feet shoulder width apart, one foot slightly in front of the other." He nudged her legs with his own. "Bend your knees. Like I said, Judo is all about balance. It's not about strength or brute force. It allows you to take on an opponent much bigger and stronger than you."

Closing her eyes, she tried to push away the gnawing fear that clawed at her insides. Focused instead on his words and the soothing warmth of his body against her back.

"Good," Connelly whispered, his breath warm against her ear. "Now, I want you to imagine someone trying to grab you from behind."

A wave of dread washed over her, making her stiffen. Images of faceless attackers filled her mind, their hands reaching for her—

"Veronica," he interrupted, voice still gentle but firm enough to snap her out of the panic tailspin. He rubbed his hands up and down her arms. "You're safe. I won't let anything happen to you."

The assurance cut through the fog of anxiety, and his touch tethered her to reality. She was safe with him. She'd always be safe with him. "I... I know."

He gave her a gentle squeeze. "You're not helpless. You'll never be helpless again. An attacker will always make a mistake, giving you the opportunity to evade or counter. You just have to learn to recognize those mistakes and take advantage. Let me show you how."

She exhaled the breath caught in her chest and nodded, clenching her fists at her sides until her nails dug into her palms. "I'm not helpless. Not anymore."

"No, you're not. Now keep your hands up." He stepped around to face her. "Do you remember the game we used to play as kids where we tried to knock each other off balance?"

The memory brought a ghost of a smile to her lips. "You were never very good at it."

"Well, I'm much better now. Judo is a bit like that. Now, imagine I'm your attacker, and I'm trying to pull you toward me. Don't resist. Just go with it."

He demonstrated by reaching out and gently tugging on her shirt. She stepped forward involuntarily.

"Good," he said again. "The key is to act quickly and decisively. First, don't panic. Take a deep breath and stay focused. Look at your foot placement. See how your front foot is right by mine. That's exactly where you want it. You step into the attack, moving in the direction of my off-balance, which is toward my forward foot. And if I were to grab you like this—" He tightened his grip on her shoulder, just enough to make her aware of it. "—you would grab my collar with one hand and my sleeve with the other. That's a standard Judo grip. Yeah, that's it. See how it keeps me from bringing my arms up? Now pivot your back foot, turning your body sideways."

She complied, blading her body between his legs. The closeness was electrifying, and the heat in the room seemed to intensify. She wondered if it affected him the same way it was her. His expression gave nothing away, but the way his breath hitched when her hip brushed his thigh told her everything she needed to know.

He was feeling it, too, but he was trying to ignore it and focus on the lesson. Which she should be doing, but every breath she drew filled her senses with him. Her chest felt tight, the protective walls she'd built around her heart starting to shake and break apart.

"Exactly like that," he said, his voice a little rougher than before. "Hook your leg behind mine, targeting the back of my knee. At the same time, pull my collar forward and push my sleeve back. This will help to further off-balance me, and as I start to fall..." He tilted back like he was going to fall. "Pull me over your hips and shoulders, rotating in the direction of the throw. That will add power to your sweeping leg and help you maintain control of the throw. Got it?"

Dammit, she had to concentrate. He was trying to help her, and all she could think about was seeing him naked. Despite the goofy rooster towel, he'd looked good. More than good. She kept fantasizing about pushing him down on the mat and straddling him, running her hands over all that hard muscle. It had been so long since she'd felt this surge of raw desire, so long since she was in such intimate proximity with a man she found attractive. She was utterly aware of his every movement, every brush of their bodies, every shared breath. It was intoxicating and downright dangerous.

Focus on the lesson, she reminded herself and took a shaky breath. Not the tantalizing scent of his body or the heat of his gaze. "Uh, yeah. I... I think so."

"All right. Let's try it slowly, step by step. I'm gonna grab you again..."

She followed his instructions, and to her surprise, he landed on the mat at her feet.

"No way." She scowled down at him. "That was too easy. You're twice my size. Were you helping me or something?"

"No, that was all you." He popped to his feet. "The goal of Judo is maximum efficiency with minimum effort. By using your attacker's own momentum, you expend less energy and still gain control. It's balance and leverage."

Unconvinced, she crossed her arms over her chest. "Okay, but what if the attacker is stronger or faster? I mean, not everyone will be as sloppy as you were just now."

He chuckled. It was a soft rumble that reverberated through her nerve endings and made her belly jitter. "That's the beauty of it. Strength and speed are a factor, sure. But technique can often outmaneuver them. Same as in chess, it's not about brute force but strategy. You're small, and they'll likely underestimate you. That's their first mistake. Use it to your advantage."

She waved him forward. "Come at me again. Like you mean it this time."

He grinned and launched himself at her. Once again, she stepped into the attack and rolled him over her hip. He landed with a hard exhale on the mat.

She swallowed, looking at her hands. She'd never felt so powerful before. "Okay. Wow."

"Again?" he asked and rolled smoothly to his feet.

"Yes." She sank into her stance and brought her hands up. "Let's do it."

"No hesitation this time. When I grab you, you lock up for an instant. That's your mistake—one that a bad guy could take advantage of. Make it fast and fluid."

He landed again, hard, shaking the knick knacks on the bookshelf. Rebel stirred on the couch, a low grumble of concern coming from deep within her chest.

"It's okay. I'm okay," he told the dog, then popped back to his feet with the grace of a panther. "Perfect. Just like that. Now we just have to practice until it's instinctive. In a real situation, you won't have much time to think. Your body needs to react naturally based on the training."

"But what if they get me on the ground?" Just saying the words sent a shiver of fear cascading down her spine. "How do I escape?"

"Don't worry. We'll practice pins and escape techniques, but I want you to focus on throws right now. Then nobody will ever take you to the ground."

"I like the sound of that. Okay. Show me another throw."

The afternoon drifted by in a blur of instruction: blocks,

holds, evasions. Connelly was patient and gentle, always making sure she was okay before continuing. Each new move gave her a sense of control that she hadn't felt in years. He taught her footwork and stance, how to fall without hurting herself, and all the ways to use an opponent's momentum against them. Each throw had a name she couldn't remember—all in Japanese—but she memorized the movements Connelly demonstrated: his body fluid as water, his strength grounded in calm assurance.

She watched him, mesmerized. He'd removed his shirt, and sweat gleamed on his torso, muscles rippling subtly as he moved gracefully around the mat. There was something hypnotic about it, his every move telling a story of survival and strength, of embracing fear and transforming it into resilience. She found herself drawn in by his energy, by the silent promise that she too could embody such power.

As the day wore on, Veronica's arms ached, and her legs were heavy with exhaustion. Still, she shook her head when Connelly asked if she was ready to call it a day.

"No," she panted. "Let's do it one more time."

Connelly nodded and positioned himself in front of her, his breathing steady and calm despite the hours of physical exertion. "All right."

Veronica steeled herself as he grabbed her once again. She'd done this enough times now that the initial shock faded, replaced by a newfound determination. She remembered his lessons and pivoted her body, hooking her leg through his just as he had shown her. There was a moment of suspended tension before he landed on the mat once more.

"Excellent." He got back on his feet with a spring in his step. "You got it. You're a natural."

"My God." She bent double and breathed out a long breath as sweat trickled into her eyes. "How are you still so energetic?"

He chuckled and tossed her a towel from his gym bag. "Years of training. Plus, I'm not the one doing all the throwing. Being the throwee is much easier."

For the second time in as many days, she laughed. She was tired, yes, but there was the spark of joy that had been absent in her life for the longest time. It felt good to laugh.

"Well, I feel like I've been hit by a truck," she admitted, pulling her ponytail free and running her hands through her sweaty, tangled hair.

"Bet you'll sleep well tonight."

She had slept pretty damn well last night with his arms around her. This thing between them—the spark, the heat...

She didn't know how she felt about it yet.

"But for now, let's call it a day," Connelly suggested, already rolling up the mat. "You've done enough for one session."

"No," she protested, "I want to keep going. I need to be able to defend myself."

He stared at her for a moment before sighing. "Vee, you've learned faster than anyone else I've ever trained. But you need to rest and let your body rejuvenate. We'll pick this up tomorrow. Go take a hot shower to loosen up those muscles. You're going to be sore."

He was probably right. Her muscles were already singing with fatigue, and a hot shower was starting to sound like heaven. "All right," she conceded. "A shower would be nice."

Alfie jumped down from the couch and padded to the door, glancing back with an expectant expression on his adorable little face. Rebel was much less equanimous about her need to go outside. She pawed at the door hard enough that it rattled in its frame.

Connelly stopped her from going to the door and pulled her in, pressing a kiss to her sweaty forehead. "No, I'll deal with the dogs. You go take care of yourself." Rebel barked impatiently and he released her. "Okay! I'm coming."

The dogs almost tripped over each other in their hurry to get outside, and Connelly's laughter filled the room before he shut the door behind them.

Veronica dragged herself to the bathroom and peeled off her workout clothes, dropping them in a pile on the floor before stepping into the steamy warmth of the shower. The jets of water massaged her aching muscles, and she let out a groan at the pleasure of it.

As she stood there, letting the warm water soothe her aching body, she replayed the afternoon—the way Connelly moved with such precision, the way his eyes sparkled when she picked up a new technique, the feel of his muscles under her hands. What it would be like to touch him, not in defense, but with affection and desire?

Touch him like she had this morning before Ash interrupted...

The memory of the kiss was so vivid, so real. She could still feel the warmth of his breath against her skin, his lips somehow both soft and hard on hers, promising so much more...

God, she desperately wanted more.

But was she ready? Could she actually take that step? She hadn't slept with anyone since before the attack. She had barely been able to masturbate without the memories assaulting her all over again.

There was one way to find out...

She closed her eyes and trailed a hand down the front of her body, dipping her fingers between her legs. Her breath hitched as pleasure ignited deep inside her belly at the first tentative touch of her fingers. She leaned against the tiled wall, the water cascading down her body while her mind kept replaying that kiss—a kiss that was all-consuming, passionate, and heartbreakingly sweet. It had sparked something in her, something she hadn't felt since... well, the last time they'd kissed.

She pictured his hands, strong but gentle, as they guided her through the training. He'd take control in bed like that if she let him.

Could she let him?

Yes. Her body was one hundred percent on board with that idea if the sudden slickness between her legs was any indication. She touched her clit, and a wave of pleasure crashed over her, leaving her legs trembling. She imagined it was Connelly's hands on her, not her own, his touch exploring every inch of her body.

Her fingers moved expertly as her mind painted vivid pictures of him undressing her, his eyes raking over her body with raw desire. She imagined the chiseled lines of his torso molding against hers, the gruff sound of his voice whispering dirty things into her ear as he claimed her. A moan escaped her as she imagined his lips tracing a path down her navel, sending sparks flying across her skin.

The bathroom was a steamy oasis, the air thick and heavy with moisture. She stood in the center of it all, consumed by the fantasy of him. Her fingers moved with purpose, tracing every curve and dip of her body, igniting a fiery heat within her. The memory of Connelly's lips on hers lingered like a tantalizing promise, and she longed to feel them again. With each passing second, her desire for him grew stronger, consuming her completely.

She craved him.

More than she had ever craved anyone else.

Her breath hitched as her fingers quickened their pace, chasing after the pleasure that was always just out of reach. She relished the memory of his scent, his touch, his taste. The sensations drove her higher and higher until she trembled with anticipation on the edge of release.

And then she fell.

The orgasm washed over her in a wild rush that left her body tingling and her knees weak. She slumped against the shower wall, gasping for breath as the water washed away her exhaustion and replaced it with a warm, languid satisfaction.

Holy shit.

She'd actually orgasmed.

She hadn't thought it was possible for her anymore.

"Veronica?" Connelly tapped on the bathroom door, his voice muffled by the wood. "Are you okay? You've been in there for quite a while."

"I'm fine," she called back, stifling a laugh. This definitely wasn't what he'd meant when he told her to take care of herself. "Just... uh, just give me another minute."

There was a beat of hesitation.

"Take your time," he finally said, the hint of concern still lingering.

She waited until his footsteps retreated from the door, then closed her eyes and sank to the floor, curling her knees toward her chest. She let herself drift in the warm silence of the bathroom, her body still humming from the sheer pleasure she'd experienced. It was a strange feeling—strange and wonderful.

She felt alive.

More than that, she felt like herself again.

After a while, the water began to run cold, and she scrambled to turn it off. She reached for her towel, wrapped it around her body, and stepped out of the shower.

The steam had fogged up the mirror. She swiped a hand over it and studied her reflection. Her eyes were brighter than they had been in ages, her cheeks flushed from the heat and exertion, and... something more.

She liked the way her muscles ached and the heady sensation of power coursing through her veins. She felt strong. And beautiful. Not because of any specific physical attribute but simply because she was rediscovering parts of herself she'd forgotten existed, or maybe they were bits she hadn't known were there in the first place.

This was the reflection of a woman who wasn't afraid. A woman who was capable and sexy. A woman who knew what she wanted and went for it.

She liked this version of herself.

And she actually *was* okay.

For the first time in a very long time, she hadn't been lying when she answered that question.

part two
light

"For there is always light,
    if only we're brave enough to see it.
    If only we're brave enough to be it."
-Amanda Gorman

chapter
twenty-two

AS THE COLD, rainy spring slowly warmed into a cool, breezy summer, things stayed quiet.

No more victims.

No more feelings of being watched.

It was almost... normal.

Ash suspected the killer realized he'd lost control during his last kill and went underground to regroup, but the sheriff also didn't think it was over. Connelly agreed. His Number One Fan wasn't done yet.

But the quiet days saw Connelly and Veronica falling into a comfortable routine. He'd wake up early to get some writing done— if he was lucky, he could get in a few solid hours before Veronica woke up and the dogs required attention. He was nearly done with the book, and he thought it might be his best one yet. The characters were scrappy and likable. The monster was terrifying and unstoppable. Only problem was he didn't know how it should end—should it be a happily ever after, or did the monster win this time?

After he finished his words for the day they'd take the dogs for a morning walk in the woods at Veronica's insistence. She claimed to find it calming, even with a protection detail trailing them.

And he couldn't deny the change he saw in her. She was calmer. She no longer flinched at the idea of stepping outside the house. She sat out on the back deck every day with a sketchbook, drawing again for the first time in years, filling the pages with sky and sea. The world was slowly expanding again for her, and as much as he hated the circumstances that brought them together, Connelly couldn't help but feel grateful for this progress. He even managed to convince her to call her Dad daily. He usually stepped out of the house to play with the dogs in the yard when she did, giving them privacy, but he hoped that whatever was broken between them was starting to heal as well.

The afternoons were reserved for practicing Judo. With each passing day, Veronica was becoming more adept at the moves. She was a fast learner, her instinctive grip on the technical aspects of the martial art surprising him.

But then again, Veronica never failed to surprise him.

In the evenings, they'd often find themselves huddled together on the couch, enveloped in soft blankets while they watched movies and the dogs snoozed. He loved those nights —just him and Veronica in a cocoon of warmth and companionship. In those moments, there was no killer, no crazy sorta-ex-girlfriend stalker. Just them, their dogs, and Veronica's vast collection of cheesy rom-coms that he'd secretly come to love. He enjoyed watching her lose herself in laughter. Her happiness was infectious, and he found himself laughing along even when the jokes were lame.

For those precious moments, the world outside ceased to exist.

And then there were those moments when he found himself just watching her. At the stove, stirring a pot of soup, lips pursed in consideration as she taste-tested the new recipe.

Curled up in an armchair by the window, reading or sketching, oblivious to his gaze. Or on one of their walks, pausing to stare at the majesty of a sunrise or the quiet beauty of the ancient redwoods.

Sometimes, when the sunlight hit her just right, he caught a glimpse of the Veronica he used to know—the one with a bravery so fierce and a spirit so untamed, it felt like staring directly into the heart of a wildfire.

Of course, that woman was gone. He knew that. She'd never again be who she was, but he loved watching her discover this new version of herself. He loved that she moved with newfound grace and self-assuredness. He loved holding her each night as she drifted to sleep. And he loved her more each day.

It was all so quietly perfect and couldn't last much longer. The world was not designed for uninterrupted bliss. It thrived on the chaos, the unpredictability, the sharp edges of existence that catch and cut when least expected. He made his living writing about those blade-like edges, after all, and he could sense one hanging over them like a guillotine waiting to drop.

Then one morning, that guillotine blade came in the form of a defense attorney and a podcaster.

They were sitting on the front porch when the unfamiliar car pulled in, Veronica tossing a ball for Rebel and he reading through his manuscript. He didn't think much of it at first. With Redwood Coast Rescue pulling double duty as bodyguards these last few weeks, new vehicles were coming and going all the time and he assumed they were just changing shifts.

But then a woman with sleek blond hair slid from the driver's seat and a man with California surfer looks and a rumpled suit climbed out of the passenger side.

Veronica stopped throwing the ball and moved closer to

his side. He closed his laptop and stood, taking her hand, giving it a reassuring squeeze.

"It's okay," he murmured for her ears alone. "See? Rebel's relaxed with them."

Rebel padded over and bumped her head against the woman's jean-clad legs for attention. Alfie trotted toward the man and sniffed his shoes.

"Hi," the woman said with a bright smile as she scratched the spot behind Rebel's ear that made the dog's leg thump. "I'm sorry to drop in unannounced but Shane"—she motioned to the man and dog team camping at the base of the driveway—"is my fiancé. And that's Clue, our dog."

Connelly looked toward their RWCR bodyguards. It had been Donovan Scott and his border collie, Spirit, earlier this morning, but they must have changed shifts since then. He could admit to himself that he was surprised Shane Trevisano had volunteered for the job. He and Shane had a history that included him getting his bell rung good by the former SEAL, but he supposed that was all water under the bridge now. And he respected the guy. Not many people could live through what Shane had and come out still swinging with a mean right hook.

Some of the tension eased out of Veronica's shoulders. "Oh. I remember you from Dr. Firestone's office. Alexis?"

The blonde's smile brightened. "Alexis Summers."

Connelly had heard that name before. "The true crime podcaster?"

"That's me. Nice to meet you."

Veronica nodded toward the rumpled suit. "And you're Cal, right? RWCR's lawyer."

The lawyer's grin was as dazzling as the southern California sun. "Yeah, I don't think we've ever been officially introduced." He stepped forward and held out a hand in greeting. "Callum Holden."

Connelly accepted the handshake. "Connelly Davis."

"I know. I've read your books."

Connelly wondered if there would ever come a point in his career that he didn't find those words utterly terrifying.

"Thanks," he replied, rubbing the back of his neck. "I hope you didn't lose too much sleep over them."

Cal's laugh was kind and warm. "Nah, not at all. I quite enjoy being kept up at night by a good book."

"Surprised you have time to read between all the womanizing," Alexis said. Her smile stayed firmly in place, but there was an undercurrent of annoyance in her voice.

Cal sighed heavily. "Oh, c'mon. You can't be mad at me for going on a few dates. Ellie rejected me, remember? She's made it very clear she wants nothing to do with me."

"Because my sister has good taste."

Cal opened his mouth like he wanted to say something more, but closed it without making a sound and backed up a step. He seemed to wilt and an awkward silence filled the air with tension.

Veronica moved closer to Connelly's side and her fingers tightened around his. He took that as a cue to break up this weird little gathering and stepped forward, gently nudging her behind him. "It was nice meeting you both, but if you're hear to see Shane—"

"Actually," Alexis interrupted. "We're here to talk to you."

The cold hand of dread curled around his heart. "Me? Why?"

"It's... kind of a long story," Cal said. "Do you mind if we come in?"

"It's about what's been happening," Alexis added. "The murders? We think it's connected to something bigger."

Connelly glanced over his shoulder at Veronica. She squeezed his hand so tightly that he swore he felt his bones shift.

"Uh, how about I meet you in town later this afternoon?" he suggested. "Let's say… The Mad Dog at four?"

The pair shared a long look, then seemed to come to some kind of unspoken agreement.

"That will work," Cal finally said. "We'll see you then."

They climbed back into the car and pulled out of the drive, stopping momentarily to talk to Shane before leaving.

"I don't like this," Veronica whispered.

He turned toward her and folded her into his arms. She was trembling. All the progress she'd made, and it felt like she was back at square one, her fear wrapping around her like a second skin.

"I know," he murmured, stroking her hair as he watched the car pull out onto the road. Shane glanced their way, his burn-scarred face twisting into a grimace of concern before he gave them a quick nod and returned to guard duty. "I don't like it either."

He hated to leave Veronica, but as the day wore on, curiosity gnawed at him. What could Alexis Summers and Cal Holden have possibly uncovered that would lead them here?

Leaving Veronica with Shane and his able canine partner, Clue, he grabbed his jacket and keys. He glanced back at Veronica once more before climbing into his car. She stood there, petite and pale against the backdrop of the front porch, clutching Alfie so tight the poor Papillon looked like he might squirm out of her hold any minute.

"I'll be back soon. Keep Rebel close and lock the door. Shane's right at the bottom of the drive if you need anything."

He waited until her silhouette had retreated into the house before he finally maneuvered his car around on the gravel driveway. He stopped at the end and rolled his window down.

Shane glanced up from the book he was reading. Of course it was one of his. Seemed like everyone in town read his books now that he lived here.

Shane stood and walked over to the car, leaning down to peer in through the window. His burn scars were even more horrific up close. Jesus, what this guy survived…

It was unthinkable.

He wore some kind of plastic mask over his scars, which explained why he'd looked so eerily shiny in the sunlight earlier. "Everything okay?"

"I'm headed to town to meet Alexis and Cal."

Shane nodded once. "Good."

"I don't suppose you'll give me a heads up what this is about?"

"Nope."

"Of course not." Connelly sighed and rubbed a hand down his face. "Listen, Veronica's shaken."

"Who wouldn't be?"

"Yeah. Can you just… move closer to the house while I'm gone? The porch, if she'll let you. I don't want her to be alone."

A smile tipped up the corner of Shane's mouth. "I don't think that will be a problem."

Connelly opened his mouth to ask why not, but was interrupted by the convoy of vehicles pulling into the driveway. He recognized Zak's truck and Donovan's motorcycle. A Ford Bronco came next with Pierce St. James behind the wheel and Sawyer and Zelda in the passenger seat. The last vehicle was a Toyota Tacoma driven by Rylan Cross.

He climbed out of his car as they all pulled up into the yard. "What the hell are you guys doing here?"

Donovan slowed his bike and killed the engine. Spirit sat

behind him in a matching helmet, her paws up on his shoulders and her tongue spilling out of her mouth in a happy doggy grin. He flipped up his visor. "Veronica won't come to therapy, so we're bringing therapy to her."

Zak leaned out his truck's window. "She's about to get an unprecedented dose of friendly intervention."

Connelly frowned. Was this the right time for an intervention? He cast his gaze back up the driveway to the house, but found only darkness staring back. No silhouette. Veronica had retreated fully inside.

"She's not going to like this," he muttered.

Donovan shrugged. "Good."

Connelly rubbed a hand over his face, feeling a headache starting to pound at his temples. This was a disaster waiting to happen. Veronica was still fragile. The last thing she needed was to be forced into something she clearly wasn't ready for.

"Look," he started, "I appreciate what you're trying to do, but—"

Donovan swung off the motorcycle and took off his helmet, revealing his close-cropped dark hair and the scars slicing across his skull from the injuries he'd sustained while a Marine. His grin was wide as he slapped Connelly on the back. "Relax, man. We've got this."

"Just trust us, okay?" Zak added. "She needs this push."

Connelly stared at the motley crew in front of him with apprehension. Each man wore an expression of resolute determination, their camaraderie tangible in the cool evening air. He knew they all cared for Veronica in their own way, but... Was this the best way to show it?

"Just... don't push her too hard," he finally said, trying to keep the worry out of his voice.

"We'll be gentle with her." Zak nodded toward the road. "Go talk to Alexis and Cal. You want to hear what they have to say."

chapter
twenty-three

WHAT AM *I supposed to do now?*

Veronica leaned against the door and stared down at the dogs. Alfie wagged. Rebel looked toward the window.

"I know, girl." She bent down to rub the dog's big head. "I already miss him, too."

After Connelly's constant presence in her life for the past few weeks, the house felt achingly empty without him.

How had she ever lived with this silence?

A sudden knock at the door made her jolt. She whipped around to peek out the window, pulling back the curtain just enough to see a fleet of cars parked in front of the house. And a group of men in her yard.

Zak. Donovan. Sawyer. Pierce.

Her guys.

And all of their dogs, too. Zak's mischievous Ranger. Donovan's bundle of energy Spirit. Sawyer's seeing-eye dog Zelda. And Pierce's mop dog Raszta with his dreadlocks held out of his eyes in a jaunty ponytail.

Her heart warred between panic and excitement for several beats. God, she'd missed them all.

Shane and his scruffy dog, Clue, walked up from the base of the driveway with a man she didn't recognize. He was the only one without a dog. Colorful tattoos covered every inch of skin on one arm. His other arm was a prosthetic.

That must be Rylan Cross, the new trauma counselor. Dr. Firestone's replacement.

The panic won out with a sudden swell of fear. It was like a physical weight pressing down on her chest, squeezing the breath from her lungs. She inhaled sharply, trying to fill her lungs against the mounting pressure, and shrank away from the window.

Another knock rattled the door.

"Veronica?" Zak's voice, muffled by the wood, did nothing to ease her growing panic. "Can you open the door?"

"We just want to talk." It was Donovan this time, his voice as gentle as she'd ever heard it.

She glanced at Rebel and Alfie, both sets of eyes concerned and watching her. But Rebel wasn't on alert, wasn't growling, and her fur lay smoothly along her spine. If the dog wasn't concerned, there was no reason for Veronica to be. Besides these guys were... well, not friends. She didn't have friends anymore beyond Connelly. But they were acquaintances and she trusted them as much as she was able to trust a man.

Which really wasn't a lot.

She first started attending the Paws for Vets group sessions at Dr. Firestone's suggestion as exposure therapy to help her trust men again. But sitting there every week, listening to their stories, had only served to ignite the flames of her anxiety. Every tale, every scar, every sleepless night they shared only reinforced her fear—that men were only ever one step away from becoming monsters.

Taking a deep breath she moved to the door, cracking it open just enough to see the gathering on her porch. "What are you doing here?"

"Since you haven't been able to come to us, we decided to come to you," Zak said.

"We've missed you," Sawyer added and Pierce, unable to speak due to the injuries he sustained in the military, nodded in agreement.

"They've been worried about you," Rylan added, stepping forward. He had beautiful hazel eyes, earnest and kind, but they sent a shiver down her spine. Those were the eyes of a therapist, trained to dissect and analyze. And he wasn't Dr. Firestone. She'd never be able to open up to this man like she had with Dr. Firestone. The thought of trying churned her stomach.

She swallowed hard. "I'm fine."

"We don't think you are," Donovan said, his dark gaze meeting hers with all the empathy she'd come to expect from him. He was arguably the scariest looking of the group—heavily muscled and tattooed with skull-trimmed hair that highlighted the scars criss-crossing his head—but he was by far the biggest teddy bear. She liked him. She'd always liked him, even when she'd been intimidated by him.

"Look, guys, I appreciate what you're doing, but..." she trailed off, unsure of what she had planned to say.

"We're not here to push you into anything," Rylan said gently.

"Then what are you here for?" The question came out with more edges than she'd intended.

Zak held out a hand to Rylan as if to say 'let me handle this' before turning back to her. "We're here because we care." His voice held an earnestness that surprised her. Zak was brash and unfiltered, the one who usually relished in pushing boundaries. But now, his eyes held a sincerity she hadn't seen before, and it caught her off-guard. "And we only want to help in any way that we can."

Sawyer's normally cheerful face was serious when he

added, "We've all been where you are now... stuck in our own heads, lost in the past."

"We know what it's like to have the world shrink around you, become a cage of fear and memories." Donovan's voice was low and soothing. "We've been there. Believe me, Veronica, we know."

Pierce signed something, his soft gaze seeming to see right through her, and she suddenly hated herself for not ever learning sign language so she could communicate with him. She looked at Donovan for the translation.

"He said it's okay if you don't trust us. We're still going to be here for you, no matter what."

Her eyes flooded with tears. Here they were, a group of rough-around-the-edges veterans who all had their own demons to battle, and they'd still come to help fight hers.

Zak bent down and for the first time she noticed the cooler sitting at his feet. "We brought some snacks, soda." He chuckled when Ranger nudged the cooler. "Hang on, mutt." He pushed the dog away. "Got stuff in here for the dogs, too. We thought we'd let them play while we hang out."

"I'm not comfortable inviting you inside."

"That's fine. Send Rebel and Alfie out. We'll just chill on the porch for a bit and let them all run. You can stay inside or join us." He shrugged like it was no big deal. "Up to you."

She hesitated. "If I come out, I'm not going to talk. This isn't a therapy session."

"We wouldn't dream of it," Zak said with his trademark smirk. "Just good company, that's all."

She stared at them all for a second longer, then looked down at Rebel and Alfie who were both glaring at her as if they were personally offended she'd ever consider not letting them join the doggie party outside. With a sigh, she opened the door wide enough to let them out.

The dogs went wild, barking and romping, their tails

wagging so fast it was a wonder nobody took flight. Spirit initiated a game of chase that sent dust flying. Alfie, with his tiny legs, did his best to keep up with the bigger dogs and the pure animal joy on his face made Veronica smile.

She watched it all from the safety of her doorway. It felt strange to see so much activity in her yard—but it wasn't entirely unpleasant. There was something about happy dogs that made everything feel a little less heavy.

Zak chuckled as he opened the cooler and passed out sodas. "All right, boys. Let's get this party started."

"Come on out when you're ready," Donovan called to her over his shoulder as he joined the dogs and pulled a ball out of his pocket, tossing it to Pierce. Zak grabbed the rope toy dangling from his back pocket and waded into the doggie chaos. Sawyer sat on the porch steps, then released Zelda from her harness so she could run, too.

Veronica lingered in the threshold, watching the men and dogs run, and something inside of her shifted slightly.

These men were no monsters; they were survivors like her —broken souls trying to mend amongst their own. She could continue holding on to her fear or give them a chance to help.

And then, gathering her courage like a cloak around her shoulders, she stepped out onto the porch.

"Here." Rylan handed her an icy can of soda from the cooler. She took it with a nod of thanks and sat on the opposite side of the steps from the men, keeping an eye on the dogs as they played.

Rylan leaned on the porch railing and grinned as Zelda threw herself into the fray. "I need a dog," he said to nobody in particular.

"Ask Zak," Sawyer said. "He has an uncanny ability to find people their perfect dog. He did it for Donovan and Pierce. Veronica, too."

"He picked Rebel for me?" The question was out of her mouth before she even realized she'd thought it.

Zak, who had been engaged in a tug-of-war session with Ranger, glanced over at them. "Yeah, and risked the wrath of my wife. Anna wasn't convinced, but I knew she was the dog for you," he said, his tone serious despite the playful growl he let out when Ranger gave an exceptionally hard tug on their toy. "Was I wrong?"

Veronica thought back to those first few days with Rebel, when she kept running off. The initial frustration, the countless hours spent chasing the stubborn dog around the woods, attempting to establish some semblance of control. It had been challenging, exhausting... and healing. The responsibility of caring for the rebellious Doberman had forced her to step out of her own mind, if only for a few hours each day. Without Rebel, she'd still be locked inside her house instead of sitting on the porch with the sun on her face.

She looked at Rebel now, a powerful yet graceful creature that was fiercely protective and loyal. A dog that had somehow known exactly what she needed, had understood her in ways no human ever could.

She watched Rebel tackle Alfie gently, her tail wagging in delight. She saw how the dog's eyes would occasionally dart toward her, as if checking on her well-being. Alfie had always had her heart, but Rebel meant more to her than she could've anticipated when Connelly showed up with the dog.

She shook her head and managed a smile at Zak. "No, you weren't wrong."

Zak grinned back at her, his arms spread wide in triumph. "What can I say? I have a knack." He pointed at Rylan. "Whenever you're ready, Ry, I'll find you the perfect dog, too."

Zak turned his attention back to Ranger, giving the rope

one last tug before letting the dog win their game. Donovan had pulled Sawyer into the fray with the dogs while Pierce signed something that made Zak laugh.

Veronica sat there watching them all and found herself smiling. Her heart felt light in a way it hadn't for a long time.

"I think..." Rylan said, drawing the words out speculatively. "You've missed them as much as they have you."

She side-eyed the trauma counselor. "Maybe."

Rylan chuckled, folding his arms across his chest. "Deny it all you want, Veronica, but I think it's clear."

Veronica merely shrugged, tearing her gaze from the chaos of dogs and men in her yard to glance at Rylan. There was a wisdom in his eyes that made her feel transparent. She frowned and looked away.

"They're good men," he added softly. "And they care deeply about your wellbeing."

"Hey, Vee!" Donovan called out from the yard, holding up a Frisbee. "Wanna give this a toss?"

She shook her head, but Donovan only grinned wider. "Come on, it's just a disc throw. Nothing scary."

Her heart pounded as she considered the invitation. She glanced over at Rylan, who was watching her with those pretty, too-knowing eyes.

"Only if you want to," he said gently.

She looked back at Donovan who was waving the Frisbee in the air as all the dogs clustered around him in anticipation. A part of her yearned to join the fun—to be part of something again beyond her own small, isolated world.

And why was she so afraid of these men? They were not the ones who had violated her. Her fear of them was irrational, but then again, was fear ever rational?

With a deep breath, she pushed herself off the porch steps and slowly walked toward Donovan. The men cheered, Pierce whistled, and Rylan thumped his prosthetic arm on the porch railing encouragingly.

God, why was she so nervous? She wiped her suddenly damp palms on her pant leg. It was a game of Frisbee in her own front yard.

"Here." Donovan passed her the brightly colored disc, his smile warm. "Give it a good toss. Let's tire these pups out."

She took the Frisbee from him, feeling the smooth plastic under her fingers. Rebel gave an eager whine, and Spirit let out a series of low yips of anticipation. Zelda tap-danced with excitement, and Ranger watched the Frisbee with the intense stare of a hunter locked on prey.

With one last glance back at Rylan, who was watching her with unmasked approval, she flung the disc as far as she could.

The dogs were off in an instant, their muscular bodies sleek blurs against the lawn as they raced after the Frisbee. Donovan clapped her on the back and said something that was drowned out by Zak and Sawyer's competing cheers. She turned to Rylan who still leaned on the porch railing. He raised his soda can in a silent toast and gestured for her to continue.

Her heart thundered, not with fear or anxiety, but with something akin to exhilaration. It filled her veins and painted a genuine smile on her face for the first time in what felt like forever. A chorus of cheers and claps erupted from the men around her each time she threw the disc and watched it spiral across the clear blue sky. It reminded her of the freedom she'd once known, pushing through the clouds and soaring above everything else. A feeling she'd forgotten. A feeling she desperately missed.

With every throw and every burst of laughter from the men she'd once considered threats, the past sloughed off her. The trauma wasn't gone—and it probably would never truly disappear—but it was lighter somehow. She had finally given herself permission to move beyond it, to reach for something more than just survival and solitude.

And she felt... wonderfully, miraculously normal again.

chapter
twenty-four

THE DRIVE to The Mad Dog was a short one. When Connelly pulled into the gravel parking lot, the afternoon sun painted long shadows across the ground.

Inside, Cal and Alexis were already huddled at a corner booth, their heads bowed together in serious conversation.

"Connelly," Alexis greeted him with a warm smile as he slid into the booth across from them. "Thank you for coming."

He leaned back against the worn leather of the seat. "What's this all about?"

Cal and Alexis shared a glance, then Cal pulled a copy of *The Shadows Within* out of the briefcase on the floor by his seat. He slid it across the table.

"The Shadow Stalker," Alexis said.

Connelly stared at them, his jaw hanging open. Were they joking? But they looked too fucking serious to be joking. He slowly reached out and picked up the book. "The Shadow Stalker is an urban legend that I turned into a horror villain. He's not real."

"Yes, he is," Alexis said solemnly. "I know he is. He held me captive."

Of course Connelly was aware of what happened to her. Everyone in town knew. She'd been abducted from in front of her motel and held prisoner in a bunker on the mountain for weeks before being set free and hunted like a deer.

"I thought Ash caught him? Wasn't it the same guy who killed Dr. Firestone?" He looked at Cal, a lightbulb going off. "Aren't you his lawyer?"

"Jaxon Thorne is not a killer," Cal said without a shred of doubt.

"Well..." Alexis touched the thin pink scar circling her throat. The move seemed almost involuntary. "At least, we know for a fact he's not The Shadow Stalker."

"But didn't he confess?"

"He recanted," Cal said.

"Bet the sheriff was thrilled about that."

Cal's bright grin made a momentary return. "I thought Ash was going to stroke out when I told him. His blood pressure shot through the roof." He got serious again. "My client has done a lot of bad, but when he confessed, he was under the influence of a significant number of drugs. He wasn't in his right mind and he felt guilty for the things he had done, so he confessed to everything he was accused of, including Dr. Firestone's murder. But he didn't do it."

"And he doesn't have the birthmark of the man who attacked me," Alexis added. "That man raped me repeatedly. He had a large birthmark on his pelvis. I'd recognize it anywhere, and Jaxon Thorne doesn't have a mark on him."

"Wait." Connelly exhaled hard, feeling as if he'd just been punched in the gut, and sat back in his seat. "The man who attacked Veronica at my house? She told Ash he had a port wine stain on his stomach or hip. She saw it when Rebel bit him and ripped his shirt."

Alexis held his gaze. "That's exactly why we're talking to you. We believe the Stalker is actually two men working together, one older and one younger. The younger one raped me and attacked Veronica. We think he's also the one imitating your books. He's impulsive, reckless, sloppy. The older man is the one who hunted me. He's cold and calculating. He's been getting away with this for decades, hiding behind the urban legend of The Shadow Stalker." She nodded to Cal, who drew a handful of pictures out of his bag and spread them out on the table. They were all images of young women with long dark hair just like Veronica's.

"These are the victims we have tied to them so far," Cal said. "Look familiar?"

"They all look like Veronica." The words tasted bitter on his tongue, and he poured himself a glass of water from the pitcher on the table. Taking a long, sobering sip, he leaned back in his seat, his gaze never leaving the faces of the women on the table. The resemblance was uncanny. The same big, expressive eyes, the same long waves of dark hair cascading down their shoulders. He could almost imagine Veronica's face among them.

"Who are they?" he asked, glancing between Cal and Alexis.

Cal picked up one of the pictures. "This is Clara Sullivan," he said, tapping the girl's photo. The young woman in the picture was smiling at the camera, her face glowing with joy. "She was reported missing five years ago."

"And this,"—Alexis picked up another picture—"is Ashley Moore. She disappeared a year before Clara. She was the youngest, only fifteen."

Each woman had a story to tell, each one more terrible than the last. Thirty-six in total. Connelly felt sick as he looked at their faces, each one filled with so much promise and life.

A chill ran down his spine as he picked up one of the photos. On the back was scrawled the victim's name, Heather Garcia, her age, 17, and the date of her disappearance, April 2,

2001. The girl shared an uncanny resemblance to Veronica as a teenager.

"Jesus Christ. She could be Vee's twin."

Alexis picked up another picture. It showed a Native American woman, who couldn't have been much over twenty, with a hard smile and sad eyes. "This was the first, as far as we can tell. Maria Ayunli Socktish. She was reported missing in June 1998 when she didn't show up to court for a hearing to get her son back from foster care. We think she's the key to figuring this out."

Connelly looked up at them. "Have you told Ash any of this?"

"Yes." Alexis's lips flattened into a grim line. "And he told the FBI, but they think we're chasing shadows, and Ash deferred to them."

"He's got a lot on his plate," Cal said. "Between the widespread corruption in his department and now these murders, he's not making the connection to what happened to Alexis. As far as he's concerned, that case is closed, and these others are all cold cases. God love him, but he's a myopic bastard. He can't see what isn't right in front of him."

"So, we're going to tie it up in a nice neat bow and put it in front of him," Alexis said. "That's where you come in."

"How can I help?" Connelly asked, his gaze lingering on the pictures scattered across the worn table as a hollow emptiness opened in his chest.

"You've studied the Shadow Stalker urban legend more than anyone," Alexis said. "We need you to help us understand him."

Something about their request felt like a violation. His novels were based on his own deepest fears and insecurities, twisted into horrifying narratives for public consumption. Digging into them felt akin to exposing all of his vulnerabilities. "But my Shadow Stalker is a fictional monster, not human. He's the amalgamation of a town's worst fears."

"And so is ours." Alexis set down a photo of May-Lynn Tapia in her red coat and one of Lucy Harper looking pissed off in her hospital bed. On top of those, she added what looked like a crime scene photo that she almost certainly shouldn't have. It showed a woman—was it a woman? Had to be, but she was so badly cut up that she no longer looked human. The as-yet unidentified newest victim. "People are scared, Connelly. "

Cal nodded. "If the younger of our killer duo is as obsessed with your book as we think, who better to get into his head than the author himself?"

He couldn't tear his gaze away from the photo of the unidentified woman. She was no longer a woman, reduced to a grotesque sculpture, her life's last moments frozen in a tapestry of horror that was more than familiar. This was more frenzied than in his book—Ash was right; the killer was losing control—but he'd penned this scene, given life to this monstrosity from the safety of his own imagination. She was an echo of what she had once been, a macabre caricature of life turned into something nightmarish. The lump in his throat solidified.

"I..." he began, only to lose his voice. He cleared his throat and tried again. "I'm gonna start writing romance novels."

Alexis gave a sad smile and gathered up the photos. "I'd read them, but right now, we need that twisted imagination of yours."

He scrubbed his hands over his face, through his hair, and locked them behind his neck, squeezing tight to combat the unease tap-dancing down his spine. He was a storyteller, not a detective. His job was to create nightmares, not solve them.

After a long moment, he exhaled the air caught in his lungs and dropped his hands back to the table. "Okay. I can do this," he said more to himself than them. "At least I can help you understand the story, the legend."

Alexis dug into her shoulder bag for a tablet and powered it on. "My sister Ellie started looking into the legend for me. She's an excellent researcher, but she couldn't seem to find much about it."

Connelly accepted the tablet when she handed it to him and smiled a little at the nursery rhyme on the screen:

In shadows so deep, the Stalker hides.
Fear his presence where moonlight dies.
Beware his bunker, hidden and dark,
Where he preys on souls, leaving his mark.
In woods so still, his hunt begins,
Fear his presence, where moonlight thins.
One by one, his tally grows,
For in the shadows, his secret shows.

He remembered the first time he'd heard the rhyme during a sixth-grade camping trip to Olympic National Park. One of the counselors had told the story of the Shadow Stalker over the campfire, and it had both thrilled and terrified him, lurking in his subconscious until he needed a monster for *The Shadows Within*. Then he delved into the legend. He'd picked it apart, exploring the meaning behind every word, every syllable, every rhythmic beat to understand the essence of the Shadow Stalker.

"Do you mind?" he asked, reaching for the tablet's stylus on the table between them.

Alexis waved a hand. "No, go ahead."

He picked up the pen and drew lines between the stanzas. "A version of this rhyme has been around since the earliest days of the Gold Rush—especially these first two lines."

Cal's brows scrunched together. "Wait." He pulled the

tablet toward him and read the first two lines out loud. "Is this about Sasquatch?"

"Could be," Connelly said and sat back in his seat, relaxing now that they were in the familiar territory of fiction again. "Or it could be about the boogeyman. A vampire. The Chupacabra. Or any other sinister figure that haunts our collective consciousness. Every culture on Earth has its own version of shadowy creatures that lurk in the dark. And it's possible the Shadow Stalker myth actually started long before the Gold Rush. Several local Native American tribes in the area have legends revolving around spirits that hide in the dark."

Warming to the topic, he leaned forward and tapped the tablet. "This rhyme is interesting because when you break it down, you can see all the layers of fear in it. Each addition was a way to frame new fears within an ancient context." He pointed at the first two lines. "There's the fear of the dark and the woods and the general sense of the unknown from the 1800s expansion west." Then he pointed at the next stanza. "And this part, here? About the bunker? These lines were added during the height of the Cold War when everyone was terrified of a nuclear apocalypse and building bunkers. Because what's scarier than a space that was built for safety being used for evil deeds? Then these final four lines about his hunt and the tally growing first appeared sometime during the height of the serial killer era in the late 70s or early 80s."

"That's fascinating," Alexis said, and it sounded like she genuinely meant it.

Still, embarrassment burned up the back of his neck. Here he was getting excited over a nursery rhyme while they were trying to track down a killer. "Sorry. I love this stuff."

"No need to apologize." Her eyes sparkled with amusement. "I totally get it. I nerd out over weird stuff all the time.

And this *is* interesting. In fact, have you ever considered doing a podcast on urban legends?"

Thrown, he sat back. "Uh, no. Can't say I have."

"My sister and I are starting our own production company, and I think you'd be amazing at it." She nodded as if making up her mind about something. "Yes, I can see that working. We'll definitely talk later." She shifted her attention back to the tablet and sighed. "But as fascinating as this is, I don't know how it helps."

"Well," Connelly said and leaned forward again. "You think this is a case of folie à deux, right? A killing duo? What if these last four lines are actually about the older killer? The lines first appeared in the eighties. If he's... let's say, in his sixties now, then he would've been in his twenties then. Prime serial killer age. It's entirely possible these lines were added about him."

Alexis's eyes widened. "So rather than hiding behind the legend, he created it? Or at least that part of it."

"The M.O. fits," Cal said.

"Did you look further back than Maria Socktish's disappearance?" Connelly asked. "What if she was just the first of this new M.O., and there were others before her?"

"I started to, but then—" Alexis broke off and rubbed her hands restlessly against her thighs. "Well. I never got the chance."

Connelly's heart went out to her. Under the brave face she showed the world, she was obviously still struggling with what happened to her. She should talk to someone.

No, he realized. Not just someone. Veronica. It would be good for them both, and he could easily picture them becoming friends.

He tucked the idea away for later consideration and refocused on the conversation. "You'd want to look for young women with dark hair—because that probably wouldn't have changed—but look beyond gunshot victims. I think he evolved into that M.O. He either inspired those lines of the rhyme or was inspired by them. His first kills would have been him experimenting, trying to find what he liked best. Strangulation, suffocation, stabbing. They wouldn't have been neat."

"Wait, wait," Cal said, pushing back from the table and grabbing his laptop from his briefcase. He typed for a moment, then slapped the table with his palm. "There it is." He swung the laptop around so they could see the old newspaper article on screen. "When I first started law school, I did a project on unsolved cases around my hometown, and my uncle told me about this one. In 1987, back when Eldridge still had a high school before they combined with Steam Valley, a girl my uncle was friends with disappeared off school property after cheerleading practice. Jennifer Anderson. She was found three days later in Lost Rocks State Park. She'd been strangled and sexually assaulted. Look at her picture. She has long dark hair and dark eyes."

"Eldridge?" Alexis asked, pulling the laptop closer to scan the article.

"My hometown," Cal said. "An unincorporated village about six miles north of here. Population, very small. And then there was this case here in Steam Valley..." He took the laptop back and typed again, pulling up another article from 1990. "My mom told me about this one. It happened when she was pregnant with me, and all the women in town were terrified, thinking some psycho was out there targeting pregnant women. Oh, here it is. Stephanie Walsh, 21. She was three months pregnant when she was killed by stabbing on June 6, 1990. Also sexually assaulted."

"And Stephanie also looks like all the rest of them," Connelly said.

Like Veronica.

Jesus.

He knew she was safe. How could she not be while surrounded by six ex-military badasses? Still, he itched to get home to her and scooted out of the booth. "I need to get back."

"Okay," Alexis said and looked up from reading the article about Stephanie Walsh. "If you think of anything else related to the Shadow Stalker, let me know."

"Will do. Keep me updated?"

"Yeah, like it or not, you're in this now," Cal said.

"I'll walk out with you." Alexis gathered her bag and also slid from the booth. "Cal, can you keep looking for more cases like these two? I think we're on to something."

"Already on it," Cal said and pulled the laptop back in front of him.

"I'll ask Ellie to look, too."

Cal gazed up with hope in his eyes. "We could work together..."

"You know she won't go for that." Alexis patted his shoulder sympathetically. "Sorry, buddy."

"Still worth a shot," he muttered.

"So your sister and Cal have a history?" Connelly asked as he and Alexis made their way toward the exit.

She sighed. "Yes, but I have no idea what it is. All I know is Ellie went from infatuation to hating his guts. Neither will talk about it." In the parking lot, she stopped beside a silver Chevy Impala and used her key fob to unlock it. She dropped her bag in the passenger seat, then dug a business card out of the side pocket.

She turned back to him and offered the card. "I meant what I said about the podcast. If you're interested."

He was. Maybe. "I'll think about it." He accepted the card and slid it into his pocket. "I also have a proposition for you."

Alexis shut the car door and leaned against it, eyebrows raised. "Oh?"

"Veronica needs female friends, and you have a lot in common—I mean, beyond what you both went through."

Her expression clouded. "Ah." She tried for a smile, but it just looked sad. "It's, unfortunately, a very non-exclusive club that no woman ever wants to become a part of, but far too many do. I'm happy to talk to her if she wants."

"If I made an excuse to leave for an evening... maybe to help Cal with his research... do you think you could swing by?"

"I've actually been meaning to do that for months." She nodded. "You know what, yeah. How about Friday? I'll bring Ellie. Make it a girl's night in."

Yes, he liked Alexis. She was smart, friendly, outgoing, and seemed to have a level head on her shoulders. Exactly what Veronica needed in a girlfriend. "I don't know that she's ever had a girls' night. She's always had guy friends."

"Well, then, she's about to discover what she's been missing."

Relief washed through him. The thought of Veronica getting some sort of support from someone other than him, someone who understood and could relate, was comforting in a way he hadn't expected. It felt like a weight had been lifted off his shoulders. "Thank you."

Alexis squeezed his arm. "You're a good friend, Connelly. Veronica is very lucky to have you."

chapter
twenty-five

THE LAST THING Connelly expected to find when he pulled up to Veronica's house was her sitting out on the front porch in the fading evening light, her hair down around her shoulders and wet from a recent shower. Rebel lay at her feet, asleep with her head pillowed on a Frisbee, and Alfie was curled by her side, his tiny paws twitching in dream-filled slumber.

Connelly stayed in the car for a moment, just watching. He couldn't remember the last time she looked so... peaceful.

Zak had been right. She'd needed today.

Rebel jumped up when his car door creaked open, her ears pricking forward and tail wagging in recognition.

He smiled as he approached the porch. "Hey, girl. Did you have fun today?" he asked the dog, rubbing her ear, but his gaze was focused on Veronica.

"She did." Her voice was quiet, but there was a strength that hadn't been there before. "*We* did."

"When did the guys leave?"

"Not long ago. Pierce and Raszta are still here, though." She nodded toward the temporary camp at the end of the driveway. "Taking the bodyguard shift tonight."

"Yeah, saw them when I came in." He followed her gaze. Pierce sat on a log beside the tent, his mop dog sprawled at his feet as he strummed a guitar. He noticed them looking his way and raised a hand in two-finger a wave. Veronica waved back with a genuine smile.

He stared at her as the soothing sounds of Pierce's guitar drifted on the ocean breeze. At that moment, she looked like the Veronica he knew from childhood— resilient, fearless, and vibrant. So different from the woman who had been locked inside herself for far too long.

Wow. Okay. What the hell had the Redwood Coast Rescue guys done or said to make her so comfortable, so open, so... at ease?

Relief warred briefly with a surprising spike of jealousy. Stupid to be jealous that she'd found comfort in the company of men who cared about her, but there it was.

"You're different," he said eventually, breaking their silence.

Veronica turned her smile toward him, and that selfish bit of jealousy evaporated. "In a good way?"

"I think so. You were okay with having them all here?"

"Not at first," she admitted with a soft laugh. "Did you know they were coming?"

"Not until they showed up."

She nodded. "I'm glad they didn't tell you. You would've tried to stop them to protect me."

"Yes, I would have."

"But I needed it. Needed that push."

"That's what Zak said, too. He called it an intervention."

"Of course he did. And I guess it was."

Connelly stayed where he was a moment longer, trying to decipher what was going on behind those hazel eyes. He wished he could read her thoughts like he used to when they were kids. She had always been an open book back then, her emotions playing out across her expressive face for the whole world to see. Now, she was a fortress.

"So," she said and shifted to face him again. "What did Alexis and Cal want to talk about?"

He joined her on the porch and sank onto the step beside her. He rubbed his hands over his face, trying to wipe away the memory of those photos. All those dead women...

He shook his head. "Tomorrow. I can't talk about it anymore tonight. It's... ugly."

She reached out and laced her fingers through his. "I hate that I couldn't go with you."

"You could have."

She shook her head and stared out over the lawn. "No, I couldn't have. I wasn't ready then." Something in her tone was different—more certain, almost defiant. "This morning, I still wasn't ready to face the world. But..."

"But what?" he prompted when she trailed off.

"But I threw a Frisbee today." Her smile was back, sudden and blinding. "I hung out with friends and threw a Frisbee in my yard. And I think now..." She drew a breath. "Maybe we can try getting dinner in town tonight?"

Connelly watched her profile against the late afternoon light, hardly believing what she'd said. "Are you sure?"

She took a moment before answering. "I won't know unless I try."

The prospect of a public outing with Veronica resounded like a victory gong in his mind. Yet, beneath the resonating triumph was an undercurrent of apprehension. He had seen her crumble under the weight of her anxiety before, but never out in the open, never in front of prying eyes that didn't understand her struggle.

"I have a better idea," he said and stood, pulling her to her feet. "Do you trust me?"

She blinked up at him, her eyes round and more green than brown in the softening light. "Always."

"Good. Let's put the dogs inside. We're going for a drive."

Anticipation buzzed through the car as Connelly drove the winding country roads, leaving behind the familiar streets of Steam Valley.

Veronica folded her hands on her lap, fingers intertwined in a grip that betrayed her nervousness. "Where are you taking me?"

He glanced at her, his dark eyes filled with mischief. "You'll see."

A few miles later, they approached a small private airport, and the sight of the runway and hangars filled her with nostalgia. She hadn't been near an airport since long before the crushing weight of agoraphobia had grounded her, and it felt a lot like coming home.

Connelly parked the car, and they stepped out into the crisp evening air. Veronica was immediately drawn to the sleek, silver aircraft resting on the tarmac. Her breath caught in her throat as she took in the streamlined design, the smooth curve of its wings promising the freedom of the open skies.

"Is that...?" she whispered, unable to tear her eyes away from the plane.

"Your very own chariot for the day," Connelly replied, sweeping his arm toward it in a dramatic flourish.

She stared at the plane, and a long-dormant ember of excitement flickered to life. The thought of taking to the air once again, of feeling the engine's rumble beneath her and seeing the vast horizon spread out before her, was too tempting to resist.

Without a word, she strode toward the plane, inspecting it from nose to tail. "She's beautiful. Is she yours?"

His grin was all crooked boyishness. "First purchase I made with my book royalties."

She smirked at him from under the wing. "But I thought you just jump out of planes. You don't know how to fly them."

Connelly ducked under the wing and wrapped his arms around her from behind. Instead of tensing at the unexpected contact, she relaxed into him. She enjoyed the heat emanating from his body, and the scent of his cologne filled her senses.

"I didn't buy her for me."

She turned around to face him. For a moment, she couldn't help but get lost in the intensity of his gaze. "Then who did you buy her for?"

"You." His thumb stroked over her cheek. "You were meant to fly, Veronica. It's time to spread your wings again."

Her heart raced with equal parts fear and anticipation, but whether that was from his closeness or the chance to break free from the prison of her own making, she wasn't sure. Probably a mix of both.

She hugged him. Tight. Leaned into the comforting warmth of his body and closed her eyes, savoring the sensation of his lips brushing the top of her head. She knew she shouldn't feel this way about him— Connelly was her friend, practically her brother. But the way he looked at her and touched her made her feel like she could conquer the world.

Could she really do it?

Could she fly again after all these years?

God, she wanted to.

She took a deep breath, inhaling the smell of his leather coat and aftershave. It mingled with the familiar scents of oil and fuel, creating an intoxicating aroma that made her head spin. She would have stood there in the hangar with him for the rest of her life, but all too soon, he pulled away. She missed the heat of him instantly and opened her eyes to see him gesturing toward the cockpit.

"Shall we?"

She had to swallow hard before she could find her voice. "Yeah. Let's fly."

As they approached the cockpit, her palms dampened with sweat, and her nerves began to fray at the edges. The plane seemed impossibly large, engines looming like great beasts waiting to be unleashed. Which was ridiculous because she had flown much bigger planes than this 9-seat turboprop. But as she climbed into the pilot's seat and strapped herself in, apprehension gave way to excitement.

She'd missed this.

She ran her hands over the controls, and the memories flooded back—all the countless hours spent in a cockpit, all the missions flown and battles won. She closed her eyes, letting the sensations wash over her, and when she opened them again, she was ready.

With a flick of a switch, the engines roared to life, sending vibrations through the plane and into the marrow of her bones. She couldn't help but let out a whoop of excitement.

Connelly's laughter filled the cockpit as he buckled himself in beside her and settled back in his seat. "The controls are all yours. Take me for a ride."

She smirked over at him. "You have no idea what you're asking."

"Go ahead." There was a dare in his eyes she couldn't resist. "Scare me."

"You'll regret saying that." With practiced ease, she taxied the plane out to the runway, the vibrations of the tarmac beneath her feet intensifying with each passing moment. She took one last deep breath before pushing the throttle forward, the plane surging with a burst of speed.

The ground fell away, and the plane lifted off into the air.

Veronica's heart soared with it, her gaze glued to the horizon. The world opened up before her, vast and endless, and she felt a sense of freedom she hadn't experienced in years. She let out a whoop of joy, and Connelly's laugh mixed with hers as they soared higher. It was exhilarating and terrifying all at once, but she kept her focus on the controls and the open sky ahead.

Freedom.

The sun glinted off the wings as they soared higher and higher, the world below shrinking to a patchwork of color and texture, with the wildly rugged mountains to the east and the Pacific sparkling in an endless blue that curved gently over the earth's surface to the west. They soared over verdant forests and fertile farmland and rivers carving meandering paths through the earth.

"Look at that view," Connelly said with soft wonder.

Oh, she was looking, drinking it all in. With as much time as she'd spent in the air, one would think she'd be used to the beauty. But she had forgotten how stunning it could be, how it could take her breath away. The world was alive and vibrant, and she came alive with it.

"It feels like coming home." She realized he was grinning at her, his eyes warm with affection. She grinned back at him. "Let's do some maneuvers."

Connelly raised an eyebrow. "This isn't exactly a plane built for maneuvers."

"All planes are built for maneuvers." With that, she pushed the plane into a steep climb, the G-force pressing her back into the seat until the engine stalled. Adrenaline coursed through her veins, igniting something in her that she had thought long lost.

Connelly didn't make a sound, but she saw his hands tighten on the armrests.

She grinned at him. "Scared yet?"

"Nope."

Of course not. Mr. Horror Writer would never admit to being frightened.

But the longer the dive went, the tighter his grip got. "Uh... Vee? Ground's coming up fast."

She pulled the plane from the stall and leveled out.

He exhaled in a rush and released his grip on the armrests. "Jesus. I might need a new pair of pants."

They were never in any danger. She was in control the whole time, but she wasn't about to tell him that. "You used to jump out of planes," she reminded.

"Yeah, but the plane was still, you know, flying when I did it."

She laughed.

The plane dipped and swerved, sunlight glinting off its sleek wings as it cut through the clouds like a knife.

She glanced over at Connelly, and warmth spread through her chest, a soft and sweet sensation she couldn't quite define. Was it gratitude? Affection? Something else entirely? She didn't know, but she was content to let it simmer and grow and thaw her from the inside out.

"Thank you," she murmured, her voice barely audible above the roar of the engine. "I never thought I'd feel like this again."

His smile was soft, his dark eyes shining with unspoken emotion. "Seeing you like this—fearless, free—it's like watching a phoenix rise from the ashes."

They continued to fly, soaring through the clouds, taking in the breathtaking views. The sky was a canvas, and they were the painters, creating new patterns and paths with every turn and maneuver. Hours passed, but it felt like mere minutes.

As the sun touched the ocean to the west, Veronica reluctantly guided the plane back toward the airport, and a sense of unease crept in, souring all of her happiness.

"What's wrong?" Connelly asked.

Of course he would notice her change of mood. He noticed everything.

"I don't want to come down," she said wistfully. "I don't want to go back to reality. It's... bleak."

"It doesn't have to be. You were born to fly, Vee, and you're damn good at it. Don't let fear rob you of this."

It was easy to make promises up here when she felt like a giant with the world at her feet. But those promises would be a lie on the ground because her fear had never been about flying. It was about living, facing the world that had hurt her so badly, that had left her broken. The fear was an insidious thing that crept in and took hold of her, leaving her paralyzed and helpless to fight against it.

"I don't know how to not be afraid," she admitted.

"Veronica." Connelly reached out to lace his fingers through hers. He waited until she met his gaze before continuing, "We all have things we're afraid of. Your fear is valid, but it can't be the only thing that defines you. You're stronger than that. You survived something horrific, and you're still here. That's a testament to your strength and resilience."

A lump lodged in her throat, and she stared at their joined hands. "What are you afraid of?"

He laughed softly. "I write horror for a living. I'm afraid of everything."

"That's not true."

"You'd be surprised," he said.

"No, but really. What scares you?"

"My biggest fear? Being buried alive."

The admission startled a surprised laugh out of her. "Oh, c'mon."

He held up his free hand. "Scout's honor."

"But that's irrational. The chances of that happening are astronomically slim."

"I know. And yet I have nightmares about it all the time. It's why I write about it in almost every book."

"To face it?"

"Yeah."

"I'm not that fearless."

"You used to be." He squeezed her hand. "But it's not about being fearless. You're allowed to be afraid. Fear is what has kept us alive since the dawn of time. I told you once before that being brave is not a lack of fear but doing the scary things despite it. And I know you can do that. Look how steady you were as we plunged toward certain death. You were a rock while I was over here silently shitting myself."

That made her smile. "I had control the whole time."

"You have control on the ground, too."

It was a revelation. She had spent years trapped in her own mind, her own fears, and now Connelly was telling her that she had the power to break free? Could she just take control and start living again?

The idea of having control over her life seemed foreign.

But... not impossible.

Was it really that simple?

Connelly squeezed her hand again, the warmth of his touch spreading through her like a balm. "You ready to land this bird?"

She had control.

"Yeah," she said softly. "Let's do it."

They made their final approach, the runway coming into view. Her heart sped up, but this time it wasn't out of fear. It was anticipation, excitement, and a newfound sense of confidence. The plane touched down with a gentle bump.

She had control.

It was a mantra she repeated to herself as they taxied back

to the hangar, as she shut down the engine and climbed out of the plane.

Connelly was waiting for her, a soft smile on his face. "You did it."

Pride bubbled up from deep in her chest. "I did."

"You're out of the house."

"I am."

And she had control.

As they walked away from the plane, Connelly slipped his arm around her waist, pulling her close. Veronica leaned into him, enjoying his warmth and strength. She looked up at him, struck by the intensity of his gaze.

"Are you okay?" he asked softly.

She nodded, unable to speak past the lump in her throat.

"You're amazing, Veronica," he said, his voice low and husky. "Simply amazing."

"I couldn't have done it without you."

"You could have." His fingers traced lazy circles on her hip. "You have it in you, Vee. You always have."

It was a strange feeling, being touched like this. She had been so closed off for so long and had built up so many walls. But with Connelly, it was different. He made her feel safe, made her want to let go of all...

She was in control.

She stopped walking, and when he turned, his mouth opening to ask her if she was okay again, she didn't let him get the question out. She surged up onto her toes and captured his mouth with hers.

He froze for a heartbeat then his lips moved soft and warm against hers, and a jolt of electricity shot through her body. She had never felt like this before, never felt the need to be so close to someone, to feel their body against hers.

But with Connelly, it was right.

The kiss turned fierce, passionate, and she poured into it all of the emotions she had been holding inside for so long.

He responded with a hunger that surprised and thrilled her, drawing her closer until their bodies were pressed together from shoulder to hip. His hands roamed over her back, pulling her even tighter until there was no space left between them.

Heat rushed between her legs, and she moaned into his mouth, wanting more.

Connelly broke the kiss, gasping for air.

"Veronica," he said, his voice ragged and raw with emotion. "Are you sure?"

She was in control.

She nodded, her eyes locked on his. "I'm sure."

Connelly stared at her, worry warring with desire in his eyes. He had to be thinking of the last time they'd straddled the line between friendship and something more— that horrible night in San Antonio when he'd asked her that same question, and everything fell apart. She'd often wondered what would've happened if he hadn't asked it. Or if she'd responded differently. Would they be happy now? Would they both still be in the military? Would they be married with three kids? Or would they have crashed and burned, completely destroying their friendship?

There was only one way to find out.

"I want you, Vee," he murmured and kissed her lightly again. "But I need to make sure you're ready for this."

She stroked his cheek. She loved that he worried so much about her, but it wasn't what she wanted from him now. She wanted his heat, his passion. "I'm ready."

It was all he needed. He lifted her into his arms and carried her back to the plane. He set her down on the wing and stepped between her legs, his eyes never leaving hers as he leaned down and captured her lips in a searing kiss. She moaned into his mouth as he cupped her breasts through her shirt, his fingers teasing her nipples to hard peaks. She ran her hands over his broad shoulders and down his back, feeling every muscle flex under her touch.

This was what it was like to be in control, to take what she wanted, and she reveled in it.

Without a word, Connelly kissed her again, harder this time, his tongue seeking entrance to her mouth. Veronica opened to him eagerly, her hands fisting in his shirt as he deepened the kiss.

But, again, he pulled away. "Are you sure you're comfortable with this?"

"Yes." She nipped at his lower lip. "Stop asking."

Still, he hesitated. "You know you're safe with me, right? I'll never do anything you don't want me to. I'll never hurt you."

"Connelly." She captured his face between her hands and stared into his worried eyes. "I trust you."

"Then get ready to fly." He scooped her back into his arms and carried her up the ladder to the plane.

She laughed as he kicked the door shut behind them. "That was so corny."

"Mm," he said, too busy kissing her to give a more coherent reply.

The plane was cramped, but it didn't matter. Connelly's lips found hers again, and the kiss was even more intense than before. He set her down on the soft leather couch along the wall, his hands lingering on her hips, and then he stepped back, his eyes raking over her body. He looked like a man possessed, his chest heaving, his eyes dark with desire.

But she wasn't scared.

She didn't feel unsafe.

This was Connelly.

He'd die before hurting her.

And she was in control.

chapter
twenty-six

THE SOUND Connelly made deep in his throat as she slipped her hands under his shirt was that of a man on the edge. It thrilled her. She moved her hands lower, dragging a finger down the bulge at the front of his pants.

"I want you," he said, his voice hoarse, but he stepped back out of her reach. "But I want to make sure you're really okay with this. We don't have to do this now. If you're not ready, we can stop and wait."

She was ready. Beyond ready, her sex already slick and aching deliciously to be filled. Even when she touched herself or used her vibrator, she never felt this needy because, alone, her mind inevitably filled with fuzzy memories she didn't want to remember. But with Connelly, her mind was clear. There was nothing but him.

"Oh my God, stop. I'm ready, but I might change my mind if you keep asking."

Panic crossed his face. "Okay, we're not doing this."

"Wait. I was joking." She reached for him, but he still stayed out of her grasp.

"I'm not." He knelt so they were eye-to-eye, his gaze

roaming over her face, and she could tell he was searching for any sign of hesitance.

"If you feel at all uncomfortable or want to stop at any time, just say the word. You're still in control. I'll do whatever you want, whatever you need, to make this good for you."

God, she adored this man. Here he was, obviously desperate to get his hands on her, his cock straining his jeans in an impressive bulge, but he was taking the time to make sure she was happy and comfortable. He was willing to wait for her. He was a good man who put his partner's needs and wants ahead of his own. It was so rare, especially in a world where women were treated as objects.

She could have made him stop.

She could have told him no.

She didn't want to.

She was in control.

She pulled him into her arms. He was shaking, and his heart pounded like a jackhammer under her ear as she hugged him. "I want this, Conn. I want this with you."

"I'll make you feel so good," he said in little more than a rumble against the curve of her neck. "So fucking good."

She shivered at the seductive promise. "I'm counting on it."

He kissed her again, a soft, gentle kiss that sent tingles throughout her body as his hands slid down over the curve of her hips. His fingers hooked in the waistband of her jeans, and he paused. "Can I...?"

She was in control.

"Please." She wanted him to touch her everywhere.

He undid the button of her jeans and skimmed them down over her hips and thighs. She stepped out of them, kicking them aside. He dropped to his knees in front of her and slid his hands up her thighs to the lacy straps of her panties.

"Red," he murmured admiringly.

She'd always been a red girl. Red lipstick, red nail polish, red lingerie. Even her hair used to have subtle, military-approved red highlights. She was glad she'd worn this particular underwear set when she'd gotten dressed that morning. She'd been feeling good today. Sexy. Confident.

Now, she felt even better.

He grinned up at her. "For me?"

"I was hoping..." She lost her train of thought as he ran a finger down the center of her panties, the sensation shooting straight through her like a lightning bolt. She whimpered and leaned into him, craving more of his touch.

He kissed her hip, then slid one finger under the gusset of her panties to stroke through her wetness. "Hoping for... what?"

"This," she gasped as her knees wobbled. "I was hoping for this."

He slid her panties down over her hips and thighs and tossed them aside.

She was naked in front of a man for the first time in years, but she wasn't scared.

She wasn't scared at all.

She was excited.

He pushed her legs apart and pressed a kiss to her mound. "You were plotting my seduction?"

"I... I wanted you to see me like this. All of me."

He groaned and buried his face in her belly, kissing her skin tenderly and reverently as he made his way down her body. He licked the sensitive skin of her inner thigh, and she cried out, her legs buckling. He held her steady, his big hands cradling her hips, and pressed a kiss to her belly button.

"You smell so good," he murmured. "And your skin is so soft. My God, you're beautiful."

He was looking at her, really looking at her, and she could

see the awe in his eyes. She was, indeed, beautiful in that moment. At least she was beautiful to him, and he was all that mattered.

When he met her gaze, his eyes were dark with lust. "I want you to know I'm not just saying this to get into your pants. I mean every word I say to you. You are so fucking gorgeous, and I can't believe you're letting me touch you. That you're letting me taste you."

And then he licked her. His tongue parted her sex, stroking up the length of her. She whimpered. The pulse of need inside her intensified until she was sure she was going to come before he had even slid his cock inside her.

He smirked against her skin. "You like that?"

"Yes," she gasped. "So much."

He chuckled and licked her again.

"I love your laugh," she said, her voice breathy and soft. She barely sounded like herself.

"I love your pussy." He buried his face in her again, his tongue stroking through her folds. He sucked her clit between his lips, and she nearly lost her mind. Her entire body felt tight with need. She wanted him to fill her so badly...

He slid a finger into her, and she gasped. He slid it out, then added a second, thrusting in a steady rhythm. She moaned and rocked against him, her hands sliding into his hair at the back of his head.

She was in control...

But she was losing it.

And she didn't care.

When he sucked her clit hard into his mouth, her legs gave out. He caught her easily and set her on the couch, then dropped to his knees in front of her again and pulled her legs up over his shoulders. Then his mouth and tongue and fingers were back, sucking, caressing, feasting. The pleasure was overwhelming, and she didn't want it to end. She didn't want to close her eyes or look away from him, to miss one second of her first real sexual experience in years.

He brought her to the edge of orgasm and held her there, his tongue stroking insistently over her clit while his fingers continued to slide in and out of her. She moaned at the onslaught of sensation, her nails digging into his shoulders to find some purchase, her body tensing as it fought the climax.

"Let go," he murmured against her skin. "I want to make you come so many times you can't stand up. I want to make you scream."

"Connelly," she said, her voice catching.

"I love the way you say my name."

"Connelly," she said again and tipped over the edge.

She was in control...

But she couldn't control the orgasm.

She couldn't control any of this. She was at his mercy, and she loved it.

The orgasm washed over her in a hot, shocking swell of pleasure. She clenched her teeth as her body convulsed, her hips bucking against his mouth. She lost track of everything but the feel of him.

"That's it, Vee. Come for me. I want to taste you."

His tongue did wicked things to her clit as he continued to finger-fuck her. She moaned, her body tightening around his fingers, her back arching as she rode out the pleasure. But even as the first wave crested, another surged.

"Connelly, please. I can't... I need..."

He stroked her faster, his fingers curling and hitting that spot inside her that made her see stars. She was going to come again. She could feel the orgasm building inside her, bigger than before, her body coiling in preparation. She was going to come over and over and over, and she might die from the pleasure of it, but at least she'd go out on a high.

When she finally settled back into herself, he was still on

his knees in front of her. He was grinning, his lips wet and swollen from her. He stroked her inner thigh with the back of his knuckles, and she shivered.

"More?" he asked.

Her entire body shook with post-orgasmic bliss. She couldn't breathe. She couldn't think. All she could do was feel.

And, as corny as it was, she did feel like she was flying again.

"Oh, God. I... I can't."

He instantly drew back. "Do you want to stop?"

Stop?

Why the hell would she want to stop when he'd just given her the best orgasm of her life? She wanted a thousand more.

She released a breathless laugh. "Hell no."

"Good." He kissed her thigh, his stubble scraping against her sensitive skin. He moved back up her body, kissing and nipping along the way. He kissed her hip and her stomach and paused to give each breast attention with his mouth and tongue. Goosebumps rose wherever his lips trailed, and she shivered in response.

He straightened and one-handedly pulled off his shirt.

She bit her lip. The man didn't have an ounce of fat on him. She couldn't help but reach out and touch. He wasn't bulky, but the muscles were lean and defined, the kind that came from hard work and steady exercise. His abs rippled beneath her touch, and an arrow of dark hair pointed her gaze to the bulge in his jeans.

He was big.

Her throat went dry. She licked her lips, but it didn't help the dryness.

He unbuttoned his pants, his eyes never leaving her face, and pushed them and his boxers down in one efficient move, stepping out of them. He stood before her, naked and unashamed, his erection jutting between his legs.

He was gorgeous.

He was perfect.

And he was all hers.

She watched as he pulled a condom from his jeans pocket and rolled it on. She wanted to wrap her hand around his cock and drive him to the edge of insanity as he had her. She wanted to run her fingers over all that hard muscle on his chest and trace the ridges of his abdomen. Wanted to grab hold of his shoulders and pull him to her and kiss him senseless while he plunged deep into her.

She needed him.

She needed this.

She needed him in her, on her, around her.

She needed him to fill her up and make her feel whole.

But she was scared.

Scared of the intensity of her desire, scared of being out of control. She was afraid that she wouldn't know what to do, that she wouldn't be able to handle it. That she would disappoint him.

He must have seen her fear because he stepped forward and cupped her face. "You are safe with me. You will always be safe with me. We can go as slow as you want. We can take all the time you need."

He kissed her forehead, and she closed her eyes. His words washed over her, calming her fear and emboldening her need.

Trembling with anticipation, she clutched his shoulders and drew him down to the couch on top of her. "I want this. I want you."

He propped himself up on his arms and cradled her head in his hands, his fingers sifting through her hair at her temples as he smiled at her, tender and sweet. "I'll be gentle, Vee."

His hands were warm on her hips as he adjusted their position and settled himself between her legs. He sank into her slowly, inch by inch, until he was fully sheathed. She gasped at the intrusion, her body tensing around his.

He stilled, and his eyes searched hers. "Are you okay?"

She nodded, and as her body adjusted to his, a spark ignited inside her. She lifted her hip experimentally, and he hissed out a breath, dropping his head to her shoulder. He began to move, slow and deep, and she let out a low moan that surprised her.

He grinned. "That's it. Let go. Let it all go."

And she did. She let go of her fear and doubt and let herself feel. Feel the pleasure that was radiating through her body. Feel the pleasure of him inside her, moving with her, pushing her to the edge. Feel the warmth spreading through her, bringing her higher and higher. He kissed her deeply, swallowing her cries as his thrusts grew in intensity. His hands roamed her body as if he couldn't stop touching her, exploring her curves as if he were trying to memorize her.

This was what she had been missing. This was the connection she'd been craving. This was life, love, passion, and pleasure wrapped up in one perfect moment.

And she never wanted it to end.

chapter
twenty-seven

CONNELLY STOPPED MOVING to watch her orgasm, even as his entire being screamed that he fuck and claim and devour her, make her his so that no other man would dare touch her again. But he resisted, held back, gentled his movements and his touch, determined to make it special for her. To make sure she felt safe and cherished.

He watched as the orgasm slowly faded and her breathing returned to normal. Satisfaction flooded through him. He'd done that. He'd given her that pleasure.

He wanted to remember this moment—the way she looked when she let go, the way she clamped down on him when he was inside her, the way she tasted when he kissed her. He wanted to remember it all so he could keep it with him always.

He started to move again, pushing into her with long, slow strokes that allowed her to ride out the tail of the orgasm for as long as possible. She was so responsive, her body quivering around him every time he filled her, gripping him tightly and pulling him deeper. His cock ached, but he ground his teeth and fought the release. He'd waited too long for this for it to be over in minutes. He wanted to last, to give her every bit of pleasure he could before he let himself go.

"Connelly," she gasped and dug her fingers into his shoulders as she raised her hips to meet his. "Oh, God."

"You can take more."

"Yes." She wrapped her legs around him and drew him down for a hard kiss. "Hard this time. Fuck me, Connelly."

The shock of those words on her lips had him freezing mid-thrust. "What?" he breathed.

"I appreciate you being gentle..."

"But...?"

"But I'm strong enough to handle whatever you want to do to me."

"I know you're strong," he said softly, staring down at her in admiration. "You're the strongest person I know. I'm just... afraid of hurting you."

"You won't. I'm not breakable. I'm a grown woman. I know my body and my limits. I want to feel you. All of you. I'm done being numb. I want to feel everything. So fuck me, Connelly. Hard and fast. Make me ache. Make me feel you for days."

Something in him snapped, and all of his good, gentle intentions vanished. He flipped her over so that she was on her knees on the couch, her back to his chest, and thrust into her again. She pushed back against him, taking him deep. He growled and withdrew and then drove into her again, then again, increasing the strength of each thrust until he was slamming into her so hard that the couch under them creaked in protest. Her fingers dug into the leather, trying to hold onto something. Her hair was in a wild tangle around her shoulders, her ass was in the air, her breasts swinging as he pounded into her.

"Conn... Oh, God," she groaned. "Yes."

His hips met her ass with a loud smack as he bottomed out inside her. "That's it, Vee. Take it all. Take all of me."

"Yes," she moaned.

Connelly had never felt so close to another person in his life. He'd never felt so consumed, so completely overtaken by another's needs and wants. His desire to give her everything she needed, all the pleasure he could, was intense. He could do anything, be anything, for her.

And he wanted it all, wanted to keep giving all until he had nothing left to give.

He thrust harder, deeper, reaching for his own orgasm, his own pleasure. He wanted to explode inside her, wanted to fill her up with his seed, wanted to watch her body accept it. He found her clit with his fingers and stroked her as he continued to slam into her. She was pushing back, meeting his every thrust, taking him deep and still wanting more. His hand and cock were slick with her juices, her body pulsing with the first small shocks of her release.

Then she came with a force that took his breath away. Her body quaked, her back arching, her head falling back as she cried out. "Connelly!"

She was so beautiful like this, wild and out of control.

Her orgasm was fast and hard and so strong he had to bite his lip to keep from screaming as her whole body tightened around him, milking him. His hips surged, burying his cock as deep as he could get as the first pulse of cum ripped from him. He exploded with pleasure so overwhelming that he swore he was coming apart at the seams. He could do nothing but thrust helplessly into her, clutching her hips as he rode the orgasm out and filled the condom.

She shuddered around him again, a violent aftershock that milked him dry and tore a strangled gasp from his throat. His heart pounded, his body sang, and a fierce, possessive satisfaction swelled in his chest.

He collapsed onto the couch, rolling so that he didn't crush her with his weight. He dealt with the condom, wrapping it in a tissue and disposing of it in a nearby trashcan. He wound his arms around her and pulled her back against his chest, burying his face in her hair as he tried to catch his breath.

"You okay?" he asked, his voice still husky.

She was quiet for a long time.

Had he been too rough with her?

"Veronica?" He started to sit up, but she held him in place.

"That was the most incredible thing I've ever experienced in my entire life," she whispered.

His chest filled with something so big and so overwhelming that he thought it might erupt. He kissed the small tattoo of wings on her shoulder, then her neck, then made his way along her jawline.

She shivered and slowly turned around to face him. She laid her head on his chest and tucked herself under his chin. "Thank you."

A laugh bubbled out of him, and he tightened his arms around her. "Jesus, I saw stars. I should be thanking you."

She didn't say anything else for a long time, just lay there, curled against him, her fingers tracing patterns across his chest.

"I think I could do that again," she said finally.

To his complete amazement, his cock twitched with interest. He was still sensitive from his release, and the aftershocks of his orgasm still pulsed through his system, but he was definitely interested in the idea of spending more time inside her.

"I might be able to help with that." He started to roll her onto her back again, but she pulled away from him and rose to her knees.

"Do we have more condoms?"

He jerked his chin toward the pile of their clothes. "I think there's another one in my pocket."

Her smile was devilish. "You came prepared."

"Correction: I came hopeful."

She crawled across his body and grabbed the jeans, her breasts brushing across his stomach as she rummaged through the pocket. She pulled out the foil packet and glanced at him with a wicked gleam in her eyes. "Want to come again?"

She was going to kill him, but at least he'd die a happy man with a well-sated cock. "Is the sky blue?"

She laughed and ripped the package open, rolling the rubber down his thickening length. He groaned and lifted his hips. He was rock-hard and ready to go again.

She straddled his hips and angled his cock up, guiding it to her entrance. She sank down, impaling herself on him. She was tight and slick, and he hissed in pleasure.

"God, you feel good."

"You do, too. I forgot how good sex could be."

He caught her hips and stilled her. "Veronica." He waited until she met his gaze, then reached up and wrapped his hand around the back of her neck. He pulled her down for a kiss— a long, deep kiss that was almost punishing. "It's not always like this. You know that. You know this between us is something different. Special. Because I—"

Love you.

The words caught in his throat. He couldn't tell her now. Didn't want her to think he was just lust-drunk and whispering sweet nothings. No, when he finally told her, she needed to believe it. She needed to know the truth of it down to the bottom of her soul.

She cupped his face in her hands. "I know this is special," she said softly. "I know. I feel it, too."

She kissed him again and started to move. He loved watching her languorously use his body to pleasure herself, loved the noises she made. She grabbed her breasts and squeezed them, pulling her nipples between her fingers. Her body was incredible from this angle, so fucking hot. He'd happily watch her do that for the rest of his life.

This wasn't just sex anymore. This was something else, something more, something bigger.

She rode him slowly at first, then faster, grinding her hips, taking him deep inside her over and over. She was beautiful and strong and so sexy, he had to touch her. "Show me what you want, Vee. Show me what you like."

She placed his hands on her breasts where hers had been. Obligingly, he circled her nipples with his fingertips, then pinched them. She let out a little moan and rode him faster, harder. He leaned forward and sucked her nipple into his mouth. He laved it with his tongue before biting down lightly.

She cried out and bowed back almost out of his reach. She was close to coming again. He loved the way she felt when she was on that edge, the way she sounded, the way she writhed in his arms. She braced her hands against his chest and leaned forward, grinding her pussy onto his cock while taking his mouth in a hard kiss, her tongue dancing with his. He groaned into her mouth and gripped her hips tightly, meeting her thrust for thrust. She was so tight, so hot, so wet, her body gripping him with each stroke. His orgasm built in a slow, steady burn at the base of his spine and spread through his body. He wasn't going to last much longer, but judging by the way she was shaking, neither was she.

Veronica broke the kiss and started to move faster, lifting herself almost all the way off him before slamming back down. Her hands pressed into his shoulders as she rode him hard, taking him in as deep as he could go, and her breasts swayed in his face.

"That's it," he whispered and caught her nipple in his mouth again. "Take what you need from me."

She was all but sobbing as she impaled herself on him again and again. "I need you. I didn't want to need you, but I do. I hate it, and I love it and—and—" She threw her head back, and her muscles fluttered around him.

"Yes," he growled. "Come on me, Veronica. Come all over my cock. I want to feel you."

Her eyes squeezed shut, her lips parted as her breath sawed out of her in short gasps. And then her body tightened around him, and she was coming again.

He watched her face as the orgasm overtook her. But then his cock throbbed, demanding release, and he arched into her. His balls pulled up tight and he erupted, his body jerking with each hot pulse. It seemed to go on forever, and he was shouting hoarsely by the time it ended, his hands gripping her hips, his hips thrusting with no rhythm.

Veronica collapsed forward. Her head landed on his shoulder. Her body still shuddered through aftershocks of pleasure. He wrapped his arms around her and held her tightly.

It was pure bliss. A moment of complete, unadulterated happiness that he wanted to remember for the rest of his life.

She nuzzled against his chest and pressed her lips to his nipple. He shuddered and slid his hands languidly up her arms, over her shoulders, then down her sides. He trailed his fingers across her belly, then down the curve of her hip. He brushed his fingertips over where they were still joined and earned a shiver from her. He couldn't stop touching her, couldn't get enough of her soft skin beneath his hands.

She sighed and opened her eyes. Her pupils were dilated, and her lips were swollen from his kisses. She made a soft, contented sound and shifted her hips. Her pussy gripped the sensitized flesh of his cock, which was still half-hard and buried inside her.

After a moment, she pushed herself up and smiled down at him. "Are you okay?"

"That's my line."

"You were screaming."

He pretended offense. "I don't scream. I shout in a very manly way."

"Very manly," she confirmed with mock seriousness, lips twitching with a smile.

Laughing, he clasped her face in his hands and brought her closer for a kiss. "I love you."

The declaration was out and hanging between them before he realized what he'd said. She stiffened.

Fuck.

The last time he'd said those words to her, her life went to hell. Would he ever be able to say them without reminding her of what happened that night?

Without a word, she lifted herself off him, and he instantly missed her heat. She sat up on her knees and snatched her shirt from the floor.

He opened his mouth to say... what? He had nothing. He closed it again. Opened it. Closed it like a fucking fish gasping for air. Finally, he managed, "Veronica—"

She held up a hand and stood to disentangle her pants from his.

"I'm sorry. I shouldn't have said that."

She bent over and picked up her bra and panties, then looked at him. "No, it's okay."

His head snapped up. "It is?"

She turned her back to him and started to fasten her bra. "I'm not saying I don't believe you. I just don't know if I'm ready to..." When she turned back to face him, the look on her face made him curse himself. She was pale, and her eyes were too wide, too bright. "I need some time."

"Right," he said, and his voice cracked on the word. He cleared his throat. "Right. Of course."

She pulled on her jeans. "We'd better go. The dogs..."

"Right. Of course." Apparently, those were the only three words he could say anymore.

She slid on her shoes and walked to the plane's door, then hesitated before stepping out onto the steps. "You coming?"

"Yeah. Uh…" He looked around blankly at his clothes. "Let me get dressed."

But he didn't move after she left. He sat there on the couch for a long time, completely naked, the condom still hanging off his now-limp dick.

Fuck. Fuck. Fuck.

He was an idiot.

He was going to lose her.

No.

Fuck, who was he kidding?

He'd already lost her.

Again.

chapter
twenty-eight

CONNELLY MADE himself scarce over the next few nights. He was still there when she needed him, still slept beside her in bed every night, but he avoided touching her, and the distance between them grew wider each day. The silence grew more deafening. He claimed he was distracted by his book, consumed with wrapping up the plot threads and polishing the manuscript for his agent, but she had to wonder if that was the truth or just another excuse to evade the minefield that lay between them.

She knew he was embarrassed and hurt. She knew she'd reacted wrong to his confession of love. It had taken her off-guard, and her initial reaction—as always—had been panic. She had spent most of her adult life erecting barriers around herself, walls so thick and high they seemed impossible for even the most determined to scale. And yet, somehow, Connelly had burrowed under them. He'd found the weak spots, those tiny cracks where a bit of her soul peeked out, and he'd gently but persistently worked his way inside her heart. And she'd let him. Because it was Connelly. Because he'd always been there for her, even when she hadn't particularly wanted him to be.

She loved him. She knew that deep down. But saying it out loud, admitting these feelings to another person, was another matter altogether. She had hidden behind her trauma for so long, had used the assault as a shield against vulnerability, and she didn't know how to let her guard down anymore. It wasn't that she didn't trust Connelly— she couldn't think of anyone else she trusted more. But her fears and insecurities had become an integral part of her identity. What remained of her if she let them fall away? And would he still love that version of her?

By Friday afternoon, she couldn't stand the tension between them any longer.

She needed to talk to him. If not for the sake of their dying relationship, then for her own sanity.

He'd taken over the kitchen table as his makeshift office, papers strewn across the top. A cup of forgotten coffee, now cold, sat precariously close to the edge. He was absorbed in his computer, typing with an intensity that made her hesitate.

Maybe she should try again later...

No. She steeled her resolve. They needed to talk this out now before she lost him completely.

She cleared her throat, causing him to jump and spin around in his chair.

"Jesus, Vee."

"Sorry, didn't mean to startle you."

"No, it's fine. It's... fine." He quickly gathered the papers and stuffed them into his laptop bag as if he didn't want her to see them. Then he closed his computer, but not before she saw a crime scene report.

"What's that?"

"Research." He shoved the computer into his bag with the papers.

He was lying. She could always tell, but she let it go for now.

"Okay." She hesitated. Drew a fortifying breath. It was now or never. "Can we talk?"

He exhaled and rubbed his temples as if he'd been expecting this. "I don't know what else there is to say. You know how I feel. You don't reciprocate, and that's fine. That's my problem, not yours."

"I'm sorry." Tears burned in her eyes, but she refused to let them fall. "I was overwhelmed. Having sex with you... that was a huge step, one I didn't know I could ever take with anyone again, and then to have you—" She broke off as the words caught in her throat. "I know it's selfish, but I can't... I'm not ready to deal with this... thing between us."

His eyes flashed in a rare show of temper. "It's more than a *thing*, Vee."

"I know!" The words came out louder than she intended, but it felt cathartic, like the release of air from a too-full balloon about to pop. "I know it's more. I know because I feel it, too. But that's how I need to think of it for now. Just a... thing. Because—surprise, surprise—I'm scared, Connelly."

As fast as the temper appeared, it vanished. "Of me?" His voice was soft, hesitant.

"Not of you." She reached out to touch his arm but pulled back at the last moment. "Of what this means for us. Of how much I stand to lose if we mess it up. I'm terrified because you're not just an abstract someone I'm scared to let in." She swallowed hard. "You're you. You're my rock. My... everything."

He stared at her for a moment, his gaze intense and probing. "So what if we don't mess it up?"

She opened her mouth but found she had no response. She exhaled slowly and tried again. "If we do, we can't just go back to being friends like nothing happened."

"No, we can't," he agreed softly. He stood up, leaving his bag and its contents forgotten on the chair. He moved toward her slowly, not in any rush to break the thick tension. When he finally stood before her, his presence filled the room, blocking out everything else.

"But we can't stay like this either." His eyes held a mix of emotions: frustration, anger, sadness, and beneath it all, a burning desire that mirrored her own. "I'm scared too. Don't think for a second that I'm not. This isn't easy for me either. Risking our friendship, potentially losing you..." He reached out to touch her cheek, and she didn't pull away this time. His fingertips were warm against her skin, and she leaned into his touch. "But I also can't ignore these feelings anymore. We've been dancing around each other for too long. So it's a risk I'm willing to take because the alternative is so much worse. The thought of never having you, never knowing what we could be... that scares me more than anything else."

Silence fell between them, but this time, it felt different. It wasn't the tense and uncomfortable silence they'd been nursing for the past week— this was a silence of anticipation, a pause in a conversation neither of them quite knew how to finish.

She stared at the man before her. Her best friend, her confidant. He was the only person who had seen every bit of her— the good, the bad, and the ugly— and still chose to stand by her side.

Connelly leaned closer. She could hear her heartbeat echoing in her ears, feel the warmth radiating from him filling all the space between them, smell the faint scent of his cologne — something woodsy and warm that always reminded her of him, even when he wasn't there. She saw the worry lines around his eyes soften as she leaned toward him. His hand moved from her cheek to tuck a loose strand of hair behind her ear, and then his fingers lightly brushed the back of her neck in a way that sent shivers down her spine.

"I love you." He enunciated each word, his gaze never

leaving hers as he drew her closer. "I always have. That's not going to change."

"I..." She swallowed hard, her mouth suddenly dry. "I..."

He saved her from answering by dropping his mouth to hers. He broadcasted his intention, giving her plenty of time to say no.

She didn't.

She couldn't.

She wanted his lips on hers, his hands on her body, his entire being intertwined with hers. She wanted to drown in the sensation of him again like she had on the plane.

His lips were warm and familiar, offering the sense of security she'd only ever felt with him. He kissed her with a gentleness that contradicted his previous intensity as though he was afraid any sudden movement would shatter the moment.

She reached up to wrap her arms around his neck and tighten their bodies together. She tasted coffee on his tongue, felt his cock hardening against her belly. Instead of inspiring fear, it made her feel... wanted. Needed. It lit a fire inside her, and she realized with a jolt of surprise that she needed him, too.

The world ceased to exist whenever Connelly kissed her. His lips demanded everything, triggering a heat to blossom inside her that swept away any lingering chill of uncertainty. She moaned against his mouth and threaded her fingers through his dark, too-long hair.

But he drew back to catch his breath and rested his forehead against hers. "God, Veronica. I want you so bad it hurts."

His voice, thick and gravelly, rumbled through her blood and sent a shiver down her spine that had nothing to do with fear.

This was Connelly. *Her* Connelly. The boy who had once played hide-and-seek with her in their childhood backyards, the young man who had looked so damn good on that tube in the Texas sun, the grown man who now stared at her with love and longing in his eyes. He was safety and warmth and comfort. Everything she had been missing in her life.

They swayed together to unheard music. He moved a hand down to the small of her back, pulling their bodies even closer together, and she could hardly breathe. He kissed her again, his tongue tracing the seam of her lips, requesting permission to enter. She opened for him willingly, allowing herself to melt into his embrace, surrender to his touch. He groaned against her mouth as his tongue met hers, and something inside her broke like a dam bursting. All the emotions she had been bottling up for years came rushing out. The tears started flowing, hot and heavy, down her cheeks, and she couldn't stop them.

"Oh, hey." Connelly pulled back and cupped her face in his big, warm hands, swiping away her tears with his thumbs. "Hey, what's wrong?"

She shook her head, unable to form words. She felt overwhelmed. Exposed. Raw. But at the same time, there was an immense sense of relief. Connelly had unlocked something inside her, something she had been struggling to access for so long.

"Shhh. It's okay, Vee." He pulled her into a tight hug, holding her close as she cried. "I've got you," he murmured as he gently rocked her back and forth. The scent of him filled her nostrils and added another layer to the comforting cocoon that was Connelly.

She clung to him, her tears soaking his shirt, her body wracked with sobs she hadn't known were waiting to be released. His arms were strong and comforting around her, his steady heartbeat thrumming against her ear. His fingers traced gentle circles on her back, a soothing counterpoint to the riotous feelings inside her.

Time seemed to stand still as she drew solace from his strength.

Finally, when she felt steady enough, she pulled back to look at him. His dark eyes held nothing but concern, framed by his too-long hair, which was even more disheveled now from where she'd been clutching at it.

"Sorry." She swiped at her eyes. "God, I'm such a mess."

"I like messes." His thumb traced the curve of her cheekbone, wiping away a stray tear. "They keep life interesting."

She closed her eyes at the contact, savoring his touch, the sincerity in his voice. When she felt steady enough, she caught his hand and turned it to brush a kiss on his palm. "I want to go to the bedroom and try this again. Without the tears this time."

"Are you—"

"If you ask me if I'm sure, I will smack you."

A soft smile played at the corners of his mouth. "Okay. But are you?"

"I've never been more sure about anything in my life, Conn. I want you."

"Good."

chapter
twenty-nine

CONNELLY SWEPT her up in his arms, eliciting a surprised squeal from her. She laughed, the sound light and free as he carried her toward the bedroom.

"Sorry, pups. You're not invited," he murmured as he kicked the door shut, leaving the dogs outside in the hallway. Alfie whined, and Rebel pawed at the door, but the world outside no longer mattered as he laid her down on the soft mattress, his lips finding hers for another searing kiss. His hands were everywhere, touching and exploring, worshipping every inch of her body with a tenderness that made her heart swell.

She undid the buttons of his shirt, her fingers trembling slightly from the anticipation. His chest was broad and warm beneath her touch, the smattering of hair there slightly rough. Her hands trailed lower, down to the waistband of his jeans. She paused for a moment, gaze meeting his.

He rolled and lay back against the pillows, cushioning his hands behind his head. His smirk was all male. "Do whatever you want to me. I'm all yours."

She liked the sound of that.

She unbuttoned and unzipped his pants, pushing them off

him. Her fingers traced a path across his abs and down to where he was thick and hard for her. His breath hitched as she wrapped her hand around his cock, stroking tentatively at first but with growing confidence. He urged her on with a soft breathless whisper of her name, his head tilting back against the pillows. His abs contracted, and his lips parted on a soft curse. She leaned down and traced her tongue over the flared head of him, taking her time in getting to know every ridge and vein that twitched under her touch.

Connelly groaned, his hips lifting off the bed. His fingers tangled in her hair, guiding her in a rhythm that had them both panting. He tasted salty and so damn good, and when she took him fully into her mouth, she couldn't stop herself from moaning around him.

His hand fisted her hair in a spasm of pleasure, and delicious pain shot through her scalp. She took him deeper, sucking and licking, as she circled his base in a tight grip and pumped him. He grew harder and harder under her touch until he was writhing beneath her.

"Fuck, Vee," he groaned.

His orgasm was sudden and intense, his hips jerking up from the bed as he filled her mouth. She drank it all down eagerly, loving the taste of him, the feel of him throbbing between her lips. He came down from his high slowly, then tugged her up to him by his grip on her hair. His kiss was rough, possessive.

"Your turn."

Before she realized what he was doing, he switched their positions, his body pressing hers to the mattress.

And there was the fear.

More of a blip than a spike, and when his mouth descended on hers, she forgot all about it. He undressed her slowly, worshipping her body with his mouth and touch like it was something sacred. He traced a path of kisses down her neck, eliciting a shiver from her. His hands roamed, learning the contours of her. She arched into his touch, wanting more. When he reached her breast, he flicked his tongue over her nipple, making her gasp. One hand slid down between her legs and found her slippery with arousal. He teased, dipping his fingers into her, eliciting a lusty moan of pleasure from her that would do a porn star proud.

She clamped a hand over her mouth as embarrassment burned through her. "Oh my God. I can't believe I just did that."

The corner of his lips twitched upward in a devilish grin. "I plan to make you do it again."

He flicked his thumb against her clit, and her legs shook like they had minds of their own.

"Conn," she breathed, clutching at the sheets beneath her to hold herself steady.

He laughed softly, and she could feel the vibrations of it against her skin. His fingers continued their rhythm, circling and dipping inside her, each motion sending waves of bliss rippling through her body. She was on fire, her breath coming in sharp gasps as she squirmed beneath him. It was too much, but at the same time, not enough.

His mouth covered hers in a searing kiss, his tongue mimicking the movement of his fingers between her legs.

"Come for me, Vee," he murmured, his voice dark and thick with desire. He nipped at her neck, sucked on her collarbone, and she arched toward his mouth, wanting more. He took his time over her breasts, pausing at each nipple, and she ran her hands through his hair, urging him on as he suckled greedily. But all too soon, he released her nipple and continued sliding down her body. He kissed her stomach and moved lower, settling between her thighs. She shivered as his warm breath caressed her sex.

Finally, he found her clit with his mouth, sucking it in

time with his fingers thrusting inside her. She cried out, arching into his touch, bucking up into it. His tongue was a master at coaxing whimpers from her, stroking and teasing until she was a needy, desperate puddle. His fingers dug into her hips, urging her to grind against his mouth, and her body complied without her conscious thought, seeking the friction she needed so badly.

Pleasure coiled tighter and tighter inside her, building to a precipice she was both terrified and thrilled to reach. The sight of Connelly between her legs, his determined gaze burning into hers—it undid her. He was relentless, his tongue and fingers driving her higher and higher until the world became a smear of colors behind her tightly shut eyes.

The way he loved her was addictive, demanding, all-consuming.

A shudder cascaded through her, pleasure curling and unfurling in a raw, primal pulse. She convulsed around his fingers, climaxing with a wild cry that echoed off the walls of the bedroom.

Connelly didn't let up, keeping his movements steady even as her body jerked and bucked beneath him. The after-shocks were just as powerful, a series of mini orgasms that made her gasp and moan long after the initial wave of pleasure had crashed over her.

Finally, he withdrew his fingers and kissed a path back up her body, his lips soft against her sensitive skin. He cradled her face in his hands, leaning in to capture her mouth in a tender kiss that tasted of her own arousal. When he broke the kiss, his dark eyes were filled with an emotion so tender it made her heart ache.

"Beautiful," he murmured, brushing a lock of hair off her forehead.

Still panting, she wrapped her arms around his neck, needing him closer. His weight pressed her further into the mattress, and his hips settled between hers, his cock nudging at her entrance.

He met her gaze. "I don't have any more condoms."

In response, she hooked her legs around his back and lifted her hips, accepting him inside. The slick slide of him entering her sent another surge of pleasure through her nerve endings. All fear and all reservations were swept away. His movements were slow and measured, showing restraint she knew he was struggling to maintain.

"Vee," he groaned, burying his face in the crook of her neck. His breaths heated her skin, sending chills through her.

She slid her hands down his back, feeling the play of his muscles as he thrust into her. Each moan from her lips seemed to drive him on, fueling his pace until they were both panting and gasping, and the bed creaked under them.

The pleasure was all-consuming. A white-hot ball of fire that radiated out from their joined bodies and burned through everything else. She closed her eyes and let it take her, let him take her. His rhythm was merciless, unyielding, demanding everything from her and giving just as much back.

Her fingers dug into the hard plane of his back, her nails scratching trails along his skin. He scooped an arm under her leg, changing the angle and hitting just the right spot to send a jolt down to the tips of her toes.

She gasped. "Conn..."

His lips curved into a ghost of a smile against her neck. "I'm here. I'm here with you. Hold on."

"Oh, God."

His breathing hitched as he thrust harder, faster. The headboard banged against the wall behind them. She clenched her muscles around him, trying to hold him deep as the tension coiled tighter and tighter...

An explosion rocked through her. He captured her lips, swallowing down her scream as she convulsed beneath him.

"Jesus. I can't..." The bite of his teeth against the pulse point was as delicious as it was unexpected. His movements became more desperate, his body riding hers with an intensity that had her spiraling toward another peak. His lips found hers again, his kiss frantic and hot as they moved together, their bodies slick with sweat.

When Connelly finally came, it was with a ragged growl vibrating in his throat. His entire body shook as he emptied himself inside her, each pulse pushing them both higher and higher until they were soaring above everything else.

He collapsed on top of her and murmured words of affection that seeped into her skin and filled her heart. He was heavy on top of her, but it was a weight she welcomed. It was comforting, grounding. She ran her fingers through his hair, savoring the feel of him—sweaty and spent—against her.

Slowly, he rolled off her, and his arm curled around her, pulling her close. They lay there in silence, entwined in a tangle of limbs and sheets. He was a furnace against her back, his heat keeping her warm even as she shivered from the aftershocks that still coursed through her body. Her heart pounded in her chest as if it were trying to escape, and yet, nestled against Connelly in the soft cocoon of the bed they'd thoroughly rocked, she'd never felt more at peace.

When he finally spoke again, his voice was soft and raw against the shell of her ear. "You are..." He began but didn't finish, leaving his words to trail into the darkness as his fingers traced lazy paths up and down her side.

"Perfect," he breathed after a long moment, finishing his sentence. "You're perfect, Vee."

Emotion clogged her throat, and she blinked hard to clear her blurring vision. There was no place for tears here. Not in this haven they'd created together, not in the post-orgasmic warmth that enveloped them.

Connelly tightened his arms around her, pressing a kiss on

the back of her neck. Her sensitive skin tingled where his lips touched, and a shiver coursed down her spine.

She rolled to face him so that they were nose-to-nose, their heads resting on the same pillow. She traced the outline of his strong, scruffy jaw with the tip of her finger. He gave a sleepy smile that was somehow boyish and devastatingly sexy man at the same time.

She loved him.

She loved him so much it hurt, but it was a sweet ache deep in the center of her.

Just as she opened her mouth to tell him, there was a knock on the front door that had Rebel and Alfie barking like mad.

Connelly's heavy eyes popped open wide. "Girl's night."

"What?"

He sat up and groped around on the nightstand until he found the alarm clock that had been knocked askew by their lovemaking. He looked at the time. "Oh, fuck."

He rolled out of bed and fumbled to find their clothes.

She watched him with bemusement. "Girl's night?"

"I thought you needed girlfriends, so I asked Alexis to come hang out with you while I go help Cal with some research." He pulled on his pants, then tossed hers on the bed and crossed to the window, pulling back the drapes to peek out.

"You did... *what*?"

"I know! I'm sorry! I meant to tell you, but then... you know, sex. My brain turned to mush."

She yanked on her clothes and crossed the room to peek under his arm at the gathering on her porch. Five women waited out there. "That's not just Alexis."

"No," he said slowly. "It is not."

"Oh my God." She dragged her hands through her messy

hair, trying to tame it. "I need to shower! I need to not look like... like..."

"Like you just had mind-blowing sex?"

She smacked his arm. "This isn't funny."

He held up his fingers a millimeter apart. "It's a little funny."

"We see you at the window," Anna Hendricks' voice chimed from the porch. "Stop making kissy faces at each other and let us in. I was promised a grown-up girl's night."

Veronica's face flamed, and she buried it in her hands. "Oh my God."

Connelly cleared his throat to stifle a laugh and turned her to face him. He peeled her hands away from her face and kissed the tip of her nose. "Go shower. I'll let them in."

He had the bedroom door open before she realized what *he* looked like. Bare-chested and barefoot, his jeans hanging low on his hips, his hair a tousled mess. "You can't go out there like that! You look like—"

"Like I just had mind-blowing sex?" He smirked over his shoulder. "I know. Because I did."

"Connelly..."

His laugh drowned out her warning. "You have two minutes to get to the bathroom before I let them in."

Searching for Shadows

chapter
thirty

VERONICA STARED DUMBLY at her reflection in the mirror as the shower water warmed. Her hair was a mess, her mouth swollen from Connelly's kisses, and she had a hickey on her collarbone. Her thighs were sticky with their orgasms, her sex sore from the literal pounding it just took, and yet she felt like she was floating on air.

"What the hell just happened?" she asked her reflection.

Connelly Davis had rocked her world. He'd rocked it so hard and so thoroughly that she was reasonably sure it had just shifted on its axis.

And now she had to play hostess to a bunch of women she barely knew?

The shower water finally reached a comfortable temperature, and she stepped in, letting the hot stream wash over her and rinse the evidence of their intimacy down the drain. She lost track of time under the steaming water, lost in her thoughts until she heard a knock on the bathroom door followed by Connelly's voice.

"Vee? You can't hide in there all night."

Dammit. She was trying to do precisely that by drawing the shower out. Hide.

She sighed heavily. Having company was the last thing she wanted. All she wanted was to curl back into bed with him and forget about the world outside.

But instead, she turned off the shower and toweled off briskly. She dressed in soft cotton pants and a loose shirt and pulled her damp hair into a messy bun. She took a deep, fortifying breath before opening the door.

She was met with a living room full of boisterous laughter, glasses clinking, and the smell of pizza filling the air.

"Vee!" Alexis waved a glass of red wine toward her. "Come meet everyone!"

Tension curled in Veronica's stomach like a venomous snake, but she forced herself to plaster on a polite smile as Alexis made introductions.

"Of course you already know Anna and Rose," Alexis said.

Rose Rawlings lifted her glass in a salute. She was the sheriff's wife and owner of The Mad Dog Pub. "Hey, Vee."

Anna was mid-bite of a huge slice of pizza. "Thanks for having us. I really needed some adult girl time."

"Poppy driving you nuts?" a curvy woman with long dark hair asked. She had a baby bump under her flowy blue top and wasn't drinking wine like everyone else.

Sasha Scott, Veronica realized, placing her name with the face. Donovan's wife.

Wait. Donovan was going to be a dad?

Anna rolled her eyes heavenward in answer to Sasha's question. "God, yes. I love that child with everything in me, but she has no boundaries right now. Sometimes Mom just wants to pee by herself."

Sasha smiled and pressed a hand to her belly. "I can't wait."

Anna pointed at her with the slice of pizza. "You say that now, but let's revisit it in seven years and see how you feel."

Alexis took Veronica by the arm and pulled her into the

living room. A woman with an explosion of blond curls and bright red-framed glasses was setting up a projection screen.

"And this," Alexis said, "is my sister, Ellie."

Ellie's smile was bright and warm. "Nice to finally meet you, Veronica. I hope you don't mind all this." She waved at the projector. "I thought we could binge the new season of Bridgerton. Have you seen it?"

"Uh... no?"

"Oh! It's so good. I've seen it twice, but I'll happily watch it again. You'll love it! The romance, the costumes, the hot men—"

Alexis laughed. "Take a breath, Elle."

Ellie's gaze shifted to the hallway behind Veronica, and she leaned in conspiratorially, her eyes sparkling behind her glasses. "But I guess you don't need fictional eye candy with *him* around."

Veronica turned and watched as Connelly emerged from the bedroom. He was appropriately dressed now in jeans and an olive green Henley. Over it, he wore his favorite cable knit cardigan with leather elbow patches. With his leather laptop bag slung over his shoulder, he looked more like a college professor than the man who had rocked her world.

He came straight to her, wrapped an arm around her waist, and pressed a kiss to her mouth that had her flushing hot from head to toe. The other women giggled like schoolgirls.

"I'll be at The Mad Dog if you need anything," he murmured. "Try to have fun."

She fisted her hands in his sweater, unwilling to let him go. "I wish you were staying."

"You do barrel rolls in planes not built for aerobatics," he reminded. "You can handle a girl's night, and I'll be back around eleven." He gave her another quick kiss and then released her.

"All right, ladies," he announced, grinning at the group as he headed to the door. "I'm gonna leave you to your girl talk and sexed-up period dramas. Behave and try not to drool too much. I just mopped."

The room erupted with laughter and hoots as the front door swung shut behind Connelly.

"You go, girl," Rose said, raising her glass in a toast. "Snagging Sexy Sweater Guy? And he mops, too? Sheesh. I'm lucky if Ash remembers to pick up his socks."

Veronica snorted a laugh, surprising herself. "What did you just call him?"

"Sexy Sweater Guy. It's what I mentally called him when he came into the pub to write before I knew his name."

"I mean, she has a point," Sasha said. "That sweater shouldn't be sexy, but on him...?"

"So hot," Anna finished, and the women all hummed appreciative agreements.

"Writers," Ellie said and swooned onto the couch, dramatically fanning herself with her hand. "Who knew, amiright?"

"You made it," Cal said when Connelly slid into the booth across from him fifteen minutes later.

"Yeah, sorry. Uh..." Connelly couldn't stop his grin. He knew what he looked like—a man who had spent the afternoon rocking the bed with the woman he loved—but he didn't care. "Something came up."

Cal eyed him with a smirk. "Looks like it came up more than once. Lucky bastard." He slid a beer over the table. "I was starving, so I took the liberty of ordering for you. Hope you like a porter and cheeseburgers."

"Porter's perfect." Connelly picked up the glass and raised it in a toast. "I only drink beer as black as my soul."

"My man." Cal tapped their glasses together, and they both took swigs of the dark beer.

The cool, bitter taste sent shocks through Connelly's system, washing away the traces of anxiety that had been gnawing at him since he left Veronica.

She'd be okay.

Zak and Donovan were both on guard duty at the base of the driveway. It was Zak's overnight shift, but Donovan wasn't about to stay away since his pregnant wife was inside. Ash's deputies—both good, solid cops—were parked on the street. The house was filled with women, most of whom knew their way around a firearm.

She was okay.

Tonight would be good for her.

And he had work to do.

He unzipped his laptop bag and pulled the computer out. "I had a thought earlier today."

"Yeah?" Cal said and also reached for his briefcase. "So did I, but you go first."

"Alexis was so sure Maria Socktish was the first victim, and even though we now know she wasn't, there might still be something to it. She was the first of the current M.O.— when he started targeting vulnerable young women with no family ties and a history of sex work and drug abuse. But assuming Stephanie Walsh in 1990 was also his victim, why was there an eight-year gap between her murder and Maria's disappearance?"

Their food arrived.

"Can I get you anything else?" Jeremy Firestone asked after placing their plates in front of them.

"I'll take another porter," Cal said and raised a brow at Connelly in question.

"No, I'm good."

"I'll bring that right out," Jeremy said. "My shift ends soon, but if you need anything after I leave, Shaina, the bartender, can help you out."

"Great," Cal said. "Thanks, Jer."

Jeremy walked away, pausing to clear an empty table nearby, and they both took a moment to doctor their burgers with condiments before continuing their original conversation.

"So..." Cal started, but Jeremy returned with the requested beer, and he closed his mouth without finishing his thought.

"Sorry for interrupting," Jeremy said and turned to Connelly. "You're Veronica Martens' friend, right?"

"I am. Connelly Davis." He held out a hand. Up close, he realized Jeremy was older than he first thought, probably closer to his own age than high school. The guy's handshake was tentative and a little clammy.

"My mom's dog... Alfie? I, um, was wondering how he is."

Man. It never occurred to Connelly that Jeremy had lost not only his mom but also his dog. "He's great. Thriving actually. Veronica adores him, and he's attached to her hip."

"Oh. Good. I—I miss him." Tears swam into Jeremy's eyes, but he blinked them back. "Uh, I found a box of his stuff that Dad missed. Some toys and stuff, but it's mostly his bowties. Mom loved to—" His voice broke.

"I'm so sorry about your mom," Connelly said, his heart going out to the guy.

"Her loss was a loss for the whole community," Cal murmured.

Jeremy nodded sharply and cleared his throat. "Uh, anyway. If Veronica wants the box, I can leave it on our porch for her. We live just a couple streets over."

Connelly checked his watch. "I can pick it up when we're done here. Around eleven, if that's not too late?"

"That should be okay. I'll let Dad know you're coming in case I'm not home yet. Have a good night."

"You, too," Cal said, waiting until Jeremy was out of earshot before finally finishing his thought. "Okay, so, why the eight-year gap between the third and fourth kills? That's a good question." He crunched on a pickle spear thoughtfully. "One I'm guessing you have a theory about?"

"I do." Connelly turned his computer so Cal could see the timeline he'd worked out. "I think his first two victims, Jennifer Anderson and Stephanie Walsh, were personal. I think he knew them both. Do we know who the father of Stephanie's baby was?"

"There's no record of it. As far as I can tell, she never even told her parents his name."

"I'd be willing to bet my next royalty check that it was him, and he killed her when she told him about the pregnancy."

"Solid theory." Cal picked up a fry, swabbed it through ketchup, and pointed it at him before popping it into his mouth. "Except for the fact that the first victim, Jennifer, wasn't pregnant. So what set him off with her?"

Connelly lifted one shoulder in a shrug. "Maybe it was as simple as she rejected him, and he didn't take it well."

"Okay." Cal nodded. "The first two victims were personal... and then there was the eight-year gap before Maria. You think he tried to stop killing."

"It's not unheard of with serial killers. Maybe he got married and had a family. Life was good for a while, and the urge to kill went away, but then something happened that triggered him again."

"Divorce?"

"Or a woman from his past reappeared in his life with a kid and threatened everything," Connelly suggested and picked up his burger. He hadn't realized how hungry he was until he took the first bite, but suddenly he was famished. The burger was big, juicy, and fantastic. He reached for the napkin holder. He was going to need a few of them.

"Holy shit," Cal said as he took a substantial bite of his burger. "I see where you're going with this. You think Maria's kid was our killer's son, and when Maria popped back up, threatening his new life, he got rid of her."

"Exactly. Do we know what happened to the boy when he went into the foster system?"

"Ah." Cal wiped his hands and mouth on a napkin, then drew a folder from his briefcase, passing it over the table. "Now it's my turn to share my thought. After our last meeting, I started wondering about the kid and looked into his whereabouts. His name was Kwane Socktish. He was held in foster care while Maria tried to pull her life together, but after her disappearance, he was adopted."

Connelly opened the folder and scanned the stack of photocopied court records. "Do we know the name of his adoptive family?"

"We do not. It was a closed adoption."

"If we're going on the assumption Kwane was our killer's son, do you think he adopted the kid after killing Maria?"

"Well," Cal said with a short laugh, "I don't have a royalty check to bet, but if I did, I would."

Connelly found a copy of Kwane Socktish's birth certificate and read through it. "No father listed."

"C'mon. That would be too easy." Cal typed something on his laptop, pulling up a map of the West Coast marked with a scatter of fourteen red dots. "I searched for kids named Kwane in the county and found nothing. Expanded the search to include the rest of California, Oregon, Washington, and Nevada, and this is all I got. Fourteen hits, but none of them were the right age." He zoomed out on the map to show more dots. "Nationwide, there are only seventy-four people named Kwane, but again, none fit our kid's statistics."

"His adoptive parents changed his name."

"Most likely."

Connelly sat back and exhaled his frustration. "There has to be something else we're missing."

They finished their meals in brooding silence, deep in thought.

"Well, fuck." Cal pushed his plate away and took a swig from his second beer. "We're no closer now than when we started."

Connelly checked the time on his phone. It was closing in on eleven. He told Veronica he'd be back by eleven. He packed up his laptop and dug a twenty out of his wallet, setting it down on the table for his half of the bill. "I gotta go. I'm sure Veronica is looking for excuses to escape girls' night by now."

"Was..." Cal hesitated and ran a finger through the condensation on his glass. "Was Ellie there?"

"She was." Connelly grinned at him. "Man, you got it bad for her, don't you?"

Cal gave him the finger, which made him laugh on his way out the door.

chapter
thirty-one

CAL SAT for a while after Connelly left, nursing his second beer as he continued looking for cold cases that fit the Stalker's M.O.

But, inevitably, his mind wandered away from murder and back to her.

Ellie Summers.

Yeah, Connelly had hit the nail on the head. He had it bad. Ellie was beautiful and brilliant and funny. He adored her freckles, and her unruly spirals of hair, and her brightly colored glasses that never seemed to sit straight on her nose. But her quirks, as cute as they were, only masked her toughness, tenacity, and fierce loyalty. She was a force of nature, unstoppable when she had a mission. He had been half in love with her by the end of their first date...

And then he'd fucked it all up.

All because of his sense of justice.

Groaning, he slapped a hand down on his laptop lid and took a long swallow of his beer. No matter how many times he apologized or tried to explain, she wouldn't hear him out. The woman was as stubborn as a mule and twice as headstrong. Cal respected that. Honestly, he did. Ellie had moved mountains trying to save her sister, and only someone with her iron will could have managed it.

But damn, if it didn't make it hard to win her back.

When he took on Jaxon Thorne as a client, he'd seen it as his duty— the cornerstone of his profession. He disagreed with the man's actions, but everyone had the right to a fair trial. That was what justice stood for. That was what he stood for.

Ellie, however, didn't see it that way. To her, he'd betrayed her sister and everything their relationship stood for by defending the man she believed was responsible raping and nearly killing Alexis.

He replayed their last conversation in his mind, her anger and disappointment stinging even now. He had hoped she'd understand why he chose to defend Jaxon Thorne, but she was steadfast in her rage. He tried to explain that everyone deserved a fair trial, even those society deemed monsters, but she simply turned away, leaving him alone in the room with his remorse.

There had to be some way he could make it up to her...

"Rose said Connelly was here."

He jumped at Ash's gruff voice and scowled up at the sheriff. "Hi to you, too. Good to see you, Ash. It is a nice night, isn't it?"

Ash's scowl deepened. "I don't do small talk."

"Oh, believe me," Cal muttered into his beer. "I'm aware."

"Is Connelly here or not?"

"You just missed him. He's on his way back to Veronica's." Cal frowned and set down his beer. Ash looked exhausted and more stressed than usual. "Why, what's wrong? Is Veronica okay?"

"Why wouldn't she...?" Surprised confusion flashed over Ash's expression before he schooled it back into its usual stoic mask. He shook his head. "No, she's fine as far as I know. Zak's on duty there tonight and reported all was quiet when I spoke to him about an hour ago."

"Okay, then. Has there been a break in the case of his super fan?"

Ash eyed him suspiciously. "Are you his lawyer?"

"Does he need one?"

"He might."

Cal curled his hand around the twenty Connelly had left to pay for his half of their bill. He'd just count that as a retainer. "Then yep. What's up?"

"You're a pain in the ass, Holden." Lines of annoyance carved into Ash's forehead with his next deep scowl. But, after a stubborn moment, he relented and took the seat Connelly had vacated. "We found Sara Parker."

"The woman who was stalking Connelly?"

"That's the one."

"Well, if she's in town, feel free to arrest her. He has a restraining order."

"He won't need that anymore. She's dead. She's the Jane Doe we found sliced to ribbons. His so-called super fan turned her into one of the scenes from his book."

Cal sucked in a sharp breath and released it with a soft "Fuck." Then he narrowed his eyes at the sheriff. "Wait. You know damn well Connelly didn't hurt her."

"I still have to question him." Ash stood. "I assume you want to be present for that? I'm going to Veronica's now."

Cal slapped down money to cover the bill and followed Ash out the door. "If Sara Parker was following Connelly, she must have gotten in the Stalker's way."

Ash cursed softly as he unlocked his Tahoe. "Don't tell me you and Alexis have roped Connelly into your conspiracy theories about The Shadow Stalker."

"It isn't a conspiracy theory."

"There's no evidence."

"There's plenty of evidence."

"It's all speculation."

Cal slid into the passenger seat, and Dante, the sheriff's big black German Shepherd, poked his nose between the seats in greeting.

"Hi, boy," Cal said, patting Dante's massive head.

Ash started the Tahoe, and they headed out of town toward Veronica's house on Bluff Road. The tension in the car was palpable. Ash kept his gaze on the road, but his knuckles were white on the steering wheel. The silence was only interrupted by the occasional squawk of his radio from dispatch.

"Look," Cal began, "I get it. You're a stick-to-the-facts, evidence-based kind of guy. That's why you're a good sheriff."

"I appreciate your support," Ash replied dryly. "But, yeah, show me physical evidence. Until then, I'm not entertaining fairy tales."

"You're chasing a killer who is recreating scenes from a horror novel," Cal reminded, trying to poke a hole in the sheriff's impenetrable pragmatism. "And you don't want to entertain fairy tales? Little late for that."

Ash rumbled something unflattering under his breath, which Cal chose to ignore. "Connelly's book is based on local legends, and The Shadow Stalker is the heart of it all."

"There's no such thing as The Shadow Stalker," Ash said through clenched teeth, staring straight ahead at the dark road. "The FBI looked at all the cold cases and agreed they're unconnected. You're grasping at straws, Holden."

"You're too focused on the legend. You can't see past the fiction to the facts underneath."

Ash was silent for a moment. "Fine," he said abruptly. "Then lay it out for me."

And so Cal did, starting with Jennifer Anderson in 1987 and Stephanie Walsh in 1990. "He seems to have taken an eight-year break, then killed Maria Socktish in 1998. By then, he'd dialed in his M.O., and the kills became more frequent. One or two victims a year that we know of, but there have been a lot of other disappearances—like Alexis and Ellie's sister, Hope—that could also be attributed to him. And it can't be a coincidence that we have the author who wrote the book on the Shadow Stalker in town, and there have been three new victims in as many months."

Cal let the silence stretch, broken only by Dante's soft, questioning whine from the back seat.

"I'm listening," Ash said finally.

"The Shadow Stalker in Connelly's book was a creature of the night, an amalgamation of fear. But what we're seeing from our research is a very calculated, very disturbed man who knows our town's lore and uses it as his cover."

"Okay. And how does the super fan fit in?"

Cal shrugged. "I think it's pretty obvious. There are two killers. One methodical, and one fanatical."

"Jesus fucking Christ," Ash muttered as he turned onto Veronica's road.

chapter
thirty-two

VERONICA HAD MORE fun than she imagined she would. The women were all smart, funny, and, most of all, kind. Every one of them checked in with her at various times throughout the night, ensuring she wasn't overwhelmed. By the time the party began to break up, she had all their numbers saved in her phone.

She'd never had a girl tribe before.

She kind of liked it.

She couldn't remember the last time she'd laughed so much.

Sasha was the first to leave, claiming exhaustion and calling Donovan to come pick her up.

"Well, of course you're exhausted," Anna had said somewhat tipsily. "You're making a whole-ass human!"

Rose was next, saying she wanted to check in with her new hire before closing time at The Mad Dog, and Anna caught a ride with her to go home and relieve the babysitter. Shortly after they left, Ellie fell asleep on the couch, leaving just Veronica and Alexis to clean up. She didn't mind, though. She'd had fun with the others but enjoyed Alexis's company the most.

Alexis had a sharp wit, and her laughter was infectious. She was surprisingly easy to talk to. She had a way of making you feel like what you were saying was the most interesting thing in the world. Despite the horrors she had gone through just a few months ago, there was a light in her eyes that Veronica found both comforting and inspiring.

"I hope this wasn't too much," Alexis said as they cleared the empty wine glasses and discarded paper plates stained with pizza grease.

"I was afraid it would be," Veronica admitted. "But it was... nice. Thank you. I know this was your idea."

"Actually, it was mostly Connelly's. My idea was to turn it into a girl's night with everyone."

A warm flush spread across Veronica's cheeks at the mention of Connelly. It brought back memories of their afternoon together and made her think of everything she wanted to do to him when he got home.

"He's a good man," she said finally.

"He is," Alexis agreed, chuckling softly as she rinsed the wine glasses. "A tad overprotective, but then again, aren't all great men?"

"Is Shane overprotective?"

Alexis snorted. "That's like asking if water's wet. He can't help himself."

Veronica laughed, the sound echoing around the now-empty room as she helped Alexis wash the remaining dishes. It felt nice, natural even. A moment of normalcy.

"Can I ask you something?" she blurted and turned to face Alexis. "How are you so... okay?"

Alexis paused, and for a brief moment, Veronica thought she might have crossed a line. But then Alexis drew a deep breath and looked toward her sleeping sister on the couch. Rebel was tucked into a tight ball behind Ellie's legs, and Alfie was snuggled into her arms like a teddy bear, only his fluffy ears visible from under the blanket draped over them.

"Ellie says I'm not. And maybe she's right." She finished drying the last wine glass, slid it into the holder on the wall, and then set the towel down. "I just... I guess I don't want him to win, you know? If I let what he did to me consume me, it's giving him exactly what he wanted. He wanted to destroy me before he killed me. He didn't get the chance to kill me, and I refuse to give him the rest of what he wanted."

"Does it help to know that he's in jail? The men who..." She swallowed hard as the word 'rape' stuck in her throat. "Hurt me were never punished, and I've always wondered if I would feel differently if they'd been caught."

Alexis hesitated a second too long.

"Wait." Veronica stared at her in shock. "He *has* been caught, hasn't he?"

She shook her head. "No. He's still out there somewhere."

"But I thought... Didn't Ash arrest someone?"

"Jaxon Thorne." She touched the thin scar on her neck. "He hurt me to hurt Shane, but he's not the one who raped me. I still don't know who it was."

"Aren't you terrified?"

"Every day," Alexis admitted, a grim smile on her lips. "And every morning, when I wake up and realize it wasn't just a nightmare. And every night, if Shane's not home and I'm alone in the darkness. And every moment in between when my heart jumps at the sound of footsteps that aren't there. But I refuse to live in that fear. I'll be damned if I let him steal any more of me than he already has." She glanced at her sleeping sister again and smiled as Ellie's soft snores filled the quiet room. "But having Ellie in my life makes it easier. And Shane." She met Veronica's gaze. "You have Connelly now. And me. And all of Redwood Coast Rescue. It's time to stop letting the assholes who hurt you steal your life."

Veronica bit back the tears that threatened to spill. "You make it sound so simple."

"It's not," Alexis replied, her voice soft and understanding. "It's the hardest thing you'll ever do."

Veronica nodded, though she found herself unable to respond immediately. The honesty Alexis showed was humbling. Maybe it was the solidarity in their shared trauma, or maybe it was just the kind of person Alexis was— raw, sincere, and brave.

"Thank you," Veronica murmured after a long silence, the words sounding inadequate in her own ears. But what else could she say?

Alexis smiled warmly, reaching out to touch Veronica's arm in a comforting gesture. "Hey, what are friends for?"

Friends.

Wow.

She actually had friends again.

Headlights flashed through the window, and they both turned toward the front of the house.

"That's probably your man," Alexis said. "Let me wake Miss Snores-a-Lot, and we'll get out of your hair."

It took both of them to pull Ellie, who was more than a little tipsy, to her feet.

"Why can't I find a duke?" Ellie slurred as they practically carried her to the door. Her cheeks were rosy pink from the wine, her hair was a frizzy riot of curls, and her glasses were adorably askew. "Instead, I find a cute lawyer—he's cute, right? With all that blond hair and that crooked smile?"

"He's cute," Alexis confirmed, straightening Ellie's glasses before they completely slipped off her face.

"Who?" Veronica mouthed over Ellie's head.

"Cal," Alexis whispered back and pulled open the door.

"Ohh."

Ellie sighed and staggered out of their grip. She whirled to face them and almost took out a floor lamp. "Cute, with a very squeezable butt." She held up her hands and squeezed the air suggestively. "But a squeezable butt doesn't make up for the fact he's a complete... ashhole." She tilted sideways and righted herself with a hand on the doorframe. "No, asshole. I meant asshole. Complete asshole. Throw the whole man out. I hate him."

At that very moment, the cute lawyer with the apparently squeezable butt walked up the porch steps with the sheriff right on his heels. He froze at Ellie's declaration, his expression like a kicked puppy.

"Hey, Ellie," he said awkwardly, shoving his hands into his pockets and shifting from foot to foot.

Ellie whirled toward his voice.

"You!" she shrieked, outraged in the way only a drunk person could be, and pointed an accusing finger at him. He flinched as if expecting it to become a weapon. "You're an ashhole—"

"Okay," Alexis cut in, drawing the word out as she grabbed her sister by the arm and propelled her down the steps. "We're going home. Goodnight, Cal." She nodded to the sheriff. "Ash." Then she waved to Veronica. "Bye, Vee. We have to do this again soon."

The sheriff waited silently until Alexis had bundled Ellie into the car, and the car was turning to leave. Then he faced Veronica, and the look on his face had her stomach knotting up.

She straightened away from the door. "What's wrong?"

"We need to talk to Connelly." His tone said it wasn't Ash, the friend, who needed to talk to him, but rather Ash, the cop.

"He isn't here."

The two men shared an indecipherable glance.

"He should be here by now," Cal muttered.

They both looked toward Connelly's rental house. No lights shone through the shifting branches of the trees.

"I'll send a car to check." Ash grabbed his radio, ordering the two deputies on the road to drive over to the house.

While they waited for the response, Veronica's gaze bounced back and forth between them. She had a sick feeling in her stomach, and it wasn't from the wine she'd been drinking earlier.

"What's going on?" Panic rose in her throat, choking her. Her eyes finally settled on Cal. "I thought he was with you."

"He was, but he left..." He checked the time on his phone. "Nearly forty-five minutes ago."

The radio crackled to life in Ash's hand. The house was empty.

"Fuck," Ash muttered and raised the radio to his mouth again. "Dispatch, this is Sheriff Rawlings. I need a BOLO for a potentially endangered missing person. Connelly James Davis, male, thirty years old. Estimated height six-two and weight one-ninety. Brown hair, brown eyes. Last seen leaving The Mad Dog Pub at around twenty-three hundred hours driving a dark blue BMW X7, Washington license plate alpha, x-ray, x-ray, two..."

Veronica's head spun as the sheriff continued rattling off Connelly's details.

Potentially endangered missing person.

Connelly had told her he'd be back around eleven, but she hadn't been worried when his arrival time came and went. After all, he often got lost in thought, scribbling down ideas on whatever scrap of paper he could find. It wasn't unusual for him to lose track of time.

"How do you know his plate?" Cal asked, sounding like he was at the end of a long tunnel.

"I have all my friends' plates memorized," Ash replied, also from the end of that tunnel.

"Of course you do. Why am I surprised?"

Endangered missing person.

Veronica's heart began to thunder in her chest, and she couldn't seem to draw enough air into her lungs. The world around her blurred and warped as she took a step back. She gripped the doorframe for support, her skin feeling too cold, too clammy.

Endangered.

"Veronica," Cal said softly, reaching for her, but she pulled back, shaking her head.

"No." She whirled on him, her voice raising several octaves with panic. "Where is he? He should be here by now. It only takes fifteen minutes to drive from the Mad Dog."

"We'll find him." Ash's voice was as gentle as she'd ever heard it. He stepped toward her, hands raised as though she were a skittish animal. "With all the shit happening around here recently, I'm just being overly cautious. It's probably nothing. He probably just stopped somewhere and lost track of time."

"No," she spat out, the fear rising like bile in her throat. "You don't understand. He wouldn't just... He wouldn't. I'm calling him." She tore herself away from her death grip on the door frame and fumbled through the house until she found her phone on the kitchen counter. Her shaking fingers slipped on the screen as she dialed, and she pressed the phone so hard against her ear that it hurt.

The ringing filled her head, echoing through her like a ticking time bomb. It rang once, twice, three times before his voicemail kicked in: *"Hey there, this is Conn... you know the drill."*

Beep.

She hung up in frustration, then redialed. One ring, two rings, three...

"Hey there, this is Conn..."

She hung up.

"Veronica." Cal's voice was heavy as he walked into the kitchen. "Stop."

"No, no, no," she mumbled to herself, her fingers frantic on the touch screen as she tried calling again.

Ring.

Ring.

Ring.

"Hey there, this is Conn..."

Everything around her seemed to stand still. The tick of the clock on the wall, the refrigerator hum, Alfie's concerned whines, Rebel's anxious pacing... they all faded into insignificance. She could only hear her own heartbeat and the ghostly echo of Connelly's voicemail.

"Hey there, this is Conn..."

She needed to feel something solid and sank to the floor to wrap her arms around Rebel. Alfie nuzzled into her lap. She held the dogs tight, trying to ground herself as she dialed again.

Her best friend. The man she loved. Her lifeline...

Ring.

Ring.

Ring.

"Hey there, this is Conn..."

"He's not answering. Why is he not answering?"

Cal's silence was telling.

She looked up at him, desperate tears blurring her vision. "Did he say anything to you before he left the pub? Did he mention stopping somewhere or... or..." She couldn't think. She felt fractured, the world around her surreal and dizzying. It was like being in free fall. The terror of not knowing where Connelly was consumed all rational thoughts.

"No. I'm sorry. I—" Cal broke off, and his eyes bugged. "Oh, fuck." He strode back through the living room and called through the open front door. "Ash! Try the Firestones' house. Connelly was going to stop there on his way home."

Ash's voice echoed back, "On it." He was back in his Tahoe, his features highlighted under the harsh overhead light as he barked orders into the radio. Veronica barely registered him, her focus still riveted on Cal.

"The Firestones?" A fragile spark of hope flared in her chest. "Why was he going there?"

He nodded toward Alfie. "To pick up more stuff for the dog."

A series of harsh curses came from the front porch, followed by the slamming of a car door and the crunching noise of rapidly departing tires.

She scrambled to her feet and ran to the door in time to see the Tahoe's blue and red lights flash on. The siren whooped as Ash peeled out of her driveway.

"We need to go there." She shrugged off Cal's touch and grabbed her keys, pulling on her coat as she ran to her car. She fumbled to hit the unlock and prayed the neglected vehicle started.

"Wait," Cal called. He tugged the front door shut, but not before Rebel shoved her way out, almost knocking him off his feet. "Jesus!"

Veronica whipped around as Rebel bolted across the lawn. "No, Rebel! Stay!"

But the dog was already gone, a black and copper blur disappearing into the dark.

"We'll catch her on the way." Cal took the keys from her trembling hands. "But you're not driving in this state."

Her protests died in her throat as he guided her to the passenger side, his firm grip anchoring her as she stumbled. She didn't even hear Ash's siren anymore, all sound fading to a dull ring in her ears. Her body felt thin and brittle like one push would shatter her into a thousand pieces.

Cal slid behind the wheel and twisted the key in the ignition. The engine coughed once but then thankfully grumbled to life. Veronica's phone buzzed in her pocket as he put the car into gear.

She scrambled to pull it out. "It's him," she breathed, a surge of relief washing over her as she answered. "Connelly?"

There was no answer. Only static.

She gripped the phone tighter to her ear, straining to hear something beyond the white noise. "Connelly? Can you hear me? Are you okay?"

"Help," he whispered, his voice weak, barely audible.

"Connelly! We're coming! Where are you?"

The connection was terrible, full of crackles and pops that distorted his words. But she thought she could make out...

The line went dead.

"Where is he?" Cal demanded. "What did he say?"

"He said..." She looked at Cal, terror closing up her throat, making speech nearly impossible. "Shadow Stalker."

chapter
thirty-three

THE FIRESTONES LIVED in a large Victorian on a quiet cul-de-sac off Main Street. By the time Cal pulled up to the house, emergency vehicles had clogged the street with lights flashing, and two deputies were setting up a barricade of sawhorses and police tape at the end of the driveway. Ash's Tahoe was among the vehicles, parked at an angle like he'd pulled up in a hurry. He stood, silhouetted against the halo of headlights, talking urgently into his radio.

A few neighbors, drawn by the commotion, were whispering at their front doors, their faces pale and fearful in the harsh lights of the cop cars. A small woman wrapped in a faded pink bathrobe stood in her yard and had a phone pressed against her ear, already firing up the town's rumor mill.

Rebel had beat them there. She was barking furiously, restrained by a deputy as she tried to break free and bolt toward the house.

Veronica barely noticed any of that. Her gaze was drawn to the large Victorian house, or more accurately, what was left of it.

The Firestones' house was ablaze. Tall flames licked against the night sky, painting everything in an eerie orange glow, while thick plumes of black smoke billowed out into the street. Firefighters were dousing the house with water from multiple angles, their efforts futile against the raging inferno.

Ash noticed them and strode over to the car. "You shouldn't be here."

Veronica tried to speak but found she had no voice.

Thankfully, Cal spoke for her. "He called Veronica."

Ash's gaze zeroed in on her. "When?"

"No more than ten minutes ago," Cal answered. "Just after you left."

"I'll contact the cell phone company and see if we can nail down a location for his phone. What did he say?"

Her lips were numb, her throat raw from suppressed tears, but she still managed to whisper, "He said... 'help.'" Her gaze strayed back to the fire. Had he called from inside the house? Was he still in there?

Ash's eyes narrowed on her. "Anything else?"

"I think... I think he said 'Shadow Stalker.'"

He growled low in his throat. "Get your dog and go home. There's nothing you can do here."

"Was he in there? Ash!" she called when he started to turn away. "Was Connelly in that house?"

He turned back, his features a grim mask. "Firemen found a body in the garage. It was in the driver's seat of Connelly's car."

"No." She shook her head. She wouldn't believe it was Connelly. She couldn't believe it. "No, no, no."

She just spoke to him.

He was alive ten minutes ago.

It wasn't him.

"Is it him?" Cal asked softly.

Ash gave a slight shake of his head. "We can't tell. It's male, but beyond that, it's too badly burned. It's like the fire started right on top of him. We'll have to wait until the autopsy for an ID."

Veronica clasped her hands in her lap and stared out the windshield at the blaze. "He's alive. I know he is."

Ash said nothing for several seconds. "I'll have Rebel brought over to you. Take them home, Cal, and don't let them leave again."

Her house was overrun again.

Alexis, Ellie, Anna, Sasha, Rose...

They had all come back. And all of their men, except for Ash, came with them.

Veronica knew they meant well, but it was too much. Too many bodies, too many voices, too much concern. Everyone spoke in hushed tones and tiptoed around her like she was a fragile china doll ready to shatter.

And maybe she was.

She certainly didn't feel strong or capable at the moment.

Alfie scampered around at everyone's feet as if unsure who to comfort first, but Rebel was uncharacteristically still, curled up on Veronica's lap, her intelligent eyes tracking the flurry of movement around them.

At some point, Anna made tea. Veronica mechanically accepted the mug, cradling it between her numb hands for warmth more than anything else. She didn't notice the tears dripping into the steaming liquid until a saltwater droplet splashed onto her thumb, and Alexis hugged her.

At three a.m., Ash finally called with an update. Cal put him on speakerphone.

"The body is not Connelly."

Everyone in the room let out a collective sigh. Veronica closed her eyes and choked back a sob of relief.

"Then who is it?" Cal asked.

"Hank Firestone."

Alexis leaned toward the phone. "How did you find out so fast?"

"The body was too old to belong to Connelly." There was a beat of hesitation at the other end of the line. "And Hank's DNA was already in our system. It flagged on several cold cases from the late 90s and early 2000s when the lab ran it. You were right all along, Alexis. Those cases were connected. Hank Firestone is the Shadow Stalker."

Alexis instantly shook her head. "He was too old to be the guy who raped me."

Shane made a sound low in his throat and wrapped his arms around her from behind.

"It's okay," she told him, kissing his scarred cheek. "Really. I'm okay. I promise."

"Cal told me there are two of them," Ash said. "We think the other is his son, Jeremy. Once the fire in the garage was out, we searched the house and found Connelly's book, filled with notes, on Jeremy's bed. It's a signed copy to Veronica."

"That's where it went," Veronica realized, remembering her search for the missing book. "Oh my God. He was inside my house."

"What the fuck?" Rose murmured. "Are you telling me I hired a killer?"

"I'm sorry." Ash's voice softened as it only ever did for his wife or sister. Then he shifted back into cop mode. "Hank Firestone owned a 2019 Ford Taurus and a 2008 Chevy Express cargo van from his job as an electrician. Both are missing."

"Jeremy drove the Taurus to work every day," Rose said.

"And he worked tonight. Maybe check the parking lot at The Mad Dog?"

"I'll send someone," Ash said.

Shortly before dawn, a state trooper found Hank Firestone's cargo van parked in an emergency turn-out on the highway with Connelly's laptop case in the passenger seat and a pool of blood in the back.

The Taurus was still missing.

Zak and the rest of the men left to search the woods around the car with their dogs, but the dogs didn't pick up any scent. There was no trail to follow. The van was empty. The forest was silent, refusing to give up its secrets.

It was as if Connelly had vanished into thin air.

By mid-morning, Zak called with another update. The forensics team had confirmed that the blood in the van was a match to Connelly's. The news hit Veronica like a punch to the gut.

"Ash is organizing an aerial search," Zak said. "We'll find him."

Aerial search.

Veronica popped to her feet. "I'll go."

When everyone looked at her like she had grown a second head, the worry shifted to mad. "I won't just sit here and wait for the news he's dead. I can fly any-damn-thing with wings. Give me a plane. A helicopter. Something."

Nobody moved or spoke.

"Fine. I'll take Connelly's plane." She pushed through the sea of bodies that had taken over her living room. Once she reached her front door, she glanced back toward the couch.

Rebel stood at attention, ears perked. Alfie sat nearby, wagging his tail uncertainly.

"Come," she commanded, and the two dogs followed her as she marched out the front door.

The cool morning air felt like a slap to her face. Around her, the world was waking up. Birds chirped overhead. A family of deer grazed at the edge of her yard. Nature carried on as if nothing was wrong.

Except everything was wrong.

The man she loved was missing.

Maybe dead.

No. She viciously shoved the thought away.

He was alive. He had to be. No other option was acceptable.

Veronica climbed into her car, Rebel and Alfie leaping into the backseat. Her hands trembled as she swerved out of the driveway.

She never noticed the Ford Taurus pull out onto the road behind her.

chapter
thirty-four

THE SWEET, pungent odor of aviation fuel and oil filled her nostrils as she opened the large doors to the hangar. The King Air 260 sat in the middle, right where they'd left it, gleaming under the fluorescent lights.

It was a gorgeous workhorse of a plane. More plane than Connelly needed, but he'd said he'd bought it for her. At the time, she'd thought it was ridiculous of him to drop several million on a plane that sat nine passengers and had a range of nearly two thousand nautical miles. But it handled beautifully and suited her needs now.

She ran her hand over the sleek wing, and tears pricked the back of her eyes as she remembered the last time she'd been here.

How he'd kissed her. Touched her. Woke up all the parts of her she'd thought long dead.

She would find him.

She wouldn't let their story end this way.

The dogs whined and paced, matching Veronica's own anxious energy. Alfie barked once sharply, and Rebel growled low in her throat. She was as ready to hunt as her human was.

Veronica quickly completed the pre-flight checks, noted

the fuel level, and texted Ash, hoping he'd see it before she took off. She picked up Alfie to carry him up the steps to the plane, then called Rebel. The athletic dog bounded up the steps without a problem.

"I'll be right back," she told them before shutting them inside and crossing the hangar to the aircraft tug parked in the corner.

The crunch of tires outside had her pausing. She expected to see Ash's Tahoe, Cal's electric blue Camaro, or maybe one of the guys of Redwood Coast Rescue. Instead, it was a car she didn't recognize.

A Ford Taurus.

The engine idled for a moment before finally cutting out, leaving an oppressive silence in its wake. She glanced around for anything she could use as a weapon, but there was nothing. Only her, and the plane with her protection K9 shut inside, and the dark figure now stepping out of the car.

Jeremy Firestone.

The world went cold around her, vision tunneling down to just him. His face was half-lit by the security light, casting deep shadows across his features. But she still recognized him —those sharp cheekbones and hollow eyes. She'd thought he had dark hair, but she'd been wrong. His hair was a fiery orange-red. If he lifted his shirt, he'd have a birthmark on his lower stomach.

This was the man she'd confronted at Connelly's.

All of her fear rushed back at once. She struggled for breath like she was drowning.

But she couldn't drown, not now.

Not when Connelly was missing, and it was up to her to find him.

Drawing on every ounce of courage she had left, she pulled her shoulders back and met Jeremy's gaze head-on.

"Veronica," he said with a smile, drawing her name out as if savoring it. "I thought it was time we meet."

"Where's Connelly?" She silently congratulated herself when her voice didn't shake because her hands certainly were.

Jeremy smirked and held up his phone. There was a countdown timer on the screen, ticking away the seconds. "Facing his fears. He has about... five hours left, give or take. Less if he panics."

"Five hours? Five hours for what?"

Jeremy's oily smirk spread wider, his dark eyes gleaming with wicked delight. "Doesn't matter."

Every fiber of her being screamed at her to run, to escape, but she remained rooted in place. She had to know where Connelly was. She had to save him.

"Where is he?" she demanded again, stepping toward Jeremy. His smile faltered for a moment, but he quickly regained his composure.

"It doesn't matter." Jeremy tilted his head, his eyes narrowing in annoyance. "He was in the way, but we're alone now, just how it was always meant to be. You're my muse. You'll be my masterpiece, and I'll finally take my place in legend. I'll finally become The Shadow Stalker."

Suddenly, it wasn't fear flooding her system but rage. It burned through her veins like liquid fire. "Like your dad?"

He scoffed. "Dad wasn't the real thing. He hid behind the name. He didn't understand its power."

"Power? Jesus Christ. It's a legend, Jeremy." Her voice carried an edge that surprised even her. The adrenaline coursing through her was a bitter taste on the back of her tongue. "It's not real. There's no such thing as The Shadow Stalker, and you have no power."

His lips curled into a snarl. She'd struck a nerve.

"You don't believe there's power in fear? Just ask Connelly Davis." Jeremy's smile returned, and she could see the glint of madness in his eyes. "Oh, right. You can't. But he'd tell you there's so much power in making others feel just how small and helpless they are. He got rich doing it. We're a lot alike, me and him. He just expresses his dark side in a more... ah, socially acceptable way. I am truly sorry he has to die. I admire him."

He prowled closer.

She held her ground. "You and Connelly are nothing alike. He can distinguish between reality and fiction."

A fierce anger blazed in his eyes, but something else flickered beneath the surface. Doubt? Fear? She couldn't tell, but she knew for sure he was underestimating her. He saw her as a victim, as prey. He didn't think she was a fighter.

He was wrong.

She took a step toward him. "And fear isn't powerful. It's weak. You're weak."

Something dark and dangerous moved behind his eyes. "Brave words." He jabbed a finger toward her as he moved closer. "But you're scared. I can smell it on you."

"Being brave isn't about being fearless. Fear keeps you alive. Connelly taught me that."

"Let's see how long that fear keeps you alive now," he said, reaching behind him and pulling out a wicked-looking knife. The blade glinted menacingly in the dim light as he twisted it in his hand with the undeniable proficiency of a practiced killer.

Veronica could feel every beat of her heart, each thump echoing inside her head, but she took another step toward him, her eyes locked on the small aircraft towbar hanging on the wall just a few steps in front of him. "Sure. I'm right here. Come and get me."

His laughter was a harsh, grating sound that bounced off the walls and echoed back to her. He lunged forward, but she was already moving. She stepped to the side, narrowly avoiding the knife blade, and caught his arm in a lock exactly as Connelly had taught her during all of those hours of Judo lessons. In one smooth, seamless move, she used his own momentum against him and flipped him onto his back. He landed on the floor with a crack of his head against the concrete.

But he didn't stay down.

She grabbed the towbar off the wall and swung it at his head as he struggled to his feet. The heavy bar made a sickening thud as it connected with his skull. She hit him again and again, and he slumped to the ground with a choked groan. He lay still, unconscious but breathing. His knife skidded across the hangar floor and came to rest at Veronica's feet. She kicked it away and held the towbar ready in case he tried to get up again.

He didn't.

But there wasn't any time for relief.

Connelly was still missing, and the clock was ticking.

She tied Jeremy up, though judging by the blood leaking out of his glassy eyes, he'd sustained serious brain damage and wasn't going anywhere except to maybe meet his maker.

Good riddance, she thought and grabbed his phone. The timer was still ticking down. She jumped on the tug and pulled the plane free from the hangar.

Once she was airborne, she set Jeremy's phone on the plane's console so she could see the clock and then called Ash from her own phone.

"Where are you?" Ash barked.

She ignored him. "Jeremy Firestone's here."

"What? Where's here?"

"Hangar four at Sierra Skyfields. You'll find him tied up with a cracked skull. He attacked me. I defended myself."

"What?" Ash said again, anger and surprise warring in that one word.

"Did Jeremy have any more of Connelly's books? Other than the one he stole from me?"

The line simmered with silent annoyance for several seconds.

"Ash!" she shouted. "Connelly's running out of time." She looked at Jeremy's phone. Under four hours now. "I need a clue. I need... something. I don't know. What books did Jeremy have?"

Ash exhaled in a rush. "All of them."

"Did he write notes in any of the others?"

"No. Just the one. Except..." He trailed off, and there was the sound of pages turning. "Wait. No, there are highlighted scenes in several of the books."

She exhaled in a rush. "Okay. Jeremy said Connelly was 'facing his fears.' Do the scenes have anything in common?"

Ash was silent for too long. She wanted to shout at him to hurry, but she knew it wouldn't help, so she bit her tongue. Alfie, sensing her unease, crawled into her lap. Rebel rested her big head on the seat next to Veronica's shoulder. She gave them both a pet.

"It's okay," she whispered to them. "I'm okay. Connelly will be okay."

"Yeah," Ash said finally. "In every single highlighted passage, a character is—"

"What are you afraid of?"

"I write horror for a living. I'm afraid of everything."

"That's not true."

"You'd be surprised."

"No, but really. What scares you?"

"My biggest fear? Being buried alive."

. . .

"—buried alive." Her choked voice joined with Ash's to finish the sentence. "Oh my God. Jeremy buried him alive."

And she'd never spot him from the air without radar.

"Holy fuck," Ash whispered.

Every breath was suddenly filled with shards of glass. She swallowed, trying to keep her voice steady. "I can't see anything from the sky. We need ground-penetrating radar. Do you have access to any?"

"Get back to the airport. I'll have it there waiting."

chapter
thirty-five

CONNELLY WOKE with a start and instantly banged his head when he tried to sit up. He opened his eyes but saw a blackness so thick it felt as if he was drowning in it. He stilled his breath, listening. All he could hear was his own rapid heartbeat pounding in his ears and a steady thump, thump, thump from overhead.

Where the hell was he?

He remembered being in the Firestone's house. He remembered finding his book on their coffee table, the chill of realization prickling his skin as he flipped through the pages and saw it was full of notes and signed to Veronica. Then there was a sound behind him, a sharp blow to the back of his head... and nothing.

No. Wait. Not nothing. He'd woken up once before in the back of a van. He'd still had his phone, had managed to call Veronica... tried to tell her...

What?

He couldn't remember.

He winced as pain sliced through his skull and reached up to probe the sore spot on the back of his head. His fingers came away sticky with blood.

Gritting his teeth against the pain, he rolled onto his side...

And hit a wall.

And another wall at his other side.

He moved his hands around in the darkness to gauge his surroundings. Cold sweat trickled down his back.

A box.

He was...

In. A. Box.

And that noise? That rhythmic thump, thump, thump. That was dirt hitting the lid.

It was right out of his nightmares.

Right out of his books.

Panic burst through him, rushing through his veins like wildfire, burning him from the inside out.

"Help!" he screamed, hammering his fists against the lid. It didn't budge an inch. His voice was a raw echo in the small space, the sound bouncing back at him.

Okay. He needed to control himself. Panic wouldn't help him now.

Calm down.

Connelly took a deep breath and held it as he tried to clear his mind. He needed to think, but the suffocating darkness made it difficult to gather his thoughts. Each breath felt more labored than the last. He tried to slow the rising panic with each inhale, each exhale. The air was getting thin, stale. If he wanted to survive, he needed to find a way out.

Suddenly, the thumping noise from overhead stopped. The silence was deafening. He stopped moving and strained to hear past his own thundering heart and sawing breaths. He couldn't be sure, but it seemed like he was alone.

The bastard had left him here to die.

And not even in an original way. He was just re-hashing what he'd already done to Lucy Harper.

Or, no.

Jesus.

Connelly realized his mistake then. He'd assumed Lucy had been the imitation of the buried alive scene because that was the second death in his book, and she was the second victim. But Lucy hadn't been buried. She'd been shot and left in a pitch-dark cave...

Because her fear had been nyctophobia—fear of the dark. The fourth death in the book.

Jeremy Firestone had saved the taphophobia scene for him. Because he'd fucking told the whole fucking world it was his biggest fear every time he wrote it into a book.

No.

He wouldn't accept this. He had jumped out of planes and survived wars behind enemy lines while caring for the injured. He could survive this. He would survive this.

He curled his fingers into a fist, drew back his arm as far as possible in the confined space, and punched upward. Pain splintered through his knuckles.

Again.

Pain.

And again.

Nothing.

The box was harder than he thought, and with a sinking feeling, he realized that it was probably metal, not wood. His breath hitched in his throat, a terrified sob tearing from his chest as the reality of his situation crashed down on him. He was trapped, and each second that slipped by was one closer to the end.

"Veronica," he whispered into the darkness. "I love you."

He imagined her beautiful smile. Her soft touch. Her heated kisses...

If he died, it would devastate her. She'd never leave her house again.

Despair gnawed at his insides, but the fear morphed into a

blinding rage. He was trapped, but he was not yet defeated. He slammed his fist against the box once again, then again, and again. Over and over until blood trickled onto his face from his already bruised knuckles.

Veronica had fought her demons, faced them head-on, and was winning the battle. He would do no less to see her again.

But seconds stretched into minutes, and minutes into hours. His strength failed him, and keeping his eyes open was becoming harder and harder. How long did he have left?

Not long, a demonic little voice cackled at the back of his mind. *Not enough time to be found.*

Desperation sunk its teeth into his soul. He was on borrowed time, breathing borrowed air. His breaths grew shallow, quick, and he could taste the bitter tang of death in the back of his throat.

Veronica.

The name was a chant, a mantra, the only thing keeping him tethered to reality. She was looking for him. He knew it. Despite life's efforts to keep them apart, they had always found each other. This time wouldn't be any different.

He had to hold on.

He hit the box again and again, but with each strike, he lost power. The darkness pressed against him from all sides like a living entity intent on swallowing him up whole. Unconsciousness began to whisper at the edges of his mind, beckoning him into its seductive arms, promising sweet oblivion. But he fought it. Fought with every fiber of his being because he knew that if he succumbed... it would be the end. He knew a final chapter when he saw it. The irony wasn't lost on him that he was facing his own end when his new book still didn't have one.

Would it have been happy or sad?

Would he have ended it with hope or fear?

It should've been happy, he thought as he slipped into unconsciousness. *Should've been a happy ending...*

Overhead, Veronica circled in the plane and watched the rescuers dig. She couldn't see much through the trees behind the Firestone house, but she could clearly see the metal coffin-sized box on the ground-penetrating radar. She checked the phone still propped among her instruments.

The timer hit zero.

"Oh, God." Air stalled in her lungs as she searched out the window for any sign that Zak and the others had reached him.

They were still digging.

"Zak," she said into the radio, fighting to keep from sobbing. "You're out of time."

"I know," came his gruff response over the static-filled line. The desperation in his voice mirrored her own. "We're going as fast as we can."

The world seemed to move in slow motion. Every passing second felt like an eternity. She mentally willed them all to move faster, work harder. She wanted to be down there with them, scooping away handfuls of dirt, but if she had stayed on the ground—if she hadn't thought to fly over the Firestones' property—they never would have found him in time. They'd needed her in the air to pinpoint his location until they arrived on the scene, and by that point, it would've taken too much time to land the plane and drive there. She didn't want to be out of contact for even a moment.

"Please hurry," she whispered as if they could hear her. "Please."

Then she saw Zak—she could tell it was him because of his prosthetic leg—wave his arms frantically toward the group of firemen standing by with a hydraulic lift. More bodies rushed toward the site, a blur of movement in the twilight.

"Almost there." Her hands clenched tight around the controls, knuckles white from the strain. She pressed her forehead against the cool glass of the cockpit window, trying to see everything. "Don't you dare give up, Connelly Davis. They're almost to you."

Radios crackled with urgent orders. Lights flashed on, garishly bright in the growing darkness, casting an eerie glow on the frantic scene below.

The radio went silent for a handful of heartbeats.

"What's happening? Zak? Ash?" Her voice rose an octave with each name. "Someone tell me what the fuck is happening!"

"Veronica." Zak's voice finally broke through the static on the radio. "We've got him. We got him, and he's alive."

chapter
thirty-six

CONNELLY STAYED in the hospital for two nights, and despite his protests, Veronica didn't leave his side. She slept in the chair next to his bed and didn't once think about the fact she wasn't in the safety of her home.

The morning of the third day, as they were preparing Connelly for discharge, Ash stopped by with news. "Jeremy Firestone just died from his injuries."

Connelly gripped her hand. "Will there be any repercussions for Vee?"

Ash shook his head. "No. The airport's security cameras caught the entire attack. It was an obvious case of self-defense, but if you're worried, you can contact Cal. He said he'd be happy to defend you."

She returned Connelly's hand squeeze with a reassuring one of her own. "Thank you."

Ash slid his notebook from his pocket. "Do you feel up to running through it all with me, Connelly?"

Connelly sighed, a look of weariness flashing across his rugged features. He released her hand and nodded. "Yeah, let's get this over with."

"I'll try to make it as painless as possible." Ash sat down at the small table in the corner by the window and opened his notebook. "Start from when you left the Mad Dog that night. What happened?"

Connelly exhaled, long and slow, and closed his eyes. "Jeremy told me he still had some of Alfie's things, so I stopped by on my way home to pick them up. He invited me inside. I was standing there in the living room, waiting for him to bring the box downstairs—and there was this smell. Like rotting meat." He paused and swallowed hard. "I didn't recognize it at first because it had a chemical undertone, but it was human decay. I'm sure of it. I noticed he had my book on the coffee table, picked it up, and started to flip through it. It was full of notes. I looked at the title page and realized it was the copy I'd sent Veronica. The one she was missing. And I just—I knew. I started to turn to leave, and he hit me over the head. Next thing I remember was waking up in a metal box. I could hear the dirt hitting the top of it..." He trailed off, shuddered.

"Did you see Hank Firestone while you were at the house?" Ash asked.

"No, I think he was already dead. I think he was the reason the place smelled."

"That lines up with the forensics reports," Ash confirmed. "It appears Hank had been dead for a few weeks at least. Under the fire damage, he was already well into the advanced stages of decomposition."

"Did Jeremy kill him?" Veronica asked. "When he spoke about Hank, there was a lot of resentment. He acted like his father wasn't worthy of being called The Shadow Stalker."

"We can only speculate at this point, but I'd say it's a good bet. Hank Firestone wasn't delusional. He didn't believe all that Shadow Stalker shit. He just liked to kill. That's why his kills were so methodical. That's why he got away with it for so long."

"But Jeremy was batshit crazy," Veronica said without a

shred of doubt. "I saw it in his eyes. He called me his muse, said I'd be his masterpiece. He truly believed he would become The Shadow Stalker of legend when he killed me."

Ash grunted. "The guy didn't stand a chance of turning out normal. Not excusing what he did, but he was groomed for this. Alexis identified him as the man who raped her from his birthmark. When I went through old rape cases, I found ten other potential matches mentioning the mark, going back fifteen years. If I can tie all of them to him, he would've been fifteen at the time of his first rape, and that victim claimed there were two of them—a younger one, who violated her, and an older one, who watched."

"My God," Veronica murmured, her hand going to her throat.

"Like I said, Jeremy didn't stand a chance. I got his adoption records unsealed, and he was Maria Socktish's son. We're still waiting on the paternity test, but I'm reasonably sure it will come back with Hank Firestone as his biological father."

"No doubt about it," Connelly said. "Jeremy looked just like Hank."

Ash nodded. "I've known him since he was a kid and had no idea he was adopted. Looks like Hank and Amelia went out of their way to keep that knowledge a secret, even moving towns from Eldridge to here after they adopted him. Friends of the family claim Hank and Jeremy went on a 'hunting trip' once or twice a year from the time the kid was about nine, and those trips line up exactly with the disappearances Alexis and Cal found. Jeremy was raised to be a killer." He closed the notebook and tucked away his pen. "I think that's all I need for now."

He was almost to the door when a thought struck Veronica. "Hey, Ash?"

He stopped and turned back, an eyebrow raised in question.

"They killed Dr. Firestone, didn't they?"

Ash's lips thinned into a grim line. "We're still waiting on forensics, but I do know for certain that Jaxon Thorne didn't do it. Despite his confession, his DNA was nowhere on the scene. The current running theory is Dr. Firestone found out about her husband's and son's extracurricular activities, and one or both of them killed her to keep their secret. My money's on Jeremy. Hank was a cold-blooded killer, but I do believe he truly loved his wife."

Veronica thought back to how Hank had looked when he gave her Alfie—unkempt, exhausted, heartbroken—and she felt a weird tug of sympathy for him. "I think so, too. Nobody can fake that level of grief. But he created a monster he couldn't control, and Dr. Firestone paid for it with her life."

"Unfortunately," Ash agreed, a hint of sorrow shadowing his stoic gaze. "She was a good woman. She didn't deserve that."

After the sheriff left, Connelly raised her hand to his lips. "I don't think I ever thanked you for saving my life."

She smiled and tilted her head in invitation as his lips brushed her neck just behind her ear. "I think you just did."

"Vee." Connelly waited until she looked at him before he whispered, "You are the most amazing woman I've ever known. When I thought I was going to die in that box—"

"Oh, don't—"

He silenced her protest with a finger against her lips. "Let me finish. Right before I passed out, you were my very last thought, and I hated that I couldn't give you the happily ever after you deserve."

Tears flooded her eyes. "Connelly..."

"But, because of you, I got a second chance, and I'm not wasting it. I love you, Veronica. I've loved you since I first saw you riding your bike across the street with that gap-toothed smile and those lopsided pigtails in your hair." He smiled at the memory and tugged on the end of her ponytail. "I knew from that moment I wanted to marry you someday, and I don't want to wait any longer."

His laptop case sat on the overbed table. He reached over and dug in the side pocket. She knew what he would pull out, but shock and wonder still coursed through her when she saw the small velvet box in his hand. Opening it up, he revealed a delicate engagement ring, the diamond sparking under the harsh hospital lights.

The tears spilled over. She tried to speak, but all she could manage was a choked sob as she threw her arms around him, burying her face in his shoulder. Connelly held her tight, whispering words of comfort and love into her hair.

"When did you get that?" She finally managed to ask between the sobs.

"Right before that weekend in San Antonio."

Oh, God. Had he planned to propose for that long? And she hadn't known, had never suspected he wanted more than friendship.

He pressed the box into her hand. The velvet was worn smooth, and she wondered how many times he'd opened it to stare at the ring over the years.

She opened it now and picked the ring out.

"I know it's not going to be easy," he murmured, kissing her neck again as she examined the stone. "I know we both have our demons... but we're stronger together. We can fight them together."

She turned and looked into his hopeful eyes and saw all the love he had for her. Saw the past they'd shared. Saw the future they could have...

And, yes, she wanted it more than anything.

She slid the ring on her finger, then, as a slow, boyish smile spread across his lips, she cupped his stubbled cheeks in her palms and kissed him. "I love you, too, Connelly Davis, and I want nothing more than to spend the rest of my life with you."

He returned the kiss with an intensity that sent a thrill through her. Warmth spread from his lips to every nerve ending and wrapped around her heart. Once the kiss broke, he buried his face in her hair and tightened his arms around her. She pressed her fingers into his back and just held on.

Finally, he pulled away and cupped her face in his hands, brushing a light kiss over her lips. "I'd like to write our story if you're okay with it. It's not horror, but I think it's worth telling."

"I've had my fill of horror for a while." She turned her hand over, watching how the diamond sparkled. "Write me a love story, Connelly."

His grin was quicksilver. "I already have."

epilogue

JAXON THORNE WAS INNOCENT.

After receiving the call from a grumpier-than-usual Ash, Cal pumped a fist in the air.

He'd known it.

He'd defended killers before and knew Jax wasn't one.

Sure, the guy had still done some pretty awful things. He'd hurt Alexis in his twisted quest for revenge, and he was going to spend time in prison for it.

But he wasn't a serial killer.

He wasn't a rapist.

He was a war veteran with severe PTSD, and the system had failed him. He'd tried to self-medicate with drugs and lost his mind, and Cal was going to make damn sure he got the help he needed while he served his time.

Cal pulled his chair out and sat heavily in it, the leather creaking under his weight. His mind buzzed with a million thoughts, jumping from one file to another in rapid succession. A sigh escaped his lips as he stared at the case files spread out on his desk.

Jaxon Thorne wasn't the only one the system had failed. Unfortunately, he wouldn't be the last.

But Cal would keep fighting for them all.

Because someone had to.

The shrill ring of his desk phone jerked him out of his thoughts. It was Ellie. He knew it before he even answered. He had expected her to call sooner rather than later, and now that it was here, he felt a strange mix of dread and relief.

"Cal." Ellie's voice came through the phone, frigid and sharp as shards of ice. "Is it true? Was Jaxon Thorne cleared of the murder charges?"

"Yes," he said.

"He's not walking free, is he? He still hurt Alexis. He tried to kill her!"

He could picture her expression—those beautiful blue eyes narrowed, lips pursed—and couldn't blame her for her anger. She'd lost one sister already and, because of Jax's actions, had nearly lost her other. It was only human to want someone to blame, someone to hate. But Jax—as messed up as he might be—wasn't the root of all evil.

"I'm aware," Cal replied, keeping his voice gentle. "And, no, he's not walking free. He will face prison time."

"Good."

Silence stretched between them then, each second pulsating with tension. He finally couldn't take it anymore and sighed.

"Ellie..." he began, but found himself at a loss for words, unsure how to comfort her when he wasn't even sure what he was feeling himself.

"I don't think there's anything else to say. Goodbye, Cal." She hung up.

Cal listened to the dial tone a moment more before slowly placing the handset back in its cradle. He ran a hand through his already disheveled hair, struggling to focus on the mound of paperwork before him. He was well aware that his decision to defend Jaxon Thorne hadn't endeared him to Ellie at all. But he also knew that he couldn't have lived with himself if he'd allowed Jax to become another faceless victim of a system that was all too quick to condemn.

His gaze strayed back to the Shadow Stalker case files open in front of him. They still held secrets, riddles, unanswered questions that would probably haunt him for the rest of his life.

But one name caught his eye, and he reached for the folder, flipping it open.

Hope Summers.

Ellie's oldest sister, who disappeared twenty years ago. She was the whole reason Alexis and Ellie had come to California and been swept up in the Shadow Stalker case. It was assumed she'd been a Stalker victim, but Hank Firestone had kept trophies, and none of them had belonged to Hope.

Cal traced his fingers over the blurry picture of Hope. She had dark hair, unlike the other two Summers women, who were both blond, but her eyes were identical to Ellie's. She'd been eighteen when she vanished. Ellie had been only six. Alexis, eight. Did they even remember her? He knew he didn't remember much from when he was that young. And yet they had left their lives behind in Chicago to come here and search for her.

A lightbulb went off inside his mind. He pulled her file free from the others and turned to his computer.

This was it. He couldn't change his job for Ellie, but he could put it to work for her. He was a damn good researcher.

He would find Hope.

And then, maybe Ellie would forgive him.

The Redwood Coast Rescue adventure continues with Cal
and Ellie's story, Searching for Hope.

Make sure you never miss a new release!
Sign up for Tonya's newsletter at tonyaburrows.com/
newsletter.

also by tonya burrows

Redwood Coast Rescue

Searching for Rescue

Searching for Risk

Searching for Justice

Searching for Redemption

Searching for Hope

<u>Northern Rescue</u>

Northern Escape

Northern Deception

Northern Salvation

<u>HORNET</u>

SEAL of Honor

Honor Reclaimed

Broken Honor

Code of Honor

Reckless Honor

Honor Avenged

<u>HORNET: Class Alpha</u>

Fragmented Loyalty

<u>Wilde Security</u>

Wilde Nights in Paradise